Anybody but Justin

The line between friends and lovers can get a little blurry...especially when you add tequila.

Gabby is serious about her search for Mr. Right, but no one can say she hasn't had a good time looking. She enjoys her numerous dates and the sex that comes with them. Until she finds herself falling for the one man she vows to never love. Her best friend and roommate, Justin. A player in every sense of the word—and a reminder of her awful past.

One night, with the help of a bottle of tequila, things get a little too hot for comfort. She moves out, intent on removing him from the line of temptation.

Justin has different plans. The tequila did more than just change how he sees his good friend. It made him realize he doesn't want to be just friends any more. He's ready for something more intimate, and he'll do whatever it takes to find out why she's running. And convince her to stay.

Warning: This book has hot sweet lovin' between friends who become lovers.

Luck be Delanie

He's lured her to paradise...and she's about to discover the price.

Long ago, Delanie made one gigantic mistake. Or committed one small felony, depending on how you look at it. Stealing a coin from a sexy stranger was just a prank to help a sorority sister get revenge. The sleeping with him part was totally unplanned. Yet she holds the memory of that one intense, passionate connection close to her heart—like the coin she still wears around her neck.

Six years later, she's invited to a beautiful resort in the San Juan Islands to not only accept a donation for an abused women's shelter, but to consider a job opportunity as well. Instead, she finds herself face-to-face with her past.

Grant has always suspected Delanie stole his rare, lucky coin. He just never knew why—or why she disappeared the morning after their hot night together. After spending years looking for her, he's lured her right where he wants her. He'll have his answers, come hell or high water.

And, if things go his way, he'll have Delanie, too.

Warning: This book contains lost lovers reunited, male masturbation, "You could have died" sex, and overall hot lovin'.

Protecting Phoebe

With her life on the line, can she protect her heart?

Phoebe's work at Second Chances, a women's shelter, has gone a long way toward her own healing after surviving an abusive relationship in college. She's moved on in every sense—except when it comes to dating.

Everything changes when Craig visits the shelter. The hot, young cop sets her pulse racing in a way that makes her consider making a move—and moving him into her bed for a casual fling. The first step: ask him out. Subtly, of course.

Craig has been attracted to Phoebe for months, so he's more than happy for the chance to get to know her better, in bed and out. His interest goes way beyond casual, but convincing her to think long term is going to take some time.

When it becomes clear her violent ex has come out of the woodwork, though, time is the one thing they don't have...

Warning: This book contains hot lovin' between an older woman and younger man, the threat of a violent ex, and a woman learning to trust a cop whose desire to serve and protect goes way beyond the badge!

Look for these titles by
Shelli Stevens

Now Available:

The Seattle Steam Series
Dangerous Grounds (Book 1)
Tempting Adam (Book 2)

Trust and Dare
Theirs to Capture

Four Play
Going Down

Chances Are

Shelli Stevens

A Samhain Publishing, Ltd. publication.

Samhain Publishing, Ltd.
577 Mulberry Street, Suite 1520
Macon, GA 31201
www.samhainpublishing.com

Chances Are
Print ISBN: 978-1-60504-571-9

Editing by Laurie M. Rauch
Cover by Natalie Winters

Anybody but Justin, ISBN 978-1-60504-524-5
First Samhain Publishing, Ltd. electronic publication: May 2009
Luck be Delanie, ISBN 978-1-60504-646-4
First Samhain Publishing, Ltd. electronic publication: August 2009
Protecting Phoebe, ISBN 978-1-60504-688-4
First Samhain Publishing, Ltd. electronic publication: November 2009
First Samhain Publishing, Ltd. print publication: July 2010

Contents

Anybody but Justin

Dedication

Thank you to Melissa at DAWN for your help and information on domestic violence. Thanks to my family and friends for your continued support, and thank you to my editor Laurie for making my books shine!

Chapter One

Oh *shit!*

Gabby dove behind a display of cereal boxes and nibbled her bottom lip. She eyed the exit some thirty feet away and wondered if she could ditch her groceries and make it out the door without him spotting her.

Her pulse quickened and she counted to ten before leaning forward just enough to peek around a box of Lucky Charms.

"Gabby?"

She snapped back and winced, glaring at the floor of the market. *Damn. He'd seen her. So much for bolting.*

Dusty brown leather shoes appeared in her line of vision as he rounded the corner. She lifted her gaze up the length of his tall body, lingering on the broad shoulders beneath his faded flannel shirt.

Her heart fluttered in her chest and she swallowed hard before tilting her head that last inch to meet the blue gaze of her old roommate.

"Justin." She forced a bright smile and switched the basket of food to her other hand. "Hey. How've you been?"

"Been all right."

His gaze, warm and knowing slid from her head to her toes in a lazy caress that made every damn inch of her body tingle. Irritation pricked and her smile grew more brittle.

And this was why she avoided him, didn't answer his calls and had basically tried like mad to forget he even existed. If she got within two feet of him, her hormones went on the fritz and her mind went spongy. Which would be fine if it were with any other guy. Anybody but Justin.

"Did you get my messages?"

"I did." Her gaze slid away again and she felt her cheeks warm in a telltale sign of guilt. "Umm. Sorry, I've been crazy busy. I recently stepped up in my position at Second Chances."

"So I heard."

The note of admiration in his deep voice had her snapping her focus back to his face.

"You heard?"

"Yeah. I'm proud of you." He shoved his hands into the pockets of his jeans and the shirt tightened across his chest as a result.

His words sent a rush of pleasure through her, but with her focus once again on his chest, she barely managed an obscure, "You are?"

"Yeah. I keep up on you, Gabby. Even if you don't pick up the phone when I call."

"Oh. No. It's not..." Her blush deepened and she bit her cheek.

"No?" He leaned forward, stretching a hand past her to snag a box of cereal off the shelf behind her.

Her gaze locked on the hint of brown stubble on his chin and for a brief second he was so close that she could smell the mixture of soap and man. Not just any man. Justin man.

Gabby swallowed hard, and she felt her nipples tighten and chafe against the cotton bra she wore.

Not good. So not good.

"Hey, look, I'll give you a call later." The lie came out in a husky rush. "We can catch up. I promised Phoebe I'd stop by the Second Chances home in a little bit. I should get going."

She moved to step around him, but he blocked her path. Her heart thudded faster.

This time when he reached out, it was to touch her. He caught a strawberry blonde braid between his fingers and slid his thumb through the strands.

"I'm going to hold you to that," he said softly.

It'd be nice if he just held her, period. Her eyelids started to flutter shut and she swayed toward him.

Choking on a gasp, she jerked away. What was she thinking? Was she completely out of her mind? This was Justin. No. No. And *hell no!*

"Of course I'll call. I will." Her head bobbed in an affirmation that contradicted the decision in her heart. There was no way she would dial his number tonight.

His lips twitched and she saw the flicker of doubt in his eyes. Finally, he gave a short nod and stepped back.

"Great. I'll...talk to you soon then."

"Definitely." She bit her lip and stepped around him, hurrying to the cash register to check out.

His gaze burned into her back and tingles of awareness raced through her body. Her palms were damp as she swiped her debit card.

One last glance back into the store showed Justin had likely disappeared down another aisle to finish his shopping.

Thank God. She fished her keys from her purse and rushed to her car.

Justin set the cereal back on the shelf and scowled. Hell, he'd only picked it up as a reason to get close to her. If only for a second.

What the hell had happened with Gabby? He hadn't seen her in six months—since she'd moved out of the house he owned without an explanation.

For two years they'd been roommates and good friends. And then she'd left and cut all contact. What happened?

You know what happened.

He headed back toward the deli, pushing back the memories of that night. The night when everything between them changed. The night that had likely motivated her to move out two weeks later.

Grabbing a pre-made sandwich from the deli, he went up to the register to pay. His gaze drifted out the windows of the grocery, even though she'd left minutes ago.

God, it was good to see her. At first he hadn't been sure it was her. Then she'd looked up, spotted him and promptly run to hide behind a stack of cereal boxes.

Same old impulsive Gabby. And she was avoiding him. He'd suspected as much since she'd stopped answering his calls and never replied to the messages he left.

He hadn't realized how much he missed her until a few minutes ago. Until she was standing right in front of him again

15

and it became clear just how much he'd lost that day she'd moved out.

She was the same Gabby he'd loved to hang out with. Cute, quirky and a bigger sports fan than half the guys he knew. He'd ditched more than one night out with the boys to sit back at the house and watch the game with her.

He handed the cashier his money and headed for the exit, stopping to hold the door for an elderly man who approached with a walker.

After the man gave a quick nod of thanks and disappeared into the store, Justin made his way to his truck.

Would she call tonight? Even though she said she would, his gut told him she'd blow him off.

Blow him off. His mind raced with images of that night and what had almost happened between them and the blood stirred hot in his veins.

He clenched his jaw and shook his head. This was bullshit. It was long past time they talked about that night. She was too good of a friend to lose over something so... Hell, who was he kidding? It was hardly trivial.

Tonight they'd talk, he decided firmly, getting into his truck to head back to the construction site. Whether she wanted to or not.

Gabby rushed into the office, letting the door swing shut behind her, followed by the reassuring click of the electronic lock.

She made her way down the hall to where she, Phoebe and Delanie shared an office. She couldn't wait to get back to her desk and get some support from her friends.

She spotted Phoebe's dark curls bent over a stack of papers. Hearing Gabby's approach, she looked up and sighed.

"You're back. Did you bring me anything?"

"Heck yeah, I did. I know what you like." Gabby tossed the chocolate bar onto her friend's desk and then went to sit down at hers. "Where's Delanie?"

"In a meeting. She'll be out in a few. Thanks for the chocolate, you're the best." Phoebe unwrapped the bar and took a bite, closing her eyes and groaning. "I needed this. It's been a crap day."

"You're telling me," Gabby muttered, and pulled out her grilled chicken breast and potato wedges.

"Hmm. What's going on with you?"

"Nothing."

"You brought it up. Don't ask me to drop it now." Phoebe's eyes narrowed and she set down her chocolate. "What happened while you were out?"

Gabby stabbed at the chicken breast with her plastic fork and sighed. "I ran into this guy—my old roommate—at the grocery store."

"And that's a bad thing because..."

"Umm. Hmm." She lifted a potato wedge to her mouth and considered how best to answer that. "We were really good friends."

"Okay."

"Like, really close. We hung out all the time, could talk about anything with each other." She paused and twisted off the lid of her soda. "We even gave each other dating advice and would talk about our sexual relationships and stuff."

"Yeah, God, I can see why you're upset that you ran into him," Phoebe teased.

Gabby rolled her eyes. "I'm not finished, you dork."

"Evidently. Go on."

"Anyway. We were roomies for two years. Life was great. Things were perfect..."

"So what happened? He screw you over on rent?"

"No." Gabby focused her gaze on the bottle of soda. "He just decided he wanted to *screw me*."

There was a moment of silence and she lifted her head. Phoebe stared at her with pursed lips and brows drawn together.

"I don't get it," she said after a moment.

Gabby shifted in her chair. "Don't get what?"

"Well, if things were so perfect between you two, why is it a bad thing that you guys fell into that romantic level?"

"Because there is no romantic level with Justin. He's a player—a serial dater. I mean, he makes George Clooney look like the marrying kind." Gabby groaned and stabbed at her chicken again. "It never mattered to me, though, because I wasn't interested in him that way."

"Or so you thought."

"Or so I thought," she agreed, her stomach twisting. "Everything changed the moment he kissed me…"

Phoebe's expression softened with sympathy. "What caused the change? Why after two years did he suddenly decide to kiss you?"

"I'm sure the bottle of tequila we were knocking back helped a bit." She shrugged. "We were watching a *fantastic* Giants game, talking about relationships and stuff…then it just kind of happened."

"Tequila's a bitch."

"Heck yeah, it is." Gabby gave a soft laugh and pulled the rubber bands from her hair, unthreading her braids.

"You said he *tried* to have sex with you. Does that mean it didn't happen?"

"It didn't happen. I stopped him before he could get my shirt off." Gabby drew in an unsteady breath. "I'm sorry. That's probably TMI."

"Not at all. You know I live secondhand through your love life."

Gabby leaned back in her chair and gave her friend a considering glance. "You know…you need to date more."

"We're not talking about me."

"Actually, you need to date, period."

"We're *still* not talking about me." Phoebe shook her head, black curls bouncing as her lips twitched. "So you didn't have sex. What happened next?"

"Well, things got weird. Like really weird." She shook her head, letting the loose waves fall over her shoulders. "We wrote the make-out session off to being drunk and never discussed it again. But I couldn't deal. At all. If he went out on a date, I was nauseous all night. If I thought about him getting it on with another girl—hell, even *kissing* another girl, I'd about throw up my last meal."

"Wow. Gabby, you really like this guy."

"Gabby really likes what guy?"

They looked up as Delanie sailed into the room and dropped a file on her desk. She sat down, ran a hand through chin-length blonde hair and lifted an eyebrow.

"Come on, don't hold out on me. What did I miss?"

"Gabby is in lust with her old roommate," Phoebe murmured. "They made out and then she moved out."

"Huh." Delanie leaned back in her chair, crossing one long leg over another.

"Stop it." Gabby groaned and took another sip of soda. "I had to move out. He owns the house—his grandparents left it to him, so it wasn't like I was breaking a lease." She lowered her gaze and picked up another potato, but barely tasted it. "I moved out when he went down to Cabo with some of his buddies for the weekend. I left him a check for my last two months and then split."

Delanie cocked her head. "What explanation did you give him for leaving early?"

"Explanation?" Gabby snorted and then bit her lip before admitting, "Well, I really didn't give him one."

Phoebe winced. "Ouch."

"Ouch?"

"Well, personally *I* would have tried to explain. Or something—"

"I know. I didn't handle it very well. And maybe I should have returned his calls or answered his emails."

"Wait, you didn't even answer his emails?" Delanie shook her head.

"I just couldn't deal with it, okay?"

"Okay, so what happened in the store?" Phoebe prodded and glanced at Delanie. "They ran into each other at the store this afternoon."

Gabby's cheeks burned. "Err, I tried to hide. But he saw me. Then, only after promising to call him later, I finally got out of there without looking like too big of an idiot."

"And are you going to call him?" Delanie asked.

"Hell, no!"

"So, apparently you *still* can't deal with it," Phoebe drawled.

"Hey. You just don't get it. We passed the point of no return. There's no going back."

"A little dramatic, don't you think?" Phoebe murmured.

"I'm not calling him," Gabby grumbled and shot a defiant glare at Phoebe. "I'm just not. So don't even try to convince me to, ladies. In fact, let's just drop the whole subject."

"Okay." Phoebe waved her hands in the air and took another bite of her chocolate bar. "I promise, I won't try to convince you. I'm dropping it."

"Me too. I need lunch." Delanie stood up and went to the mini fridge in the corner.

Gabby grunted. Justin had probably gone through a slew of girlfriends in the six months since she'd moved out. The man loved to argue that celibate had the same meaning as celebrate. Which made absolutely no sense.

"I mean, there's just no point in calling him," she said to defend herself. "It'd just be weird. And I don't do weird."

"Oh, are we still talking about this? Sorry, I thought you said something about dropping it. I must have misunderstood." Phoebe's eyes widened in mock innocence and she crinkled her chocolate bar wrapper, tossing it into the waste bin. "I'd say the point would be salvaging two years of friendship you had with this guy."

"It's too late."

"It's never too late," Delanie argued, returning to her desk with a yogurt and a sandwich.

"Trust me on this one." Gabby grabbed the rest of her lunch and went to put it in the fridge, muttering under her breath, "It was too late the minute he touched me."

Chapter Two

After jerking the ties on her sneakers tight, Gabby straightened and jogged in place. She slapped her palm against the round metal crosswalk button one more time and brushed the sweat off her forehead with the back of her hand.

The electric sign switched to indicate it was safe to cross and she sprang forward to resume her steady running pace. Adrenaline rushed through her blood as her feet pounded the pavement and Fergie sang from her iPod.

She'd been running for a half hour and had about another ten minutes. Or, if she went by her playlist, another four songs.

The sun verged on setting and the streets were filled with drivers rushing to get home from work. She drew in a breath of San Francisco air and increased her pace, wanting to push herself the last bit before she turned back toward her apartment.

She closed her eyes for a moment to savor the first few chords of the Daughtry song that came on. When she opened them, another jogger breached her peripheral vision from behind and she moved to the right to let him pass.

Instead of moving beyond her, he came up beside her and slowed his pace.

What the hell? She frowned and cast a sideways glance his way, then nearly tripped over her own feet.

"Hey."

She read the greeting on Justin's lips and pressed the stop button on her iPod.

"What are you doing?" she demanded, not slowing her pace.

"Jogging," he replied, his grin widening. "What are you

doing?"

Her pulse quickened and it had nothing to do with the exercise this time.

"You don't jog," she pointed out, resenting the fact that she sounded winded and he didn't.

He looked completely at ease and hadn't even broken a sweat.

"I thought it was a good time to start." He shrugged and kept pace with her.

"How did you—" she drew in a deep breath, finding it a little difficult to carry on a conversation at this point in her run, "—know I'd be jogging here?"

"I didn't. It was a long shot. I knew this used to be your standard route, but you could've changed."

Apparently she should've changed. Jerking her attention from him, she focused her gaze straight ahead and ground her teeth together.

"We need to talk."

"I told you I'd call you."

"You wouldn't have."

He'd read her that well, had he? She should have known.

."I'm not talking now. I'm running." Her jaw clenched and she picked up the pace, hitting play again.

Any further conversation he might have tried to make got drowned out by her music. For a moment, she hoped he'd take the hint and just turn right back around and leave her the heck alone.

Instead, he stayed abreast, continuing to match her steady pace, but made no effort to talk further.

She drew in an unsteady breath, silently cursing him out for putting her in this position. Literally. They were so close, the hard muscles of his arm kept brushing against her shoulder— each touch sending the heat radiating off him straight through her body in tingling waves.

By the time she started to become okay with the fact that he wasn't leaving, they'd arrived at her apartment.

When she slowed, he did so as well, casting a curious glance at the building beside them.

Gabby hit stop again and pulled the earbuds from her ears.

Justin braced his hands on his hips, breathing in deeply—

finally, he looked a little winded!—and eyed the complex with narrowed eyes.

"This your new place?"

"Yeah." She pulled the rubber band from her hair and redid her ponytail. *Leave. Just leave. Please don't ask—*

"Mind if I come up and see it?"

Her chest expanded with the slow breath she drew in, but she forced a small smile.

"Not at all. Come on up." She turned away from him, her pulse quickening and her mouth drying out.

This wasn't happening. It just couldn't be. She'd successfully avoided him for months now, hoping he'd take the hint.

And yet here he was, about to step foot into her new apartment.

She was all too aware of how close he stood behind her as they reached her door, and her fingers trembled as she grabbed her key from the pocket of her shorts.

"You okay there?" His question feathered across her ear and she winced, overshooting the keyhole and scratching the wooden frame.

"I'm fine." She clenched her teeth and directed the key into its target location with more force than necessary.

With a silent harrumph to celebrate her success, she twisted the handle and pushed the door open.

Justin followed her inside, his gaze moving around the average-sized apartment with open curiosity.

Her furnishings were sparse, just the one love seat and kitchen table she'd had when she'd lived at his house. Jesus, it seemed like just yesterday. And, at the same time, it seemed like a millennium.

His gaze followed her as she tossed her keys onto the table and walked to the kitchen.

The soft curve of her ass swished beneath the nylon shorts she wore, her bare, tanned legs stretched out beneath the hem.

He forced himself to look away from her backside, especially once he felt the familiar rush of blood to his dick.

This is Gabby. You know it's a bad idea. It was a bad idea that one night, and it's still a bad idea.

23

Checking out women was hardly anything new for him. He loved women and everything about them. Their softness, the sway of hips in their walk, the smell of them, the enticing sounds they made when he found just the right spot to—

"Do you want some water?"

He blinked and thrust a hand into his hair. "Yeah. Thanks, Gab."

If he hadn't been staring at her back, he might have missed the tensing in her shoulder. She sounded normal, uttering a breezy, "No problem."

His brows drew together and he bit back a sigh. She obviously felt uncomfortable around him. Damn it. Why?

She turned from the sink and left the small kitchen, the glass of water outstretched in her hand.

"So, what have you been up to?" she asked, her gaze avoiding his.

The moment he took the glass from her, she moved past him into the living room a few feet away.

"Working." He followed her to the love seat and sat down. "The normal stuff."

Partying. Dating entirely too many women, yet spending too many nights alone and missing something. Missing Gabby.

She made a barely audible *harrumph*, but when he glanced up, her expression was carefully blank. That was odd, she never hid her emotions from him. And yet, from the moment he'd run into her in the store this morning, she'd had one big wall up.

He took a long drink of water and then set the half-empty glass on her coffee table. He stared straight ahead for a moment, debating what to say. He was here in her apartment. Damn it, he needed to say *some*thing.

"So, why'd you move out the way you did?"

Gabby spit her water back into her glass and coughed. "Excuse me?"

"You're stalling. Why can't you just answer the question?"

"Justin…" She set her glass down on the table next to his and offered an abrupt shrug. "We'd discussed the possibility I'd be moving out—"

"Someday in the nowhere-near future," he said tersely. "The deal was we'd shake up the living arrangement when one of us got serious with someone we were seeing."

She gave a soft laugh, but it didn't hold humor. "Right. And we both know you're not the type to get serious."

Tension rolled through his muscles and his jaw flexed. He turned in the seat to look at her. "What does that mean?"

Pink filled her cheeks and she swallowed hard. "Nothing, Justin. I wasn't being serious."

"You wouldn't have said it if you didn't mean it."

"Look, please forget I said it. I was just kidding."

But she hadn't been. At least not entirely. He drew in an unsteady breath, his head swirling with the memories of all the time they'd spent together.

Both of them had dated a lot, had rarely held a relationship that lasted longer than a couple of months. They'd discussed their dating habits many times. Had laughed about it.

And yet, this time she'd flung the words at him as an accusation—there'd been no teasing.

His gaze dropped to where her hands were fisted on her lap. Impulsively, he reached out and caught her wrist, sliding his fingers downward to force her hand open again and then holding it. It was a gesture that wasn't uncommon for them, and yet she attempted to pull her hand free.

"Look at me, Gab."

Her shoulders rose with the deep breath she dragged in, and then she tilted her head to give him a sideways glance. Her eyes were carefully schooled. He knew that look. She'd come to poker night too many times with the guys for him to not recognize that *you won't get shit out of me* look.

"I want you to be completely honest with me," he said quietly and tightened his grip on her hand—her dainty, soft hand. His brows drew together. Had her hands always been this feminine?

"Okay." She arched an eyebrow. "Are you going to ask it?"

He shook his head, wondering how the hell she was managing to get him so damn flustered.

"Yeah. I'm gonna ask it," he said gruffly and then focused his attention on her face again. "Did you move out because of that night?"

The only sign that he'd shocked her was the slight widening of her eyes. But then she narrowed them just as quickly and a sardonic grin slipped across her mouth.

"That night? Ah, Justin, you're going to have to be a lot more specific than that. We lived together for a couple of years."

"Damn it, Gab. Don't pull that crap on me. Anyone else might buy it, but I don't." He scowled. "You know exactly which night I'm talking about."

Her fingers arched against his hand, but he didn't loosen his grip. The slight smell of sweat from their run lingered in the room, with the overlying scent of her lotion. Some melon thing she'd worn the entire time he'd known her. It had never seemed seductive before, but now...

She lowered her gaze from his and her tongue swept across her bottom lip before retreating safely back into her mouth.

Desire stirred low in his groin and his next breath in wasn't quite as steady. Jesus. He still wanted her. The idea rocked him to his core.

Bad idea, Justin.

"Are you telling me—" He leaned forward and caught her chin, his face just inches from hers. *Very bad idea, Justin.* "—that you don't remember this?"

The need to remind her of that night consumed him. Her eyes widened in trepidation, just before he lowered his mouth down onto hers.

So soft. So sweet.

When she would have pushed him away, he moved his palm to her back and held her still, moving his mouth against hers.

Half a year. How had he gone a half a year without her? And why had it taken two years for them to reach this level of intimacy?

His tongue teased the crease of her mouth open, and then slid inside to taste her.

The angry sound she made morphed into a frustrated moan and finally one of surrender. Her tongue moved out to meet his—almost angry in the bold strokes she made to tease him.

Justin's blood pounded through his veins. His entire being focused on the smell of her, the press of her breasts against his chest, and the soft sounds she made as she kissed him back. Sounds that alternated between pleasure and frustration.

Her hands slid up to his shoulders to wrap around his neck, pressing her body snugger against his. The scrape of her hardened nipples against his chest sent another rush of blood to his cock, bringing it fully erect. He groaned, grateful for his loose running pants.

He explored her mouth thoroughly, teasing the hidden spots before returning to spar with her tongue. His hands, which had been resting on her waist, slid up her ribcage to just under her breasts.

He barely hesitated before sweeping his thumbs up to stroke over the tight peaks of her breasts. He lifted his lips from hers just a fraction to allow her strangled gasp, before he captured her mouth again.

All rational thoughts on why he'd come here tonight—*because it couldn't have been for this, could it?*—abandoned his mind. The need to touch her naked skin, to taste the salty sweet softness of her flesh, swept through him.

He deepened the kiss, caught her nipple between two fingers and pinched, all while easing her onto her back on the couch. It was a move he'd mastered in years of seducing women.

Tonight it failed.

Gabby wrenched her mouth from his, shoving him so hard he fell off her and onto the floor.

"*Stop.*" She scurried off the couch and across the room from him. "What was that, Justin? What the hell *was* that?"

He winced, picking himself up from the floor. His balls ached and his dick still throbbed with the need to be buried inside her. Inside...Gabby. *Shit.*

His stomach clenched and he thrust a hand through his hair. Her question was a good one. What the hell *had* he been doing? Seeking out a repeat performance for the night that had likely killed their friendship?

Feeling like the biggest ass on the planet, he lifted his gaze to look at her. Her nipples were outlined against her tight shirt, her lips swollen, and her eyes held a mix of anger, desire and...fear.

"Gabby—"

"If you set out to prove that I want to screw you silly, then congratulations, Justin." Her laughter sounded a bit unsteady and she folded her arms in a protective gesture across her breasts. "Fine. I want you. I won't apologize for that or deny it."

The air in his lungs refused to leave. His chest tightened.

Gabby wanted him too. Gabby—

"But there's no way in hell I'm going to act on it," she finished flatly. "Because that would make me stupid."

Chapter Three

Gabby watched the myriad of emotions flicker across his face. Surprise, disbelief, and then finally annoyance.

Of course he was annoyed. Justin wasn't the type of guy who got turned down.

Disappointment burned in her stomach, but she refused to dwell on it. Even as her swollen breasts ached from his brief touch and the promise of so much more. So much she could never accept from him. Friendship, yes. A sexual relationship? No. *Hell no.*

"I don't understand." His jaw flexed. "I didn't set out to prove anything, Gab. I didn't plan for any of this. But since you're being so damn blunt, I think I'll just return the favor."

Her pulse jumped in anticipation of what blunt could mean with him. "Please, don't—"

"I want you, too. I want you in a way I haven't wanted a woman—"

"Stop right there, Justin."

"I *can't.*" He stood abruptly and lifted his hand toward her.

She flinched and reared back from him. Her face burned as she realized what she'd done.

Surprise swept across his face and then confusion. He lowered his hand and didn't stop her as she moved a step backward.

"Did you think I was going to hit you?" he asked, disbelief thick in his tone.

"No." Her cheeks warmed further. "No, of course not."

He didn't look convinced by her response; his brows still remained knit together.

"Gabby? What am I missing here? Why are you so afraid to take this thing between us to the next level?"

"Because I can't trust you!"

Her hoarse words hung in the air—increasing that invisible barrier between them. She could've sworn she saw a flicker of hurt on his face, but then it was gone.

"How can you not trust me? Jesus, Gab, you know me inside and out. I considered you my best friend—"

"That's just it," she said quietly and closed her eyes briefly. She hadn't wanted to go here with him. Hadn't wanted to have to admit it. "I *do* know you, Justin. I know you entirely too well."

"Please don't tell me you're going to give me some crap line about how sleeping with me would be like sleeping with your brother?"

"No!" She laughed and some of the tension left her body at his ridiculous question. "I wouldn't have been all over you like white on rice a minute ago if I remotely had that brother vibe while kissing you."

A smug smile flitted across his face before he straightened it and cleared his throat.

"Okay, so what's the problem? Why don't you trust me?"

"Because I know how you are with women." She turned away and walked back into the kitchen. There was no way she would let him see the vulnerability she knew would be naked on her face. It was an effort to keep her words light. "You sleep with a woman for a few weeks...maybe even a month or two, and then it's over. You move on."

"Gabby..."

"I don't want to be one of those women, Justin. I won't."

There was no response right away. Was he mad? Disappointed? She stared out the small window in the kitchen and drew her bottom lip between her teeth.

"I don't know why you're casting stones from a glass house," he finally said. "In the two years we lived together, you never once had a long-term relationship."

"Maybe not," she admitted. "But there were a helluva lot more women passing through the house than men, Justin."

"Not that many more."

She turned, startled at the sudden tightness in his words.

When she looked at him again, his expression had turned surly and his hands were shoved into his pockets.

"What, did you keep track or something?"

He didn't reply, which sent a wave of butterflies through her stomach. He wouldn't have kept tabs on the men she'd dated, would he? By all appearances, he'd barely noticed when she did date different guys.

"We're more alike than you think. I don't see how it could hurt to just see where this thing between us goes."

Why did he keep pressing? Her pulse sped up and she ran her tongue over her lips. No way. It was simply too crazy to contemplate.

Twice now Justin had touched her in a way that went beyond platonic. That was two times she'd gotten swept away on a rush of desire, but more so, had felt the tugging at her heart. Of wanting to let someone in. Lord, he already had one foot into the door of her heart, having been her best friend.

But Justin was not a man she could fall in love with. She just couldn't. It wouldn't end right at all. The best-case scenario, she'd end up with a broken heart. The worst case...she'd end up like her mother.

"I'm sorry, Justin. I won't risk our friendship."

"Friendship? What the hell friendship is that, Gab?" His words turned harsh. "You moved out like some damn felon on the run. Don't return my calls, my emails. It was sheer luck I ran into you at the market today. What kind of friendship do we have exactly?"

He was right. His words sent stabs of guilt into her gut and she knew it was mirrored on her face.

"You pretty much blew off our friendship six months ago." He paused. "What are you running from?"

You. The possibility of us. The words lingered thick on her tongue and she was hesitant to say them aloud. Fortunately, she didn't have to.

The firm knock had them both glancing toward the door to her apartment.

He glanced back at her. "Are you expecting someone?"

Gabby drew in an unsteady breath and gave a slight nod. "Yes. I have a...I'm going out tonight."

Understanding dawned in his eyes and he rocked back on

his heels.

"I see."

She swallowed hard, knowing there was no reason for her to feel guilty. Absolutely none. She had the right to date whoever she wanted. So why did she feel like the biggest witch right now?

Another knock came from the front door—sharper this time.

"I need to get that," she muttered and moved toward the door.

Justin turned to follow after her. "I'll leave."

She winced, but didn't protest. It wasn't as if she could invite him to dinner with her and Steve.

Before opening the door, she turned to face Justin again.

"I'm sorry," she said quietly.

His gaze darkened and lingered on her lips. "I'm not."

Another heated flush swept through her. There was no doubt just what he wasn't sorry for.

He leaned forward and his breath feathered against her ear.

"And I won't be sorry next time, either." His lips brushed her ear, sending a rush of shivers down her spine. "Remember that, Gabby."

She stepped back, his bold promise making her unsteady as her hand wrapped around the knob of the front door.

"Just go," she whispered, and then tugged open the door.

Steve stood on the other side of the door, still dressed in his suit and tie from his day job. His eyes widened in surprise at Justin, who strode past, giving Steve a curt nod before disappearing down the hall.

"Who was that, Gabrielle?"

"An old friend," she said with a forced smile. "We used to be roommates. We just went jogging together to catch up."

Steve stepped into her apartment, his brows drawn together in a frown. "You lived with him?"

"Yes. No need to worry, we were just good friends." *Until six months ago.*

She kept that little bit to herself.

"All right then." Steve's expression relaxed and he smiled. "I've been looking forward to seeing you all day."

She'd completely forgotten about their date tonight. And

when he leaned in to kiss her, she turned her head so that his lips brushed across her cheek harmlessly.

"I'm sorry," she stuttered, knowing he would get suspicious. "I'm still all sweaty from my run. Do you mind if I grab a quick shower?"

"Not at all." He straightened with a nod and loosened his tie. "I'll just sit and watch the news."

Of course. The news. Who watched the news when the game was about to come on? Justin would have considered it a crime to pick the news over the game. And she totally would have to agree.

Oh, God, what was she thinking? This was not about Justin. This was about Steve. A respectable man with a stable job. Who made it very clear he wasn't looking for anything temporary. This man wanted long term. He was the kind of man most women wanted to marry. He was everything Justin wasn't.

"All right." She bit back a sigh. "Help yourself to anything to drink. I'll be out in a few."

"Thanks, Gabrielle."

She went into the bathroom and shut the door, letting her head fall against the wooden frame.

This was a mess. A total mess. After months of trying to move forward and get her life in order, she'd finally come to the point where she'd wanted to change, wanted to have her first stable relationship. But now that was all shot to hell.

Justin had managed to firmly plant himself back in her life—and worse yet, her heart.

The next morning, Justin went into work with a bitter taste in his mouth and a headache that wouldn't quit. He almost wished it were something as simple as a hangover, but no, it was a helluva lot more complex.

Or then again, maybe it was a hangover of sorts. A hangover from his encounter with Gabby last night.

He should have known she'd be dating someone else. Someone new. But what was up with the guy in the suit? In the years he'd know Gabby, he never would have pegged her to get involved with someone so...so damn starched looking.

As Justin had left her apartment, the man had stared at

him like his constipation pill had just kicked in.

What could she possibly see in him?

Stability.

The word sent another wave of bitterness up his throat. Gabby wasn't about stability. She was about having fun. Or at least she used to be.

When she'd been melting in his arms last night, it had seemed perfect. What he'd kept telling himself was a bad idea suddenly seemed like the perfect solution.

They were two of kind. The fact that they hadn't fallen into bed earlier was a damn shame. One he intended to remedy. The question was how to convince Gabby.

"Hey, boss, need you to check out something on the site."

Justin glanced up as Henry, one of his electricians, appeared in the doorway.

"You okay, boss?"

"Yeah. Sorry. Got a lot on my mind." He sighed, trying to clear his head from all thoughts of Gabby.

"Whatever you did, send her flowers."

"What?" Justin glanced sharply at the older man.

"Send the girl flowers. She'll get over it." The other man grinned. "It's been working for me for the last twenty years."

"How do you know it's a girl problem?"

"It's always a girl problem. Unless it's a boy problem."

Justin sighed in exasperation and scowled. "It's not a boy problem."

Henry laughed. "Didn't think so. Not with your reputation."

"Do I have a reputation?"

The smile wiped from Henry's face and he cleared his throat. "No. No, course you don't." His gaze darted back outside the trailer.

Justin grabbed a hard hat and put it on with a sigh. Apparently he *did* have a reputation.

Twenty minutes later he returned to his trailer. Between the problem with the wiring and Gabby, it was just too much to deal with without his cup of morning Joe. He went to the coffee pot to pour himself a cup.

"I would have gotten that for you."

He glanced up to see his secretary, Haley, standing in the doorway, notepad in one hand and a pen in the other.

34

"Thanks, no need." He gave her a brief smile and glanced away.

He'd been extra careful lately not to encourage the woman. Haley had never come right out and said anything to him, but she made it very clear in other non-verbal ways that she'd be open to visiting with him outside a construction zone.

The idea held little appeal to him, though. Odd, since she was an attractive woman who seemed nice enough.

And it wasn't just Haley. For a while now, no woman had seemed to grab his interest.

"I was just about to make a lunch run to that Greek restaurant down the road," Haley said, watching him from beneath her lashes. "Want anything?"

"Thanks. I'll pass."

"You sure? They're fabulous."

"I'm not big on Greek food. Thanks, though."

Greek food screwed with his digestive system. Gabby had known that, which was great, since she couldn't stand the stuff either.

His chest tightened at the thought of her. He needed to do something to show that he wouldn't give up. Something to show her how much she meant to him. Maybe Henry was right and he should send some flowers.

The idea fell flat in his head. Gabby wasn't a flowers type of woman. She'd always made cracks about how guys were so predictable and boring with their methods of wooing.

If anything, flowers would just annoy her further.

Unless... An idea popped into his head and he grabbed his car keys, deciding it was time to take his lunch break.

"You've got flowers."

Gabby glanced up from her computer, her brows snapping together as she stared at the flower-loaded vase Phoebe held out to her.

"Flowers?"

Guilt had her gut clenching. Poor Steve. He was probably trying to make amends after last night. Hoping she'd change her mind.

Seeing Justin again had put her on the edge all night.

She'd snapped at Steve more than once, getting really bitchy when he'd tried to engage her in a conversation about the stock market.

Ugh. Who talked about the stock market over a dinner celebrating their five-month anniversary? Then again, who made big deals over monthly anniversaries?

Well, maybe some people did, but she certainly wasn't one of them. And then he'd brought up that *one* thing that had really killed it for her...

Gabby held out her hands to accept the vase from Phoebe, wishing she were the type to appreciate flowers more.

"I wish someone would send me flowers," Delanie murmured. "Lucky girl."

"What, the senator doesn't send you flowers?" Gabby drawled, mentioning Delanie's recent high-profile love interest.

Delanie rolled her eyes and turned back to her computer. "If he does, I'm sure they're picked out by his secretary. Nothing like what you got."

It wasn't until Gabby held the flowers in her hand that she realized it wasn't your average vase.

"Oh my gosh." She set them on the desk and pressed her fingers to her lips, giggling. "These flowers are in a beer mug."

Phoebe smiled. "Yeah, you just noticed? I couldn't stop laughing when I signed for them."

Gabby leaned forward and sniffed the white mini carnations popping out of the mug that gave the appearance of beer head—she had to give him props for being creative with the vase and flower choice.

"You know," she murmured. "I never would have pegged Steve to send such a fun bouquet of flowers."

"Maybe he didn't," Delanie suggested suddenly.

Gabby gave her friend a skeptical glance and reached for the attached card.

"Nobody else..." she trailed off, her nail pausing in its unsealing of the envelope. Her pulse quickened.

No. He wouldn't have. Would he?

She slid her nail all the way across and popped up the fold of the envelope so she could retrieve the card.

He would.

Phoebe gave a soft laugh. "Judging by your expression, I'm

going to guess they're not from Steve."

"No. They're not."

"The old roommate?" Delanie asked, her face lighting up.

"Yeah. I don't get it."

There was a knock on the door and the receptionist peeked her head in.

"Delanie, you have Amelia from the safe house in the other room waiting to talk with you. Do you want me to tell her it will be a few minutes?"

"No, thanks, Laurie. Tell her I'll be right there." Delanie sighed and stood up from her desk. She gave Gabby a pointed look. "I want to hear everything when I get back."

Gabby rolled her eyes and waved her away. "There's nothing to hear."

After Delanie had disappeared, Gabby glanced back at the card and frowned.

"Okay, wait a minute. It's signed *See you tonight. Justin.*"

"You're going out with him tonight? Hey, you've been holding out on us."

"No! I'm not going out with him. I have no idea what he's even talking about."

She shook her head and dropped the envelope to the desk. Something slid out from the envelope, flat and rectangular.

Her pulse sped up even faster, and she gasped, reaching for it.

"What? What'd you find?" Phoebe peeked over her shoulder. "A ticket?"

"Not just a ticket. A ticket to the Giants game tonight."

"Oh wow. This guy not only sends you flowers in a beer mug, he sends you tickets to a baseball game? Gabby, I do believe you've found your soul mate."

"Stop it," she muttered, smoothing her thumb over the ticket and almost salivating as she recognized the box seats Justin purchased every year. "I shouldn't go."

"Of course you should. And you will. This man *knows* you. He knows you won't be suckered by a dozen roses and the promise of a candlelit dinner. But hot dogs at a baseball game?"

And I'm easy like Sunday morning. Gabby pulled the rubber band from her ponytail and scowled, knowing her friend was right.

"What time's the game?"

"Seven-fifteen."

"Perfect. You'll have plenty of time to get ready once you leave here."

Gabby groaned. "It isn't right, Phoebe. Justin is on my *don't go there* list."

"Why not go there?" Phoebe sat on the edge of Gabby's desk, her lips pursing. "I mean, just who do you think you're convincing anyway? It's so obvious you're hooked on him."

Chapter Four

Gabby's stomach dropped, her throat tightened at Phoebe's all-too-accurate observation. "It doesn't mean anything."

"Sure it does," Phoebe said softly. "And that's why you're fighting it so much."

The phone rang, saving Gabby from answering. Grateful for the interruption, she reached for the receiver. From the corner of her eye, she saw Phoebe slide off her desk and walk back to her own.

She hung up the phone a minute later and sighed.

"Bad news."

Phoebe glanced up from the paperwork she was going through and lifted an eyebrow.

"How bad?"

"That was Lacy from down at the safe house. Becky Martinez went back to her husband this afternoon."

"No." Phoebe's face crumpled with devastation and she leaned her elbows on the desk, burying her head in her hands. "Oh God. We try so hard to help them..."

"Hey." Gabby stood up and crossed to her friend's desk.

The helplessness and bitter disappointment hit her hard, but not as much as it did Phoebe, being that she was an abuse survivor. She didn't know much about Phoebe's past, only that she'd been in a bad relationship in her college years and it was why she'd come to work for Second Chances.

She placed a hand on Phoebe's shoulder and said quietly, "You know how hard this is. Sometimes it takes a couple of times. The good news is we'll still be here when she wants to come back."

"If. If she comes back," Phoebe said thickly. "Good God. When she first came in here… I'm surprised she only had a few scars."

"I know."

Second Chances had a registered nurse working for them, but Loretta's injuries had been at the point of her needing to be admitted to the hospital. She'd adamantly refused when the gentle offer had been made to take her there.

"I'm sorry." She squeezed Phoebe's shoulder again.

"I know." Phoebe nodded and lifted her head, her smile weak and her eyes watery with obvious tears of frustration. "Thanks, Gabby."

"No problem. Can I get you some water? Chocolate? Anything?"

"Well, there is one thing."

"Anything," Gabby said fervently. "I'll drive down to Ghirardelli's and get you the biggest—"

"I don't want chocolate." Phoebe rolled her eyes and gave a soft laugh. "I just want you to promise me something."

"What's that?"

"Promise me you'll go to the game with Justin tonight."

Gabby's stomach flipped with butterflies. "Are you sure you don't just want the chocolate?"

Phoebe narrowed her eyes. "Come on. It's not like you weren't going to go anyway."

"You're right." Gabby walked back to her desk and picked up the ticket, sliding it between her thumb and forefinger. "I can't say no to the Giants, you know that too well."

And so did Justin, which meant it looked like her fate for the night was sealed.

She sat back in her chair, refreshed her email and hoped she wasn't making a very stupid decision. She'd settle for semi-stupid though.

Justin lifted his painfully overpriced beer and took a swig, shaking his head.

She wasn't going to show. The game was just minutes away from starting and Gabby had yet to make an appearance.

Disappointment clenched his gut and he cursed under his

breath, reaching for his beer.

She must have been serious about keeping her distance from him—he'd never known her to miss a game before. Especially when it was a free ticket.

He'd known it was a risk, that she might very well chuck his flowers—which would be a damn shame since they'd been like the anti- flowers bouquet—and not use the ticket.

The hype of the game kicked off as the players ran onto the field and the announcer began calling their names.

Shit. He glanced at his watch and sighed.

"This seat taken?"

Tension rolled through his body and he jerked his head up, shielding his gaze from the setting sun with his hand.

"Didn't think you were going to come," he admitted gruffly and let his gaze rove over her. Her silhouette showed a toned body, the jeans and pink tank top showing the soft side of her curves.

"You know me better than that." She sat down onto the seat next to him and lifted one eyebrow, her mouth pursed. "You play dirty, Justin. You knew the minute you put that ticket for tonight's game in there, you'd hook me."

"I'd hoped."

She'd left her hair down under the white and pink Giants cap. The reddish blonde waves fell around her face, softening her look from the usual braids or high ponytail she wore.

Her lips were shiny with gloss and the realization surprised him. Gabby had rarely worn makeup when they'd lived together. She'd never needed to, though.

But tonight, everything about her indicated that she'd made an extra effort with her appearance.

He met her eyes again and saw both nervousness and maybe excitement. Their gazes locked and her expression grew more nervous. Her tongue swept across glossy lips as her attention skittered to the baseball field.

"Traffic was awful, or I would have been here sooner."

"You haven't missed anything. They only just announced tonight's lineup."

"Oh good." Some of the tension visibly eased in her shoulders and a smile curved her mouth. "This is going to be a good game."

"It is." He tore his gaze from her and glanced out over the field. "I'm glad you came."

"Thanks for the ticket..." she hesitated, "...and the flowers."

"I know you're not a flowers fan—"

"No, they were great. Phoebe and I got a kick out of them. I would never have guessed they even made flowers like that." She bit her lip, appearing to want to say more. "I'm...I should just make sure you realize—I'm here tonight as your friend, Justin. Nothing more."

"That's only because we haven't actually become lovers yet," he couldn't resist teasing. Though, if he admitted it, he was pretty much serious.

Her eyes widened and flickered with both disbelief and amusement.

"You're terrible." She shook her head, but her words were spoken on a laugh.

"How was your date with the suit last night?"

"I thought we were here to watch the game."

"I'm watching." He lifted the beer to his mouth and took another sip, his lips twitching.

The first player from the opposing team went up to bat and they both went silent, switching into game-watching mode.

They clapped and screamed, encouraging the pitcher, who immediately threw three strikes. The batter walked from the field, kicking the ground in disgust.

"He has a name, you know," Gabby said as they watched the next batter make his way to home plate.

"Who does?"

"The suit. It's Steve."

Justin gave a slight nod, keeping his eyes on the player at bat.

"When did you meet him? Obviously—Yeah! That's two!" His attention shifted briefly as the pitcher threw another strike. "Less than six months ago. Unless you were dating him when..."

She glanced at him sharply. "When I lived with you? No. I met him the month after I moved out."

His muscles tensed and he was careful to draw in a slow breath. Five months? For either of them, that was almost considered a long-term relationship.

He just barely managed to bite his tongue before he could ask if she'd slept with him. That was not his business—and Gabby would probably tell him as much in a very non-polite way.

"Oh damn!" She groaned as the batter hit a pop fly into centerfield.

"He'll catch it." His confidence was proven when the centerfielder caught the fly ball with little effort. "What happened to your faith in our team, girl?"

He nudged Gabby lightly in the ribs and she laughed and gave him a soft swat on the shoulder. It was so familiar. So much how they'd used to be. He missed it. Missed her.

"I have plenty of faith in our team. It's just been a while since I've been to a game."

Over six months, he'd wager. Seeing as he'd always been the one to bring her.

"I'm going to grab a beer real quick."

Justin urged her back into her seat when she tried to stand. "I'll grab you one. Sorry, I should have offered earlier."

Her brows puckered. "I can get it, Justin, it's no problem."

"I invited you here tonight, Gab. I'll get your beer." He stood up and moved past her, giving her bare arm a quick squeeze.

The minute his fingers touched her soft skin, his chest locked. The blood rushed south in his body and his gaze dropped to the soft curve of her breasts barely peeking above the tank top. Her nipples showed tight through the thin fabric.

She inhaled quickly and flashed him a brief smile, sliding her arm away from him.

"Thanks, Justin. I appreciate it."

"No problem." He clenched his fists and strode up the stairs to the concessions.

Some things felt the same between them, but others were brand spanking new. Like the mutual attraction. Would he ever get used to it? And even more so, could he convince her acting on it was the right thing to do?

This was such a bad idea. Gabby tucked a strand of hair behind her ear and then pressed her palm against her belly, which seemed to be making somersaults with her lunch.

Sitting next to Justin, having his hard thigh brushing

against hers and smelling his familiar aftershave, was making her mind and hormones go into complete twitter mode.

She should never have promised Phoebe she'd go to the game tonight. What had she been thinking? Besides—*Homerun!*

Gabby rose to her feet, screaming and clapping along with the rest of the stadium as the batter knocked one out of the ballpark.

Excitement bubbled through her veins and she gave another loud scream of support.

"Ah, damn, I missed a homerun?"

"Yes! It was awesome, too." She took the beer he handed her and, still buzzing on excitement, pressed a kiss to his cheek.

They both tensed, and when she finally thought to pull away, he'd already slid a hand around her waist to hold her close.

She dragged in an uneasy breath and closed her eyes. Every inch of her aware of how hard his body was against her softness. Her knees went weak and she gripped his forearm, biting back a sigh when he nuzzled her hair.

The crack of the ball connecting with the bat resounded before the crowd exploded with excitement.

Justin pulled back from her, muttering a barely audible curse.

She sank back down into her seat, her hand shaking slightly as she took a sip of the beer. *It was just a hug, Gabby, calm yourself.*

Despite her internal pep talk, she knew how delusional she was. That hug had been loaded with familiarity, sexual tension, and oddly enough, tenderness.

The rest of the game passed in a blur, a mild distraction, but nowhere near the intense eye candy she was used to it being. No, her mind was somewhere else completely. Leftfield, just not in the baseball sense.

"I don't suppose I could convince you to go get something to eat?" Justin asked as they filed out of the stadium with thousands of fans.

She hesitated, but her stomach gave a soft growl at the idea of food. Salty peanuts somehow hadn't qualified as dinner.

She just didn't want this to turn into a date. Or maybe it

already had. Biting her lip, she gave a quick nod and figured out how to make it less date-like. "Sure. I can buy."

"Not a chance."

"It's only fair. You bought the tickets."

"I have season tickets. I had to bring someone."

Her lips twisted. Of course. When she'd first met him years back in school, the season tickets had been one way he'd weeded out his women. If a girl couldn't get down with a Giants game, she didn't last very long.

At some point, he'd stopped bringing other women on dates and he'd just started taking her. Not that she'd had any problem with that. Hell, it had been a free baseball game with her best friend. But then they'd barreled past that *do not cross* line and everything had just turned damn complicated.

Sitting next to him tonight, she'd almost felt like one of the girls he'd dated from all those years ago. The best friend status was a memory that drifted further away each time Justin gave her one of those *I wonder what you'd look like naked* looks.

"Okay, we can do Italian or greasy spoon. Those are the only two places I know that'll still be open and serving food."

"Italian," she answered without even considering the other option. "I'm totally down with some pasta."

"Still a garlic freak?"

"Heck, yeah. I'm no vamp."

"You're a total vamp," he murmured, and caught her hand to pull her back from a particularly rowdy group of fans barreling through the gates.

Gabby's stomach tightened and she gave a flat laugh—not like Justin could hear it over the screaming fans. His comment had most likely been a joke. Her a vamp? As in sexy, femme fatale? Not freaking likely.

When was the last time she'd worn a dress? Probably her cousin's wedding years ago. She almost regretted putting on the small amount of makeup tonight. It meant she was trying. Trying to impress Justin.

"Why don't I drive?" he offered. "We can come back for your car after we eat."

She gave a short nod and her heart skipped when his fingers tightened around hers. Why was he still holding her hand?

It doesn't matter. This wasn't sexual. It wasn't romantic. It was just two friends hanging out.

Right.

Justin opened the door to his truck and she climbed up easily, all too used to riding up front with him.

"So how come you had an extra ticket tonight?" she asked and immediately wanted to kick herself.

"I've had an extra for a while."

His admission had her eyebrows lifting. Did he honestly expect her to believe that he hadn't taken random women to the game once she'd stepped out of his life?

"You didn't take anyone?"

"We're only a few months into the season. I brought a co-worker once or twice."

But no women?

"So tell me more about Steven."

Gabby flinched. Why the heck did he have to pick that subject to change to?

"What do you want to know?"

"What does he do?"

"He's an investment banker."

"Interesting."

"Is it?" She glanced at him sharply.

He shrugged and backed out of the parking spot. "If you're into that kind of thing."

"He's a good guy," she said defensively.

"I'm sure he is."

Gabby folded her hands across her chest and cleared her throat. *Don't even ask.* "What about you? Who's your newest girl?"

And you asked. Stupid!

"There isn't one."

Gabby snorted. "No, really. Who is she?"

When he didn't reply, she glanced over at him. His fingers had tightened around the steering wheel and there was a subtle tick in his rigid jawline. He seemed almost embarrassed and maybe even a tad frustrated.

"What's up? You drink an anti-love potion or something?" she attempted to tease him. "Usually you have women crawling all over you. Don't tell me that's changed."

"I won't."

She looked away at his admission. Of course it hadn't. The man was sex personified. He always had—

"They're just not the right woman."

Her heart sped up and her palms dampened. Woman. He'd said woman, versus women. *It doesn't mean anything, Gabby, not a darn thing.*

"How's the job going?" she asked quickly, deciding it was her turn to change the subject.

He gave a soft laugh, almost like he'd known she'd gotten all atwitter by his response.

"The job's good. I'm a construction manager now. Don't know if you knew that or not."

She whipped her head to the side to look at him, her jaw falling open slightly.

"Seriously, Justin? When did this happen?"

"Few months ago." His mouth curved into a smile, and she could see how proud he was.

"That's fabulous! You didn't think that'd happen for another year or two at least."

"I know."

"Justin," she squealed and reached out to pat his leg, her excitement for him momentarily making her forget the wisdom of her move.

"Thanks, Gab. I knew you'd be excited for me." His hand covered hers and squeezed, trapping her palm against the muscles of his thigh.

Tingles of awareness rocketed through her body and, instead of pulling her hand free like she really knew she should, her fingers flexed against his leg.

"You deserve the position. You worked your ass off to get that bachelor's degree."

He didn't reply, but his thumb brushed across the back of her hand.

"We've both really kind of stepped it up this year career-wise, huh?" she murmured.

He nodded and pulled the truck into the parking lot of a small restaurant nearby.

People milled around outside, waiting to get seated. Apparently they weren't the only ones who'd had the idea to grab food.

"Hmm," Justin's brows drew together and his mouth twisted. "I don't suppose I could talk you into letting me cook you something back at my place?"

She drew in a slow breath. The idea both had appeal and shot off every warning signal in her body.

"Doug would love to see you."

"Doug…" Her mouth curved into a smile. "Oh, man, do I miss him. How's he doing?"

Justin snorted. "Pain in my ass."

Gabby nudged him in the ribs with her elbow. "He is not. You love that dog."

He grunted in response, but she could see the fondness in his eyes. Loved his dog was an understatement. There was no word to describe how much Justin cared for the mutt they'd found barely alive on the side of the road a year ago.

"So, what do you say?" he asked again. "I don't think we'd even find parking here, let alone get a table anytime soon."

"Justin…"

"It's only dinner, Gab. We can do quesadillas and Doritos."

Just like the old times. She folded her hands in her lap and glanced out the window. *Such a bad idea, Gabby. Say no. Tell him—*

"Okay."

Chapter Five

From the corner of her eye, she saw some of the tension ease from his body and the smile flit across his face. He threw the truck in reverse and backed out of the parking lot.

A few minutes later they were speeding down the highway toward Justin's house and the place she'd called home for two years.

By the time they pulled up in front of his house, Green Day was playing on the radio and they'd passed the time discussing the game.

Before she could grab her purse off the floor and open her door, Justin had already climbed out to do it for her. That was one thing she'd always appreciated about him. His manners. He'd been raised by his grandparents—southerners who'd moved to San Francisco—and from all accounts, they'd made certain their grandson knew how to treat a lady.

"Thanks," Gabby murmured, taking the hand he offered to help her down.

At the brush of his fingers against hers, more tingles swept through her and a warm heat grew low in her belly.

"Come on. I want to show you something." He didn't release her hand, just tugged her along after him as he bypassed the front door and took her into the backyard.

The gate swung shut behind them, banging loudly, but she barely noticed as her gaze swept the scene in front of her, lit up by a nearby street lamp.

"Oh my God, you've been busy."

"Well, I hired a landscaper," he confessed, squeezing her hand. "The new position left me with a little extra money."

"Justin, you can see...you've got a *view* of the city!"

"A little one." His grin expanded until he looked like an excited kid. "I was thinking about adding some kind of fountain back in the corner there. And I'm already checking into getting the hot tub repaired."

"I still owe you for that," she muttered, guilt clenching in her belly at the memory of that summer night. "I told Vic not to bring the beer bottle in with us, but he snuck it in anyway."

Justin's fingers tightened around hers for a moment, but then he gave a short laugh. "No problem. The thing is so old, it may just need to be replaced."

Gabby snuck a glance at him, wondering briefly if she'd imagined the bite of jealousy in his tone. But that would be silly. She'd dated Vic for two weeks, tops.

A low and familiar bark came from inside the house, growing more frantic by the moment.

"I think Doug figured out you're here," Justin stated sardonically, one of his fingers doing a light and feathery caress over her inner palm. "If I don't bring you inside, he may just bust through a window."

A shiver slipped down her spine and she bit her lip to keep from sighing. Damn. Why did her body heat and respond to him the minute he touched her? It took away all control, made her feel all too helpless to this impossible attraction toward Justin.

"Well, we shouldn't keep him waiting then." She pulled her hand free, knowing she'd do something stupid if she let him hold it a second longer, and walked quickly toward the house.

At the back door, she waited, keeping her gaze lowered to avoid meeting his questioning glance.

His keys jingled as he unlocked the door. He'd barely pushed open the solid wood door when Doug came bounding out.

His fat paws slapped against her chest, nearly knocking her down. Fortunately, Justin moved back to catch her.

"Doug! Easy boy," she cried in between giggles. The mutt, a cross between a black lab and a St. Bernard, ignored her and continued to bounce around her, swiping her with big sloppy kisses.

"All right, Doug. Let her catch her breath." Justin snagged the dog's collar and pulled him away gently. "You can go inside, Gab. I'll let him run around outside for a second."

Still breathless from laughing, she hurried into the house

and pulled her baseball cap off, setting it on the dryer.

Her glance drifted around the laundry room before she walked down the hallway that led to the kitchen. The sink only had a few dishes in it, what looked to be from this morning.

She snorted and shook her head.

He'd always done that. Left the dishes until before he went to bed. She, on the other hand, couldn't stand a dish just hanging out in the sink. Because, come on, how long did it take to just rinse the plate off and shove it in the dishwasher?

Heavy footsteps on the wooden floor announced Justin's entrance into the house. She held her breath, glad her back was to him.

"Doug misses you."

She gave a soft laugh and some of the tension eased from her shoulders. Doug padded past them and into the living room.

"I miss you too."

Inhaling sharply, she closed her eyes at his surprising confession. Why was he doing this? Pushing this? Didn't he know how close she was to breaking? To just giving in to this pull between them?

"I thought we were making quesadillas," she said warily and turned to face him. The intensity on his face made her stomach do back flips and her pulse pick up in a panic. "Justin...maybe me coming here tonight was a bad idea."

"Sorry." He thrust a hand into his hair and shook his head. "Sorry, Gab. Sometimes I just say things without thinking it through. You know me."

Impulsive. Always had been. And it used to be such a fun and endearing quality about him. Now it was almost a hazard.

"I'll grab the tortillas and cheese." He moved past her to pull open the fridge. "You still like pepper jack?"

"Love it." Her focus shifted downward when he squatted to grab something off the bottom shelf. His jeans tightened over his butt and she bit back a groan.

Justin had always had a great ass. That was one of the things all her friends would comment on when they dropped by.

"And to drink I have soda, beer, milk or...water?"

"Water." She'd need to keep her willpower in check tonight. So, definitely no more alcohol. "Too many peanuts at the game."

She turned away, needing to focus on something besides Justin's butt and the butterflies that had taken up residence in her belly. She went in search of the frying pan and placed it on the burner. She flipped on the stovetop and then pulled out a knife from a nearby drawer.

Justin set the block of cheese next to her, his fingers brushing her wrist. More tingles spread through her and she drew in an unsteady breath.

"You okay?"

His soft question brushed against the curve of her ear.

No, she wasn't okay. She hadn't been okay since Justin had showed up in her life again yesterday morning.

"Fine." She forced the word out, knowing it sounded a bit brittle and overly bright.

She took the brick of cheese from him, ignoring the way his lips curved into a knowing smile.

"So, if I told you that I have the ingredients for guacamole, would you make some?" he asked, still standing all too close while he unsealed the bag of tortillas.

"Only if you make your salsa."

"Deal. Though mine's twice as hard to make."

"Hey, you didn't have to agree to my terms."

"I'm a sucker for your guacamole."

"I remember." She finished slicing the cheese and put it away in the fridge. "Okay, where's the avocado?"

"Here. On the windowsill." He leaned past her to grab them.

The familiar smell of his soap and aftershave tickled her nostrils and she closed her eyes, taking a moment to just breathe him in.

His elbow brushed against her breast and the heavy ache low in her belly bloomed into something even hotter. She swallowed hard, her nipples peaking beneath her top.

A barely audible groan escaped her pursed lips, but the way Justin's body went abruptly rigid, she knew he'd heard it.

Maybe it was being back in the house...or likely it was just Justin. But in that moment, it was too much. The desire for him, to let him touch her and to touch him in return. It swept through her like some powerful force of nature.

"Avocado." His unnecessary statement came out hoarse as he dropped the fruit in front of her.

Gabby stared at it for barely as second, before she backhanded the avocado and sent it wobbling to the other end of the counter.

There was a heavy pause before Justin muttered, "You don't want guacamole?"

"No." She turned and he stood so close that her breast brushed his arm again.

Heat flared in his gaze before he looked pointedly at her mouth.

"What *do* you want, Gabby?"

She swallowed hard, turned off the stove, and then reached up to cup his face, letting her thumbs stroke over the stubble on his cheek.

"You know what I want," she whispered, still unable to admit it aloud.

His arm snaked around her waist, pulling her to him a moment before his mouth crushed down on hers

Justin's heart thundered in his chest as the almost crippling desire he had for Gabby consumed him. She was going to let him make love to her. She'd given him the green light.

He slid his hands down to her ass, lifting her, and she immediately wrapped her legs around his hips.

His tongue plunged deep into the warmth of her mouth to explore the hot and moist interior.

The rub of her breasts against his chest had his cock hardening further, nestling snug against the softness of her bottom.

He moved them toward the bedroom, groaning when she sucked his tongue into her mouth and squeezed her thighs tighter around him. He kicked open the half-closed door to his bedroom, then kicked it shut again. He moved them toward his bed, stumbling over his work boots.

He fell onto the bed, rolling to take the brunt of the fall, which brought Gabby on top of him.

Straddling him, she tore her mouth off him and sat up. She reached for the hem of her shirt, jerking it above her head.

The V of her black satin bra pushed her breasts together to display an impressive amount of cleavage. His mouth watered and he lifted his hands to tug away the cups of the bra.

Her pert breasts fell free, the light pink tips already textured and hard for his mouth. She was so damn pretty, sensual in a subtle way. A way most men probably wouldn't discover until they had her naked.

He opened his mouth, needing to tell her how sexy she was.

"What about Steven?" How the hell had he allowed himself to ask that instead?

She gave a soft laugh as she reached up to pinch her nipples lightly. His cock twitched and he drew in a harsh breath at the sight.

"I broke up with him."

"You did? When? Why didn't you say something?" he choked out.

"Last night." She lowered her body downward, until her breasts were just above his face. "At dinner—"

He captured one pink tip between his lips, causing her to break off as he suckled her deep. Christ, she tasted sweet. He smiled, loving the way she gasped and writhed above him.

"At dinner," she continued breathily. "*Oh*...told me why...*oh God*...oral sex could never be part of our relationship. He has a clitoris phobia."

Her nipple popped from his mouth with a loud suctioning sound. He stared at her for a moment, astounded by her statement.

"Are you shitting me?"

She sighed and drew a finger down the center of his chest. "You think someone can make this stuff up?"

"What an idiot," he growled and grasped her hips, rolling her again until she was beneath him.

Her green eyes narrowed slightly as she stared up at him and her tongue swept across swollen lips. "My sentiments exactly. So I immediately ended it."

Justin drew in an unsteady breath, his chest tightening at the playfulness and desire in her gaze.

He ran the palm of his hand over her stomach, taking a moment to dip his finger into her navel.

"You should know that I'm nothing like The Suit, and am actually quite fond of the clitoris." He skimmed his hand across the waistband of the jeans riding low on her hips.

Her stomach rose as she sucked in a breath, her lips curling into a challenging smile. "I know you are."

"You do?" He dipped a finger below the waistband, smoothing it back and forth against her silky skin.

Her hips lifted slightly against his light touch. Further aroused and amused by her response, he moved his hand to cup her pussy through her jeans.

"Mmm. You told me." Her lashes lowered, veiling her gaze. "And I heard you once or twice...with other women. It certainly sounded like you knew what you were doing."

She'd heard him. The idea of it both intrigued him, and yet sent a rush of regret through him.

"Yeah? You didn't get weirded out?"

"No. I got horny," she admitted bluntly with a soft laugh. Her lashes fluttered upward again. "And then later I got jealous."

Justin blinked in surprise, the naked vulnerability in her gaze at her admission momentarily robbing him of response. She had no reason to be jealous. Those times with other women had just been an outlet for the one woman he couldn't have. Gabby.

He hadn't been with another woman since that night with her. He opened his mouth to tell her, but lost all thought when she covered his hand, pressing his palm harder against her swollen sex.

"But I have you right now," she whispered. "And that's all that matters."

The vulnerability that had slipped over her stunned him. It wasn't her. Gabby was a rock. Nothing shook her.

The urge to reassure her rushed through him and he lowered his head to drop a kiss on her stomach. He bracketed her waist with his hands and brushed his lips across her bare flesh.

Her body trembled under his mouth and her fingers slipped into his hair to clutch him.

Dipping his tongue into the crater of her navel, he deftly unsnapped her jeans and tugged down the zipper.

She lifted her hips off the bed and slipped her hands down to help push off her pants.

Justin tugged them the rest of the way down her legs and

tossed them to the ground, never taking his gaze off her. How could he? Damn, she was sexy.

Her skin was pale, dotted with freckles in areas that he'd have a good time kissing. Her slim hips were covered by black satin panties cut high on her thighs and her breasts spilled over her bra.

It wasn't enough. He needed to see all of her. See Gabby completely naked, with no secrets.

Catching the edge of her panties between two fingers, he tugged them down. The curls of her pubic hair sprang free, and he couldn't stop a small groan of excitement.

Once the panties were free from the tangle of her legs, he took a moment to stare down at her. So many women he'd been with had shaved completely, or waxed their pubic hair into something freakishly angular.

And here was Gabby, trimmed just enough, but still all woman. The tight red curls shielding her pussy glistened with her arousal.

"Gabby," he murmured. "You are so damn sexy."

She made a soft sigh and shifted, revealing the darkened pink lips of her labia.

Justin slid up her body, wanting her mouth again. Needing to reassure and have that connection with her again. She was ready for him, sliding her hand into his hair and parting her lips.

His mouth covered hers, the kiss harder this time. More fervent and deep. He slipped one hand down her chest to unsnap the clasp of her bra, tugging the satin free and tossing it aside.

He palmed one breast, moving his hand back and forth over the hardened nipple. His tongue moved against hers as he slipped his knee between her legs to press snug against the wet, swollen mound of her sex.

She gasped raggedly into his mouth and ground her body against him. He sucked her tongue into his mouth, drawing on it while she began a rhythmic grind against his knee.

Her hands slammed into his shoulders, pushing him away.

"Please, oh God, please, Justin," she pleaded, writhing beneath him. "It's too much. I just want you inside me."

He gave a soft laugh and braced himself above her with one

arm. His gaze drifted down her body, now naked and vulnerable to his gaze.

"No way, Gab. No way am I rushing this," he stated huskily and traced a finger from her collarbone down to the curls below her hips. "I refuse to settle for a quickie when this is so damn long overdue between us."

Chapter Six

"You're so stubborn." She gave a pained groan and arched her hips against him.

Possessiveness rushed through him.

"Don't act surprised." He lowered his head to her breast and drew the flat of his tongue over one textured peak. "Mmm. You taste good, Gabby."

"Do I?" She clasped his head between her hands and he watched her eyelids drift shut again. "Mmm. I bet you do, too. Mind if I have a turn?"

"Maybe later." He captured the tip between his teeth and flicked it with his tongue.

Any witty response she might have formed died on her sharply drawn breath.

"Like that do you?" He drew the nipple fully into his mouth and suckled it, alternating hard and then soft.

From the sounds she made and the way her body jerked, it was clear she enjoyed it more when he drew harder.

Wanting the proof of her body's response, he slipped his hand down her stomach and past the springy curls. When he delved one finger into the folds between her legs, hot moisture greeted him.

She gasped, her body clenching around his finger. He lifted his gaze and found her watching him. Her eyes were glazed with pleasure, her gaze moving over his face.

"For so long," she whispered. "I've wanted this. And I knew it was a bad idea, but it didn't matter. I wanted your mouth on me, your fingers inside me."

His chest swelled with a mix of pleasure and

possessiveness at her admission. He lowered his gaze to where his finger slowly penetrated her.

"I've wanted to touch you," he muttered raggedly. "Since about five minutes after you moved into my house."

There was a pause, heavy with shock. "Really? But you never...why didn't you?"

"Because you were my roommate. Became my best friend. I didn't want to fuck that up." He groaned as her body clenched around his finger again. "Jesus, Gab. You're so hot. Wet."

Using his other hand, he parted her labia and exposed the hard button of her clit. His mouth watered at the sight. He wanted to draw it into his mouth, wanted to hear the cries of pleasure she'd make when he sucked on her.

He slid back down her body, dropping kisses on each of her hips before pausing to nuzzle her curls and breathe in the musky scent of her.

Moving lower, he slid his tongue into the slit between her legs. The sweet moisture that fell on his tongue hardened his cock to the point of pain.

He moved his mouth upward, already losing control. He drew her clit into his mouth and gave it one firm suck.

Gabby's hips rose at least an inch off the bed and she cried out. He pushed her back onto the bed and circled the button with his tongue, slow and then fast, pausing to draw on it every few seconds.

She tugged at his hair, both pushing at him and holding him against her. Her thighs tightened around him and he knew she was on the brink. A second later she went rigid and gasped before her body shook beneath him.

He gentled his mouth to a light suckle on her clit, teasing her damp curls with his fingers.

"Please," she begged weakly, tugging his head up. "Justin, please."

Part of him wanted to please her again, bring her to a second orgasm, but the quiet urgency on her face convinced him she needed much more than that at this point.

Her hand closed over his erection through his jeans and cemented his decision.

A soft growl escaped from his throat as he slid back up her body. He brushed his mouth over hers, letting her taste herself.

She threaded her fingers into his hair and kissed him back feverishly. When he lifted his head, he was out of breath and desperate to bury himself deep inside her.

He stood up and stripped out of his clothes in record time, reluctant to be away from her any longer than necessary.

"You're bigger than I thought," she said softly.

Justin started to laugh but choked when she reached out to stroke his cock. He managed to grab a condom while her thumb rubbed against the moisture on the head.

"Gabby," he warned through clenched teeth. "Slow down, honey."

"Speed up," she countered and swung her legs off the edge of the bed so she was facing his erection. "Let me put it on."

She stole the condom from his fingers and ripped it open.

"Hmm, might need a little more lubrication first," was the only warning he got before she took him into her mouth.

"Jesus." He grasped her head, intending to push her away. He closed his eyes, his fingers curling into her hair instead.

Gabby was sucking his cock. How often had he fantasized about this in the last few months? He couldn't possibly stop her yet.

She moved her tongue over him, bringing him deep a couple of times before he felt his sac tighten.

"No more," he ground out and pushed her back.

She laughed softly, her hands fumbling over his cock to place the condom on him. Once the task was complete, he eased her backward onto the mattress and climbed between her spread thighs.

Her lips curved into a sexy pout. "And why do you get to be on top?"

"Because I got here first." He nudged her thighs open wider and pressed her knees back toward her hips.

His cock probed the slick folds of her pussy, sliding in just barely. He stared at where they were almost joined, before lifting his gaze to hers.

Gabby stared at him, all teasing and lightness gone. In its place, the heat of desire and an intense trust.

His blood pounded harder and he swallowed with difficulty. Without breaking eye contact, he pressed steadily into her.

Her body clenched around his cock, her hot, slick moisture

easing his deep drive into her channel.

"Damn, you're small." His jaw clenched. He should have known she would be by the slightness of her body.

She lifted her hips to press into his foreword thrust, and he slid in to the hilt.

The breath locked in his throat and for a moment his eyes crossed from the sensation.

"Justin." His name floated on a sigh. Her fingers gripped the bedspread.

He didn't move for a moment, just stayed deep inside her, his cock pulsing. Only when she tightened around him and gave a frustrated whimper, did he draw out and begin a slow slide back inside her.

He found a rhythm that Gabby matched easily. It started as a slow and languid thrusting, before turning into something far more fervent and the sounds of his sac hitting her ass resonated in the room.

Her heavy breathing turned into low moans, putting what little control he had left at risk. His grip on her legs tightened and he pounded into her faster.

"Yes." She gasped and closed her eyes. "Just like that."

A growl of possessiveness ripped through him and he thrust blindly into her. Her moans echoed, reverberating in his head. The sensation of her slick heat squeezing his cock ruled him.

Reaching down, he found her clit, swollen and wet, and pinched it.

Her moan switched to a guttural scream and the walls of her pussy gripped him as she came. More moisture coated his dick as she trembled.

Watching her face, the complete abandon and pleasure, sent him over a second later.

His sac tightened and he exploded mid-thrust, his fingers digging into the softness behind her knees.

Wave after wave of pleasure rocked him through his orgasm. A few minutes later, with his thighs still shaking, he lowered her legs to the bed and slid on top of her.

"Jesus, Gabby."

"No kidding," she muttered, biting his shoulder and then kissing the same spot. "That was...yum."

"Good way to put it." He rolled to the side, his heart still pounding from his climax. "Why the hell did we wait so long to do that?"

"I haven't a clue."

Gabby let out a shuddering breath. Her stomach felt as if butterflies had taken up permanent residence. She wiped her palm down her face, but it did little to wipe the smile from her face.

There was a softness around her heart, a hope for possibility that she'd never really let herself feel before. The possibility of Justin.

"Are you hungry?" He nuzzled her neck, pressing a kiss to the pulse she knew must be all aflutter.

"A little bit," she admitted.

"Me too. How about we go make those quesadillas now? You know, since you made me forgo them earlier?"

She swatted his shoulder and giggled. "If you think for one minute that I'd believe you'd choose food over sex, you're completely delusional."

"Well, never over sex with you, Gab." He grinned and climbed off the bed, holding out his hand.

Her heart sped up and her stomach flipped again.

"You coming?"

"Sure." She placed her hand in his and his long fingers closed around hers.

They opened the door to the bedroom and Doug bounded in, barking with excitement.

"Don't think he appreciated being locked out too much," Justin commented, leaning down to rub the dog's ears.

"Apparently." She patted Doug on the head and moved past him toward the kitchen, her stomach growling.

Justin followed her and retrieved the cheese from the fridge again.

"Thank God tomorrow's Saturday," she murmured. "I'm going to be exhausted in the morning."

"Will you stay here tonight?"

His question knocked the wind from her sails. She opened her mouth to answer, but wasn't quite sure what to say. Stay here. Sleep in his bed. More snuggling. God, the idea had appeal.

"Do you hear that?"

His sudden question saved her from having to answer the other one.

"Hear what?"

"I think your phone is ringing."

"My phone?" Her brows drew together as she pushed past him to retrieve her purse from the laundry room.

She yanked out her cell phone on the beginning of the fourth ring and answered.

"Hello?"

"Gabrielle, is that you?"

Gabby grabbed onto the washing machine, her knees almost gave out at the trembling voice on the other end of the phone.

"Gabrielle, are you there?"

"Yes, I'm here, Mom." She closed her eyes.

A lump settled in her stomach, a premonition that this would not be a good phone call. Her mother didn't just call to chat after not talking to her daughter for several years. Especially after midnight.

"What's going on?" She lowered her voice, her hand squeezing around the phone.

"I...I left him. I left your father tonight."

Shock and disbelief warred inside her, but she pushed the emotions aside. She had too much training with her day job to let them interfere with what needed to be done.

"Okay. Where are you now?"

"Ugh—well, I'm at a payphone at the mini-mart down the street from the house."

"Stay where you are. Go inside and wait if you can. I'll be there in twenty minutes to pick you up." She drew in a slow breath. "And please, Mom, don't leave."

She snapped the phone shut and ran a hand through her hair.

"What's going on?"

She spun around, pressing a hand to her chest in surprise. Justin stood in the doorway to the laundry room, naked and seeming unconcerned by the fact. Not that it mattered; she was sans clothes right now as well.

Her gaze drifted over his body, needing the second of distraction. But it didn't put her any more at ease. If anything, the knot in her stomach doubled.

Hearing from her mom gave her the gentle reminder as to why she'd sworn never to sleep with Justin. *Don't think about that now.*

"I need to go," she muttered. "That was my mother."

"Your mother?" His brows drew together and his look grew more troubled. "I thought you didn't see your mother anymore?"

"I haven't. Not in over two years." Her stomach clenched and a wave of anxiety threatened to overtake her, but she stuffed it down. *Later.* She could think about all this later.

She moved past him to grab her clothes from his room.

"It's after midnight, Gabby. What's going on?" He caught her arm before she reached the door to his room. "Where are you going?"

"I need to go pick her up."

"This time of night? You don't even have your car."

"I'll...call a cab. Look, I have to go." She tugged her arm free and hurried to find her clothes, pulling on each item with rapid speed.

When she turned to grab her shoes, she found him half dressed.

"What are you doing?" she asked sharply.

"I'll drive you."

"No. Justin—"

"The hell if I'm going to let two women drive around San Francisco alone after midnight in a cab."

She glared at him and then shook her head, knowing it was pointless to argue with Justin once he got his mind set on something.

Giving a terse nod, she grabbed her shoes.

Five minutes later, she'd given him directions and they were speeding down the highway toward the neighborhood where she'd grown up.

"You gonna tell me what's going on?" Justin asked, breaking the silence that had settled since they'd gotten into his truck.

She swallowed hard and glanced out the window. No, she really didn't want to tell him. That was a part of her life she kept to herself. No one knew about it except Phoebe and Delanie. Even then, confessing to her friends had been hard enough.

"Gabby, it's me. You know you can tell me anything."

Not this.

She bit her lip, deciding on truth with omission. "My mother left my father tonight."

He didn't say anything for a moment, and then, "Is this a good thing?"

"Yes." The word was almost a whisper. "A very good thing."

How many years had she lain in her bedroom, the blanket drawn over her head and her face stuffed into the pillow? Praying again and again that God would give her mother the strength and wisdom to leave her father.

The truck bounced into the parking lot of the mini-mart and Gabby blinked, shaking herself out of the past.

Her stomach dropped when she scanned the parking lot and didn't immediately see her mom's petite form.

"Is that her inside?"

At his words, her gaze flew to the inside of the store and the woman hovering around the alcohol section.

"Shit. I'll be right back." She fumbled with her seatbelt then jerked open the door to the truck and jumped down to the pavement.

By the time she got inside, her mom already had a can of beer in her hand.

Gabby rushed forward, snagging the beer from her grasp and then pulling her into a hug.

"This isn't going to help things, Mom," she muttered.

Her mother stiffened in her embrace and then let out a ragged sigh, her body going limp against Gabby.

"You okay?"

When her mother didn't answer, Gabby pulled back to get a good look at her. Despite all her training and hands-on experience in her job, it didn't make it any easier seeing the bruises on her own mom's face.

The gash above her right temple needed tending to and the bruises appeared to be at least a couple of days old.

Gabby gripped her mother's hands and squeezed. "I'm proud of you, Mom."

Her mother's expression wavered between uncertainty and fear.

"Mrs. Davison?"

Gabby went rigid at the sound of Justin behind her. Damn. Why couldn't he just wait in the car?

Her mother's gaze skittered over Justin warily and then back to Gabby.

"I called your dad," Arleen said in a soft voice after a moment. "He's on his way to pick me up."

The air rushed from Gabby's chest as if she'd been slugged.

"No. No, Mom. Please don't go back to him," Gabby pleaded, her voice hoarse from frustration and disappointment. "Please, Mom."

Justin stepped forward and took her mother's arm in a gentle grip.

"Tell you what, Mrs. Davison." He gave her a smile that Gabby knew had a damn near-perfect success rate at getting what he wanted. "Why don't we go have a cup of coffee and you can think about it."

Her mom hesitated. "I don't know..."

"If you want to go back to your husband after coffee, I promise we'll return you to your home."

Like hell they would! Gabby shot him a furious look, which he countered with one that clearly said *trust me.*

"Just coffee?" her mother hedged.

"Just coffee."

Gabby held her breath, her body zinging with tension. Any moment her father would pull up to the store and then the shit would really hit the fan. Chances were the police would get called.

After another moment, her mother nodded.

"Great." Justin nodded at Gabby and escorted her mother out to his truck.

After setting the beer back in the fridge and apologizing to the cashier, Gabby hurried out of the store and into the backseat of Justin's truck.

Just as they were pulling out of the parking lot, she recognized her dad's beat-up Toyota pulling in.

Her body sagged in relief at the near miss and she was damn grateful she'd let Justin talk her into taking his truck.

66

A cab would have been too obvious and her dad would have followed them all over San Francisco to get his wife back.

Justin turned the radio to an easy listening station and started to make small talk about the weather they'd been having.

Gabby swallowed hard, more appreciative toward him by the minute. He was putting her mom at ease now. And, if she admitted it, she likely wouldn't have even gotten her mother out of the store without him.

She leaned back in the seat and closed her eyes, weakened by the relief of having her mom in the truck and out of harm's way. For now, at least.

There was a lot of traffic out, even this late at night. The white noise of the other cars rushing by them lulled Gabby back into a calm state.

When she opened her eyes again she found Justin watching her in the rearview mirror, even as he continued to make small talk with her mother.

She gave him a half smile before turning to look out the window. What must he think right now? Clearly he had seen the condition of her mother and appraised the situation. Had handled it quite fabulously, actually.

Her stomach rolled with unease. She'd hoped to never have to share this part of her life with Justin. Why hadn't she considered the fact her mother would obviously be walking around with fresh bruises?

Justin pulled into a twenty-four-hour diner and parked the truck. They all filed out and went inside.

She squeezed into a booth next to her mother, hoping like hell Justin would be able to pull off what she'd never been able to do. Convince her mom not to return home.

An hour later, she could easily believe that Justin was a twin of The Pied Piper.

Not only had he sweet-talked her mother into not returning to her husband, he also had her agreeing to check into the Second Chances house.

Gabby put in a call to Nicole, the lady working the graveyard shift at the house, and told her the situation with her mother and to expect them.

She'd had to leave Justin at the administrative office and borrow his truck, because there were strict rules about who was allowed to know the location of the house.

By the time she'd settled her mother into the safe house, and picked up Justin again, it was almost three in the morning.

She could barely keep her eyes open, even as her head spun with the events of the night.

When Justin took the exit to his house, she was too tired to protest. Her car was still down by the stadium, and she didn't trust herself to drive when she was this out of it anyway.

"We'll grab your car in the morning," he murmured, as if reading her mind and breaking the silence they'd maintained since they'd dropped off her mother.

"Okay." She gave a weak nod and yawned.

He reached out a hand and threaded his fingers through hers. Her pulse tripped, and she clutched his hand like it was a lifeline.

"You should have told me earlier."

Her gut twisted and a sour taste rose in her throat. She didn't even pretend to not know what he was referring to.

"It isn't exactly something I want people to know, Justin."

He was silent for a moment. "How long has it been going on?"

She gave a harsh laugh. "Since I was a kid."

"And she stayed with him." His response wasn't a question, more of a statement of incredulity.

"She loves him. It's not uncommon for a woman to stay."

And it wasn't, working at Second Chances had proven that to her on multiple occasions.

"Did he ever..." Justin's fingers tightened. "Did your father ever hit you?"

"No." Her response wasn't exactly the truth. Her father had lifted his hand to her once, when she'd dared confront him about what he was doing to her mother.

With the slap across her face had come the motivation to leave home. It hadn't mattered that she'd only been seventeen and just about to finish high school. Fortunately, she'd had a friend whose family had been willing to take her in.

For years after, she'd tried to convince her mother to leave, but ultimately it had hurt her relationship with her and they'd lost contact.

She felt Justin's gaze on her. He probably didn't believe her reply, which just made her feelings for him deepen a bit more. He'd always been a little too perceptive.

He pulled the truck in front of his house and turned off the engine. Once again, he was out of the truck and had her door open before she could do it herself.

He slid an arm around her shoulder, pulling her snug against him as they went inside.

Doug barked happily, dancing around them, eager for attention, but Justin led Gabby straight back to his bedroom.

She tugged off her clothes, the task difficult since her fingers shook with exhaustion.

Justin, half undressed already, made a sound of sympathy and stepped forward to help remove her clothes.

Even though the gesture should have made her feel like a helpless child, she appreciated it. She leaned into him and let her body go pliant as he manipulated her out of her clothes.

When she was naked again, he brushed a kiss across her forehead. "Go lie down, I'll grab the lights."

She gave a sluggish nod and stumbled to the bed, crawling onto the mattress and letting her head flop onto the pillow.

A moment later, the lights went out and then Justin's footsteps approached the bed, the mattress dipping under his weight.

When he pulled her into his arms, she didn't resist, just buried her head against his chest and breathed in the familiar scent of him.

The hair on his chest brushed against her cheek, but didn't bother her. If anything, it made her feel smaller, more feminine and protected. And after the emotional roller coaster she'd been on tonight, she kind of needed it.

He brushed another kiss across her forehead and smoothed a hand up and down her spine.

A yawn popped her jaw. Her muscles went lax under the calming strokes of his hand and comfort of his embrace.

How long ago had it happened? she wondered drowsily as she teetered on the brink of sleep. When had he stopped being just a really good guy friend, and become the guy she loved...

Chapter Seven

Gabby woke when Doug started to bark in the other room. She lifted her head and groaned when she caught sight of the time.

Not even six.

Beside her, Justin stirred, and she glanced down to find him watching her. He'd done so much for her last night. For her mother. Her throat tightened with emotion and she bit back tears, instead trying to just focus on how nice it was to wake up in bed with him. With Justin.

His naked chest and shoulders were visible above the sheet, large and muscled. Heat stirred low in her belly as she thought about the way his body felt while on top of her last night.

"Doug must've spotted the paper boy," Justin said softly. "It's early, Gab. You should go back to sleep."

She licked her lips and gave him a sleepy smile. "I don't know if I can fall back asleep just yet."

He lifted an eyebrow. "No?"

"Well, now that I'm awake and you're right here..." She reached out and trailed a finger over his chest. "I'd kind of feel remiss if I didn't take advantage of you."

Heat flickered in his lazy gaze that dropped to her breasts. "Hmm. And we wouldn't want that, now would we?"

"It'd be an awful waste."

"Sure would."

Gabby scooted over and moved on top of him, settling a leg on each side of his waist. Too tired to sit upright, she slid forward so she lay across his chest.

"Mmm. I like this," Justin murmured and slid his arms around her. His fingers chased a lazy pattern up her spine.

Tingles raced through her and she grew damp between her legs. She nuzzled his neck and breathed in his scent. Traces of soap and sweat. All male.

"I like this, too." She pressed her hips hard against his to escape the teasing of his fingers.

He laughed softly and slid his hand down to cup her ass, squeezing the flesh. Her eyes closed and she bit back a groan.

"Touch me," she pleaded.

His chest lifted below her as he drew in a slow breath and then his hand slipped lower, moving down between the cheeks of her ass to tease the folds of her pussy.

"Here?" he murmured against her forehead.

"Yeah." She parted her thighs wider and he slipped a finger inside her. "Yes. Mmm. *Justin.*"

"Were you dreaming about me, honey? You're already soaked."

She bit her lip and smiled against his chest. "Justin, all you have to do is smile and I get wet."

His cock jerked against her ass and she laughed.

"You've got some mouth on you, Gab." He added a second finger to her pussy. The sounds of her wetness filled the room as he fingered her.

"You know, I bet you'd like my mouth on *you*," she murmured and lifted her head to look at him, while her hand reached behind her to wrap around his cock.

"I bet I would." His hot gaze narrowed. "And why don't you swing your pussy around up toward my mouth while you're doing it."

Her pulse tripped and she licked her lips. "I think I can handle that."

Gabby slid off his chest, turning her body around so she faced his feet. Her breasts rubbed against his thighs as she wrapped her fingers around his cock.

Justin gripped each side of her hips and a second later his tongue speared into her pussy.

A guttural groan spilled from her throat and her eyes floated shut. She leaned down, her hair falling across his leg as she licked the head of his cock.

His fingers slid over her ass, while his tongue swept over her slit to find the swollen bud of nerves at the top.

Her hips bucked and she gasped, lowering her mouth again to bring his length into her.

Justin moaned and the sound vibrated his lips against her clit. Pleasure jolted through her veins, spurred her to find a faster rhythm as she moved her mouth on him.

He flicked his tongue over her nub, again and again, while his hips lifted his cock deeper into her mouth. She cupped his sac, massaging him harder now.

The dizzying pleasure swept higher inside her, twisting in her head like a chaotic tornado of sensation. He pushed a finger deep inside her and she exploded. Lights went off in her head as her body trembled.

She felt Justin's sac tighten in her hand and then his cock pushed deeper against her throat. He let out a low groan and came, slow and warm in her mouth.

Still shaken from her own climax, she swallowed all of his release, squeezing his legs until his body went still beneath her and his mouth left her body.

Gabby pressed her cheek to his thigh and let out a ragged breath.

"That was pretty amazing," she muttered.

"I'll say." Justin still stroked her ass. "Come here. I want to hold you."

She twisted around until she lay on the bed again, her head resting on his chest and his arm around her.

"Think you can fall back asleep now?" he asked drowsily.

"I don't know." She gave a soft sigh and closed her eyes. "You keep rubbing my back and maybe."

His chest shook with a quiet laugh. "Try to rest a bit. You barely slept."

"I'll try..." She drew in a deep breath, her body heavy and sated from her release and exhaustion.

With the steady rise and fall of Justin's chest and his continuous rubbing of her back, it only took her a few minutes before she fell back into slumber.

The slobbering tongue across her face woke her. Gabby propped herself up in bed, pushing Doug back with a sleepy laugh.

"Morning, boy." She ruffled the dog's ears and glanced to her right, noting the other side of the bed was empty.

Where was Justin?

The toilet flushed and her gaze drifted toward the bathroom. A second later the shower turned on followed by Justin belting out an old Alice in Chains song.

"The man still can't sing," she muttered under her breath and climbed out of bed, stretching her muscles.

She checked the clock and her eyebrows shot to the ceiling. Oh jeez, it was almost noon! She'd been hoping to get back down to the Second Chances house before lunchtime.

Scrambling for her clothes, she dressed as quickly as possible. She sighed, wishing she had time to have a nice leisurely breakfast with Justin. Thank him profusely for last night and everything he'd done.

Maybe she'd take him to dinner tonight.

Her stomach flipped with butterflies, warmth spread through her and a smile twisted her mouth. She placed a hand over her stomach and bit her lip to keep down the giddiness.

Lord, she was acting like a simpering teenager.

She slipped into her shoes and grabbed her purse, then headed into the living room.

Justin's computer was humming quietly on the coffee table and she cast it a thoughtful glance. Maybe she'd send off a quick email to Delanie and let her know about the situation with her mom.

Dropping her purse on the couch, she made a quick detour to his laptop. She was about to open another browser, when her gaze landed on his email.

There was a letter up from Lilly23.

Close out of his email, Gabby, it's none of your business.

Even knowing she should just look away, her gaze drifted over the body of the email.

Dirty. So dirty. Her stomach rolled. The woman was openly discussing a night they'd spent together. The things she'd done to him, that he'd done to her.

Close the damn screen, Gabby.

Beep.

She jumped at the little bell that dinged on his computer and then saw the source of it as a little white chat box popped

73

up. It was a message from Sweetcheeks4U.

Hey sexy, you're online! I owe you breakfast in bed and since you're up and I'm up...why don't you come over? Do you still have that key I gave you?

Her throat tightened with a sudden lump, her stomach churning double-time now. She stood up, her hands shaking.

What had she been doing again? Her thoughts swirled in a jumbled mess in her head. Oh yes. She was going to email Delanie. Her gaze fell to the laptop again.

An open email from one woman, discussing their sex life.

She shook her head. *Stop it.*

Another woman IM'ing him to invite him for breakfast and obviously so much more.

"I can't deal with this," she whispered. Grabbing her purse, she ran from the house, slamming the front door shut behind her.

She came to an abrupt stop on the front porch, her mouth gaping as she stared at the driveway. Her car. It was still at the stadium.

Her pulse tripped and a panicked whimper escaped. She should just go back inside and wait for Justin to get out of the shower, and then ask him to drive her to her car.

Justin. She closed her eyes for a moment, her throat thickening with tears.

That email. The IM.

You knew this about him, Gabby. You knew what kind of man he is. Only somewhere along the line, she'd changed her mind. Convinced herself he was different. He had changed.

She opened her eyes again, blinking away the moisture.

And now it appeared that he hadn't. And now she'd just become another notch on his proverbial bedpost.

"God, I fucked up," she whispered and strode off the porch. She'd walk to the grocery store and call a cab to take her to the office.

No way was she going back in the house to face Justin. She just couldn't. Not yet. Not until she had her emotions under control enough to tell him he couldn't be a part of her life anymore.

She increased her stride, until she was almost jogging. A cab appeared on the horizon in the oncoming lane, and she scrambled across the street to wave it down.

A few minutes later, when her pulse had begun to slow and they were speeding toward her office, the tears of anger finally fell.

Justin turned off the shower and grabbed a towel, wrapping it around his waist.

Despite the late night they'd had, he wasn't really tired. In fact, he was in a pretty good mood. And the woman responsible for it was curled up in his bed right now, dead asleep.

His mouth curled into a smile as he considered the ways he could wake her up. The memory of last night, their lovemaking, flickered through his head.

Too long. They'd waited entirely too long to bring their relationship to this level.

He grabbed a comb and ran it through his damp hair, staring at the image in the mirror. He loved her. He'd suspected it for the last six months. One big clue had been that his desire to date other women had been completely extinguished.

There'd only been Gabby. In his head and in his heart. Last night had cemented that realization for him.

He set down the comb and pulled open the bathroom door, eager to touch her again. His gaze drifted to the empty bed and his brows drew downward.

She'd woken up?

He crossed the room, heading for the kitchen. She'd probably just gone to make coffee or fix them some breakfast.

But arriving in the kitchen, he only found Doug, chowing down on the bowl of food he'd been fed earlier.

Where was she?

Some of the tension eased from his body and he sighed. Her mother. She'd wanted to go see her mom first thing.

He knew that was likely the case, but something still didn't add up. Her car wasn't here. She would have had to call a cab. Why didn't she just wait for him to get out of the shower?

His gut clenched and he shook his head. Picking up his cell phone, he dialed her number. As had been the result so many times in the past six months, she didn't answer. Her voicemail eventually picked up, instructing him to leave his name and number.

He left a quick message, not caring that he sounded a bit terse and on edge. Hell, she'd put him on it. What was the deal?

He walked to the fridge then tugged open the door and stared absently inside.

In the two years they'd lived together, he'd never suspected the secret she'd kept hidden about her mother. His throat tightened and he shook his head. What kind of childhood did she have?

Just remembering the distrust and bruises on Gabby's mom's face sent a wave of anger through him. Gabby told him last night that her dad had never hit her, but he wasn't quite sure he believed her. He knew the little signals she'd make when she wasn't being one-hundred percent truthful.

He gave a soft curse. God, he wanted to see her. Talk to her more about it this morning, without the exhaustion and when they were both functioning on a normal level.

Why hadn't he insisted on going to the Second Chances home last night instead of letting her talk him into waiting at the administrative office?

He could understand her reasoning. It was protocol. The location of the house wasn't just given out to anyone. And unfortunately that meant he had no way to get a hold of her this afternoon.

Which meant he was shit out of luck. At least for a few hours. She'd drop by later. She would.

Realizing the fridge still remained open and he was no closer to making a decision on what to eat, he reached in and grabbed the eggs.

If he didn't hear from her tonight, he'd drop by the administrative office tomorrow.

Justin pulled up in front of the office of Second Chances and climbed out of his truck. His gaze slid over the parking lot and he bit back a sigh, not seeing Gabby's car anywhere.

Still, he'd come all the way down here. He may as well see if she'd come into the office today. She hadn't returned his phone calls—and he'd left more than one message.

He'd even dropped by her apartment, and even though he'd seen her car outside, she hadn't answered the door.

If he were a smarter guy, he would've taken the hint. She was completely blowing him off. Everything. Their friendship. The night they'd become lovers. *Him overall.*

He walked to the glass door to the complex and rang the buzzer, since the doors were kept locked.

Almost a minute passed before a woman with short blonde hair approached. The door swung open and she gave him a slight smile.

"Can I help you?"

"I'm looking for Gabby, has she been in today?"

"I'm sorry, no..." She hesitated and something like sympathy flickered in her eyes. "I can leave her a message if you'd like."

"I realize she doesn't work Sundays," he persisted. "But I know her mother was taken to the safe house a couple of nights ago, and I just thought maybe she—"

"I'm sorry, sir." The woman's gaze became shuttered and her tone cooled. "I'm really not able to discuss this with you, which I'm sure you understand."

The air hissed out from between his teeth and he gave a sharp nod. Christ, this had gotten him nowhere.

"Of course. If you could..." He thrust a hand into his hair. Hell, he wasn't convinced that Gabby wasn't sitting in the back office avoiding him. But why? "If you could just tell her Justin stopped by and is looking for her."

The woman's expression turned speculative as she gave a slight nod.

"Of course. Have a good day, Justin." Without any further pleasantries, she pushed the door shut, the electric whir informing him that it had locked again.

He turned away and glanced back over the parking lot. What the hell could he do now?

His chest tightened and frustration ate heavy in his stomach. She was in there. He'd bet his last dollar on it.

Justin strode back to his truck and sat down inside. He'd just wait for her, she'd come out eventually.

It wasn't even a half hour later when the door to the building opened. Gabby was halfway across the parking lot before she looked up and saw him.

He watched her eyes widen and her steps falter, but he had

to give her credit for not turning to run back inside.

When he stood just inches from her, he could see the nervousness and regret in her eyes.

"What are you doing here, Justin? I thought you'd left." She folded her arms across her chest.

At least she made no pretense at having known he'd been at the door awhile ago.

"We need to talk, Gabby."

"Do we?" She cleared her throat and lowered her gaze. "Okay, maybe you're right. We should."

His pulse jumped and some of the tension left his shoulders.

"First, how's your mom?"

She looked up and he saw the relief in her gaze. "She's good. Still at the safe house—which is good. I was half afraid she'd leave soon after we got her in."

"That's great. I'm glad to hear it."

"Me too." She nodded. "I just hope she stays."

Justin paused, relieved that she was at least talking to him. "Why don't we go have lunch? We can talk—"

"I'd rather not blow my lunch hour on this." Her shoulders tensed. "What I need to say will only take a minute."

What *she* needed to say? The tension crept right back into his muscles. There was something about the way she'd said those words and how she wouldn't meet his gaze.

"Okay. Go ahead then."

"I think we both know that sleeping together was inevitable. It was bound to happen at some point—though I really did try to avoid it," she said, her voice lacking much emotion. "But now that it's happened, I can admit we made a mistake."

"A mistake?" The word hissed from his throat. His gut twisted. Was she serious?

"And at this time…" she went on, but seemed to hesitate over the next words. "I'm really not comfortable seeing you anymore, Justin. In any context."

In any context. He blinked, completely at a loss at her statement. In any context translated to *get out of my life.*

"Gabby, you can't be serious. We're—"

"I've said what I needed to say," she interrupted warily, lifting a hand, but still not meeting his gaze. "I was hoping to do

78

this in a less abrupt manner, but you've kind of backed me into a corner."

"I see." His mouth tightened and a small tic started in his jaw.

"Maybe someday down the road we can talk."

"Don't count on it. Like you just pointed out, you already said what you needed to say," he muttered and shoved his hand into his pocket, wrapping his fingers around his keys. "Have a good life, Gabby."

Her head snapped up now, her eyes wide. He wasn't sure if there was a hint of moisture in her gaze, because she blinked before he could analyze it.

Not like it mattered. He turned away from her and strode back to his truck.

Last night had meant nothing to her. She was the fucking love of his life, and to her he was a mistake.

He kicked a rock across the parking lot and climbed into his truck, gunning the engine.

He backed up and, as he sped out of the parking lot, he lifted his gaze to the rearview mirror. Gabby stood exactly where he'd left her, watching him leave.

A bitter taste rose in his mouth and he drew in an unsteady breath, wishing his heart didn't feel like it was being gouged out with a dozen dull spoons.

He tore his gaze from her image and focused on the road ahead of him. Looking back sure as hell wouldn't do any good.

Chapter Eight

Delanie glanced up when Gabby returned to the office. "That was fast. I thought you were going to grab us some sushi?"

"Oh. Right." Gabby pressed a hand to her forehead and frowned. Her heart raced so fast she was feeling a bit lightheaded.

How had she gotten those words out to him? How in the *hell* had she said those words to Justin?

Phoebe stood up and cleared her throat. "Hey, I'll grab the sushi for us, okay, ladies?"

Delanie gave her a grateful look. "Would you mind? Thanks, Phoebe, you're the best."

"Yeah, thanks," Gabby managed to muster, but the thought of food made her nauseous.

Once Phoebe had disappeared, Delanie turned back to her. "You don't look so hot, are you okay?"

"Fine," she muttered and shook her head. "No. Not fine. Justin was out there when I left."

"Still? I thought he'd gone."

"Me too," she muttered. "Otherwise I sure wouldn't have gone outside."

"So are you going to explain what's going on? Why you're avoiding him like the plague?" She folded her arms across her chest. "Or am I right on the mark by guessing you guys slept together?"

Gabby sat down on the edge of Delanie's desk, her throat working against the emotion. "Right on the mark."

"And so I'm also going to guess, by your gloominess, that

this doesn't automatically mean you're going to get married and procreate until you're blue in the face?"

"Right again." Though the idea had so much appeal, it made her want to throw herself on the ground and start crying.

Because that just wasn't possible. Especially after what she'd just said to him. The thought of the words she'd hurled at him made bile rise in her throat.

"Why is he so bad for you, Gabby?" Delanie set down her pen, which she'd been twirling between her fingers. "I mean, I get that you said he wasn't the settling down kind...but for some guys, maybe it just takes one woman to change all that."

Gabby rolled her eyes and sniffled. "You've been watching way too many chick flicks."

Delanie lifted an eyebrow and drawled, "You know I prefer action."

"I know. Sorry."

"Seriously, though. You don't think he can change?"

Gabby hesitated. "I found something yesterday morning."

"Oh God, were you snooping?"

"No! He, umm, just had his email open."

"You *read* his emails?"

"Just one." She bit her lip. "It was from some chick describing their time in bed."

"Okay...but maybe it was an old email? Maybe they had sex a long time ago."

"Oh." Gabby paused and her brows knitted. "I suppose...I didn't think of that."

"Okay, Nancy Drew. Since you were scoping out his emails, did you check his sent items? To see if he replied?"

"What? No, the email was open. I..." Gabby broke off and gave an exasperated sigh.

"That email may not mean anything."

Gabby gave her friend a disbelieving look. "There's more, though. Another girl sent him a suggestive IM while I was sitting at the computer."

"Okay. Look, Gabby, I know it looks bad. But you have to remember something. Justin used to date a lot. You both had no qualms about being involved with many people over the years. Maybe he's changed and the women from his past haven't gotten the hint?"

Gabby's pulse quickened at the possibility. "Do you think?"

"Maybe. What did Justin say about it when you asked?"

"I didn't."

"You didn't ask him?"

"No! I ran out the door before I could screw up any more than I already had."

"You mean by screwing Justin?"

"Right."

"You need to just talk to him, Gabby. He can probably explain. I've never seen you like this over a guy."

"Like what?"

"Twitterpated."

"Twitterpated? Is that a word?"

"I don't know, grab a dictionary. But really, talk to him about this." Delanie sighed. "Seriously, Gabby, when I went to the door he looked...so incredibly desperate. Anxious. Like a guy looks when he's afraid he's lost the love of his life."

The lump in Gabby's throat grew and she lowered her gaze. God, what she wouldn't give for Delanie's words to have one ounce of truth.

"He doesn't love me, Delanie. We were really good friends. Really good friends who discovered we're also compatible in the sack." She shook her head. "That in no way means we're the stuff they write fairytales about."

"You never know." Delanie steepled her hands on her desk and balanced her chin on them. "What's really going on here, Gabby? You're shooting down every possible solution with an excuse. Why won't you even give you guys a chance?"

Frustrated, Gabby admitted flatly, "Because he's too much like my father."

Delanie's mouth tensed. "You think Justin would hit you?"

"No, of course not," Gabby said softly, her mouth curving downward slightly. "Justin would never hurt me. Not physically anyway."

"Then how's he like your dad?" Delanie asked and then went silent for a moment. "I don't mean to pry, I just don't know a lot about your parents, Gabby, other than that your father was abusive to your mom."

"My father has been unfaithful to my mother for probably their entire marriage. He could never be happy with just one woman." Her gut twisted, the admission sounding odd on her lips. Had she ever talked about it, really? "Initially he didn't hit her that much. The first time I remember it happening was when she spoke up about him being with another woman."

Delanie reached out and grabbed her hand, squeezing it. "Gabby..."

"She actually learned pretty quickly. Maybe only once or twice did she bring it up to him after that. But it was like, after that first time, the seal was broken." Gabby's jaw clenched. "If dinner was late. If she asked him to turn down the volume on the television. After a while it didn't matter, anything could set him off..."

Delanie's fingers tightened around her. "And it took her this long to leave him?"

"She still loves him. After all he's done to her. I tried for years to make her leave, I really did."

"There's not a lot you can do for someone like that, Gabby. Except be there when they're ready."

"I know." Gabby lifted her gaze and thought of Phoebe. Their friend had gone through it herself, had admitted how hard it could be to leave an abuser.

Delanie cleared her throat. "So, do you think that because Justin dated a lot—and let me remind you that you did too— he's just like your father?"

"God, you and Phoebe are like my therapists," Gabby muttered. "I just know my father left big, negative impressions on me about men who have a hard time committing."

"But Justin hasn't committed to anyone yet. Once he does, it's possible he'll never touch another woman again besides his wife." Delanie gave her a pointed look.

Gabby snorted.

"Seriously, Gabby. I mean, if you're going to rule out all the men who've dated lots of women, you've just lost a big chunk of the penile population."

"Jesus." Gabby groaned and started to braid her hair, anything to distract her from the valid points Delanie may or may not have been making.

"Just talk to him, Gabby. *Please.*"

"It's too late...I did talk to him," she admitted. "Outside. I basically handed him a hand basket and told him where to go with it."

"You didn't."

"I did."

"*Gabby.*" Delanie bit her lip. "Are you sure that was the right move?"

Gabby blinked, her eyes suddenly filling with tears. She never cried. This was freaking ridiculous!

"No. But I already said some pretty crappy things to him. And the way he looked at me afterward..."

"Okay, so tell him what you just told me. About your father."

"I can't."

"Then you've lost him." Delanie sighed, obviously exasperated.

Delanie was right. If she didn't talk to Justin, try to explain things, then she had lost him. And the idea of it made everything inside her swirl with misery.

She couldn't paint all men with her dad's brush. Once she really sat down and thought about it, she knew Justin wasn't like that. And she also knew she didn't want to lose him. At all. But—oh God—was it too late?

"Hey, Gabby. I have a confession of my own."

Gabby looked up at Delanie's sudden announcement, pushing aside her own fear of having already lost Justin.

"Oh?"

"Yeah." Delanie bit her lip. "I haven't told Phoebe yet, because I feel awful."

Gabby studied her friend closely and saw the guilt on her face. "What's going on?"

"I took a call a couple of hours ago. There's a resort up in the San Juan Islands in Washington State. Apparently the owner has heard of Second Chances and wants to donate to our organization."

"You're kidding!" Gabby cried, eyes widening. "That's great news, why would you feel guilty about it?"

"Because I've been invited up to spend a week touring the resort. To discuss the details, sign some papers, and..." Delanie glanced away, her cheeks turning pink. "Consider a job offer as the resort's marketing director."

Gabby leaned back on her heels and her lips parted. "I

didn't know you were considering a new job."

"I'm not. I mean, I wasn't." Delanie hesitated. "But the idea of working in marketing has so much appeal, it's why I majored in it. And...God, I just feel so guilty even considering it."

Gabby shook her head and placed a hand on her arm. "Don't feel guilty."

"I haven't taken the job yet and likely won't. But I want to go up there to see the place. Accept the donation on behalf of Second Chances." She paused. "And consider the possibility of the job. But how do I tell Phoebe?"

Gabby knew Phoebe and Delanie had gone to college together, had been close. And after Phoebe had left her abusive relationship, they'd both come to work at Second Chances together.

"Delanie, I really think she'll understand if you decide to go." Gabby smiled. "And you don't even have to tell her about the job part. If you decide not to take it, no harm done. If you do, deal with that bridge when you come to it."

Relief flickered in Delanie's expression. "Thanks, Gabby. You're right."

The door opened again and Phoebe came inside, carrying their lunch. Gabby gave Delanie a quick wink and hurried back to her desk.

Phoebe crossed the room, unusually quiet as she set the brown paper bag on the desk.

"Thanks for grabbing lunch," Gabby said and grimaced. "Seeing as I couldn't seem to complete the task myself."

"No problem," Phoebe murmured and sat down in her chair, staring at her desk, seeming lost in thought.

Gabby and Delanie exchanged a glance, before Gabby asked, "Everything okay?"

"Sure." Phoebe gave a quick nod and then hesitated. "I just...I'm sure it's nothing, but I could've sworn I just saw Rick outside the sushi restaurant."

"You saw Rick? Did he approach you?"

By Delanie's sharp response, Gabby guessed Rick to be Phoebe's abusive ex.

"No. In fact, I know I'm just being silly." Phoebe gave a laugh that didn't hold much humor. "It was just for a second, and when I looked again he was gone. Besides, he moved to

New Jersey a couple of years ago."

"Okay..." Delanie drew out the word slowly. "Just promise me you'll be alert, you know, just in case it was."

Gabby nodded, feeling a faint stab of concern. "I agree. Be alert."

"Of course," Phoebe said, but her expression had closed off, a clear indication she was through discussing it. She dug into the paper bag and pulled out two black containers. "California Roll for Gabby and Dragon Roll for Delanie."

Gabby crossed the room and scooped it up. "Thank you, Phoebe."

"You're welcome." She stood back up and muttered, "I'm running to the bathroom. Be back in a few."

Gabby watched her go and frowned. "Think she's okay?"

"I hope so." Delanie shook her head, opening her box of sushi. "Because I will kick that man's ass to China and back if he shows up in her life again."

Gabby laughed softly. "You're a great friend, Delanie. To both of us. Thank you for the talk earlier. I needed it."

Delanie glanced up, her eyes brightening. "Justin?"

"Yeah." Gabby bit her lip, knowing she needed to see him tonight. Try to explain things. He deserved that much. And God, please let him understand and take her back. "I'm going to talk to him tonight."

"Good. I'm glad, Gabby. I think he's the one for you."

"I do too," she admitted softly. "I just hope...it's not too late." Her lips twitched. "And he has a damn good explanation for those emails."

"Trust him, Gabby. Trust him."

Gabby took her food back to her desk, knowing that despite all her fears about the idea of them together, she did trust him. Which made her freaking out this morning even more awful. She'd go to him tonight and explain. Apologize. Help him understand that she'd completely failed that first instance of trust...

But how much did Justin trust her?

She glanced at the clock, her stomach rolling. In a few hours she'd have her answer.

Justin took another swig of beer and scanned the email again. Without hesitating, he hit send and then sat back on the couch.

Done and dealt with.

Not much more to do tonight other than get shit-faced in celebration of a broken heart. Not like he'd admit that to anyone—hell, admitting it to himself made him feel like the biggest idiot on the planet. Mainly because he'd brought this on himself.

He'd continued to pursue Gabby when she'd flat out told him she didn't want to get involved.

Standing up from the couch, he scratched his chest and shook his head. He'd just figured that once they finally slept together, she'd change her mind and see things the way he did. That though they rocked on the friends level, they were destined for so much more.

He walked to the fridge to grab another beer, but hesitated when Doug let out a sharp howl from the front room. He barked again, but this time it was more of a happy bark, which was followed by a series of ecstatic yelps.

Was it even possible?

He shut the fridge and walked slowly into the living room. Not even three feet from the door, he froze when someone knocked on it.

Doug jumped off the couch and ran to the door. He sat in front of it and then turned to stare at Justin, his tail slapping the ground in a rhythmic declaration of happiness.

Justin's gaze lifted from his dog to the door. Drawing in a slow breath, he took the last few steps and swung it open.

The fog had rolled in, bringing with it a mist that hinted at rain.

And Gabby stood on the doorstep, her arms wrapped around her middle, almost defensively. Her lower lip trembled and her eyes held a mix of fear and regret.

"Gabby," he breathed her name on a sigh, his gut clenching. "What are you—"

"My father slept around on my mom. One affair after another. If my mom protested, he'd beat her up."

Justin drew in a ragged breath at her broken confession. The sudden glaze of tears in her eyes made them shine greener under the porch light.

"I need to know you're nothing like him, Justin." Her voice cracked. "I need to know that I would be enough for you."

His chest tightened and he had to force himself to swallow against the lump in his throat.

"Because I love you," she whispered almost inaudibly. "I didn't want to. But I do."

"Gabby," he said thickly and stepped out onto the porch and slid his arms around her, pulling her against him. *She loved him.* It was hard to stand upright, his muscles almost went lax with her confession.

"I didn't handle things well today," she went on, dragging in a watery breath. "I was so hung up on my own insecurities."

"Gabby," he pushed her away slightly and lifted her chin with one finger. "It's okay."

"It's not. I just—"

He closed his mouth over hers, sliding his tongue deep to taste her sweetness. To claim her. To reassure her.

She tensed in his arms, making a frustrated groan. But after a moment, when he softened the kiss, her body went pliant against him and she made a soft sigh of surrender. Of relief.

He lifted his head, his heart pounding harder.

"Never," he said fiercely, his own voice shaking now. "Ever doubt that you're not enough for me." He pushed a strand of hair off her forehead and kissed a tear off her cheek. "I would never cheat on you, Gabby. And I sure as hell wouldn't hit you."

"I know," she gave a wobbly nod. "I had no right to judge you on your dating habits—you were right. I was just as guilty. We were both just searching for...*the one.*"

"Exactly. And even though we didn't know it, we'd already found what we were looking for." He moved his thumb over her swollen bottom lip and gave a crooked smile. "You were living right under my roof. I think I've been in love with you for longer than I realized."

She closed her eyes and buried her head against his chest. The moisture from her wet cheeks dampened his T-shirt.

"Will you answer me something, honey?" he murmured, stroking her back. "Friday night we crossed that bridge from friends to lovers. You left early Saturday morning. Did you just wake up regretting it?"

She stiffened in his arms and he thought he heard her curse under her breath.

After a few seconds she pulled away and looked up at him, guilt clear on her face.

"I'm not proud of this, but I looked at your email," she confessed. "I only read a bit, but it was enough..."

Justin lifted his head and looked past her, visualizing what she would have seen. The email he'd put off responding to for weeks. The one from a woman he'd dated almost a year ago and who he'd recently run into at a bar. He'd had the email open so he could reply. No wonder she'd freaked out.

"Gabby, about that—"

"No, it's my fault for looking."

"Let me finish. About five minutes before you showed up at my door, I'd just replied to it. I'd been putting it off."

Her hand slid up to cup his face, her fingers moving back and forth over the stubble. Her gentle touch combined with her slight body pressed flush against him sent a ripple of desire through him. His body hardened and he drew in an unsteady breath.

"It doesn't matter, Justin," she said softly.

Another thought kicked in. "You saw the IM too, huh?"

"I did, but seriously, I know—"

"I'm sorry you saw that, Gab. Let me explain."

"You don't have to—"

"But I *do* have to explain. To you and to them. To any woman who contacts me." He drew in a slow breath. "I explained that I've fallen in love with somebody else and am giving up the dating scene."

"You said that?" Her gaze searched his.

"I did." He stepped back from her and took her hand. "Come inside and I'll let you read the email. The IM—"

"I don't need to read them," she cut him off, her body relaxing in his hold. "I trust you, Justin. If you say they're nothing, I trust you." She licked her lips and her expression relaxed into something a bit sultrier. "If I follow you inside, the last place I want to go is to your computer."

"Yeah?" He traced a finger down her arm. "Where do you want to go? To your apartment to start moving your things back here?"

"Maybe later. Right now I think I'd like to, hmm, *go to heaven...in your bed*." Her attempt to hold back a giggle failed.

"That's a terrible line." He scowled and lifted her up. She wrapped her legs around his waist, nuzzling his neck.

"It *is* a terrible line, and you're *so* guilty of using it in the past."

"Am not," he lied, grinning as he stepped inside and kicked the door shut behind them.

"Dude, you told me *every*thing," she reminded him and wrapped her arms around his neck. "But, Justin?"

"Yes, honey?"

"I think for the first time in your life..." she pressed a kiss to his lips and then sighed, "...that line might actually work tonight."

"You think so, huh?"

"I do." She winked. "But I'm game if you want to prove it."

"With pleasure, Gabby." He tightened his grip on her and headed to the bedroom. "With pleasure."

Luck be Delanie

Dedication

Thank you to Melissa at DAWN for your help and information on domestic violence. Thanks to my family and friends for your continued support, and thank you to my editor Laurie for making my books shine!

Chapter One

"I like your tattoo," a deep voice came from behind her. "The last time I saw it I was taking you from behind."

Delanie choked on the wine she'd just taken a sip of, her fingers almost crushing the stem of the glass.

No. It wasn't possible. Goosebumps broke out over her body even as quick heat spread inside her. She could feel the owl tattoo on her shoulder blade tingle under his gaze.

What was more shocking? His words or the man who had just spoken them? God, it was a toss-up.

She drew in a slow breath, afraid to turn around. Her heart pounded furiously beneath her breasts and her palms dampened.

The coin she'd stolen from him six years ago hung on a pendant around her neck like a beacon. Thank God it was beneath the neckline of her sundress and well out of his view.

"Do you remember that night?" His warm breath tickled her ear.

Hot shivers raced down her spine as his words evoked images of the night they'd spent together. The air locked in her throat and she bit her lip, trying to halt the bombardment of erotic images.

Of course she remembered. That night was a firebrand on her mind. But admitting she hadn't forgotten could only bring trouble. *It couldn't possibly be him standing behind me,* the silly voice of denial screamed in her head.

Without turning around, she could sense the tall, hardness of his body just inches from her. Could feel his blue eyes burning a trail over her.

Another tremble wracked her body.

Get yourself together, Delanie. You're not a silly co-ed anymore. And he has no idea what you did the morning after your night together.

She focused hard on the sparkling blue water that lay beyond the trees. She'd always heard Washington State was beautiful, and this island and resort in the San Juan Islands was a genuine paradise.

Funny how she'd considered herself a lucky woman getting invited to such a posh resort. How wonderful that not only was she here to accept a donation to the Second Chances shelter, but to also consider an offer as the resort's marketing director.

Her lips twisted. She should have known. Paradise always had a price.

"Still thinking about that night?"

Annoyance pricked at his mocking tone. Knowing she couldn't very well keep her back to him forever, she forced a bland expression onto her face and turned around.

Her bravado slipped a notch the moment she saw him, but she forced it back by lifting her chin higher. "I think you have me mistaken with someone else."

"Do I?" He lifted an eyebrow, his mouth twitching with obvious amusement.

She swallowed hard.

Grant Thompson looked just as good now as he had six years ago. Scratch that, he looked better. The tall, lean, college athlete had turned into a sexy grown man. His face was harder now, more angular with the loss of the boyish roundness.

His hair, once more red than blond, had settled into something in between. But those eyes...those eyes were just as blue and piercing as they had been all those years ago. On that night she'd been stupid enough to bounce the bed springs with him.

She felt the warming of a blush and bit her cheek.

"Excuse me." She stepped past him, but he reached out and caught her elbow, swinging her back around. Hot tingles raced up her arm where his fingers touched.

"Wait, Lanie—"

"Well at least you got my name right this time." Her voice shook as she tugged herself free from his grip. She stumbled backward and eyed him warily.

That heart-crushing moment would remain engraved in her mind forever. Right after bringing her to a sweet morning-after orgasm, the jerk had called her Janie. *Janie!* And then to add insult to injury, he'd fallen back asleep before they could even finish making love. Wait, sex. Of course a guy like Grant wouldn't consider it *making love.*

"I'm sorry about that." Grant's jaw hardened, all amusement vanishing. "That mistake caused a helluva delay in finding you."

"Sorry? As if that—" She broke off and narrowed her eyes. "In finding me?"

He tilted his head and gave her a considering look. "Is that why you left so suddenly that morning?"

Guilt stabbed low in her gut, and she reached to touch the pendant under her dress. Before her fingers connected, she jerked her hand away and tucked a strand of short blonde hair behind her ear instead.

Careful, girl. You're on dangerous grounds right now.

"Look." She let her gaze slip away from his. "I don't know what kind of twist of fate brought us together, but I'll catch the first ferry back to Anacortes."

"It was me." He stepped closer, blocking her path back into the building.

Her heart almost stopped at the three words. "Excuse me?"

"I'm the twist of fate." His mouth tightened. "Finding you was the first piece of good luck I've had in years."

She almost dwelled on the luck comment, but the fact that he was claiming to be the twist of fate resonated louder.

The urge to flee increased and she shook her head, glancing around the patio. Her stomach clenched as she realized they were alone now.

"Grant..." She ran her tongue over suddenly dry lips and his gaze darkened as he observed the small movement.

"Lanie." He stepped forward and she took a step back, her pulse jumping.

"Delanie," she muttered without thinking. "I haven't been called Lanie since college."

"Fine. Delanie."

The waves crashed against the rocks below as he backed her up against the guard railing.

"When does the next boat leave?" she queried, her heart fluttering harder in her chest. "I can arrange to be on it."

"You don't understand. I don't want you to leave." His hands curled around the rail on each side of her body.

The faint smell of soap and cologne tickled her nostrils and the heat of his hard body mingled with hers.

"It took me six years to find you."

Six years faded to nothing with him standing so close. A tremble rocked her body, and her nipples tightened, chafing against the lace of her bra.

She bit back a groan. "Please..."

"The last thing I'm going to do is put you on a boat home, Delanie. We have a lot to talk about."

Her stomach dropped and her mouth went dry. Oh. God. He *knew*.

His lips hovered just inches above hers and he used the tip of his thumb to trace the seam of her lips. The blood pounded through her veins and it became a struggle just to drag air into her lungs.

All outside noise disappeared and their gazes locked. The vision of that night so many years ago ran through her head, trapping her in a vortex of memories and sensation.

Her gaze moved to his mouth. She wanted him to kiss her. Wanted him to eliminate those few inches between them and cover her mouth with his. But that would be crazy. Ridiculous.

Her eyelids drifted shut.

"Ms. Williams, we can check you in now."

The heat of his body disappeared. She blinked her eyes open again and Grant had stepped away from her, annoyance clear on his face.

"Thank you, Burton." He shifted his attention from her to the approaching employee.

Smoothing her hand down the front of her dress, Delanie tried to regain some of the composure she'd lost in the past few minutes. She had to be completely insane. Talk about a close call. She'd been fully prepared to let him kiss her.

"Please remember that Ms. Williams is to be placed in room two in the north building."

Her gaze jerked back to Grant in surprise. Why was he ordering around the employee like he owned the place?

The blood drained from her head and she gripped the railing to steady herself. Oh God. He probably *did* own the resort. Was Grant the sponsor who had seemed too good to be true? Was he the one offering her this job?

Her stomach dropped and all her hopes and expectations disappeared.

"Of course, the room is already prepared." The employee gave a quick nod. "If you would just follow me, Ms. Williams."

Eager to put as much as distance as possible between herself and Grant, she hurried after the employee.

"Delanie."

Her name spoken softly on his lips had her stumbling to a halt again.

"Yes?" She drew her bottom lip between her teeth, glad her back was to him once again.

"Have dinner with me tonight."

"This is supposed to be business—"

"I know." Footsteps sounded on the patio and then he walked past her. "I'll come by your room at six."

She stared at his retreating back, her eyes widening when he suddenly tripped and stumbled into one of the patio chairs.

"God damn bad luck," he mumbled before disappearing inside.

Why did he keep bringing up luck? She shook her head and dragged in a deep breath, clenching her fists at her side.

"Ms. Williams?"

"Yes. Sorry, I'm coming."

Delanie stared out the open French doors of her suite. The cool breeze from the straits swept into her room, lifting the gauzy white curtains around her.

The décor of the room ranged from white wicker furniture to a plush bed set high on the far side of the room.

The resort was the ultimate paradise. It had also just become her personal nightmare.

Grant Thompson. Just thinking his name made her knees a bit weak again. And she was not a weak in the knees type of woman. But nothing could have prepared her for the emotional punch she'd taken when she'd turned around to find him standing there.

He wasn't supposed to show up in her life again. Ever. Fate didn't have that perverse a sense of humor. She groaned. *Obviously it did.*

It had been one night. One night when she'd been young, stupid, and horny as any sorority girl in lust could be.

She picked up her cell phone and debated who to call. She'd been spending more time with Franklin lately, but the idea of calling him made her stomach churn. Besides, it'd be a little weird to discuss her old lover with her current almost lover.

Biting her lip, she called Second Chances, the battered women's shelter where she worked. She pushed aside the immediate guilt over the fact that she hadn't mentioned to her friend that she'd considered taking a new job. Not that it mattered now...there was no way she'd accept a job at a resort Grant owned.

"Second Chances, how can I help you?"

"Phoebe? Hey, it's Delanie. Is it at all possible to get me on a flight back to San Francisco tonight?"

"Tonight?" Phoebe asked sharply. "What do you mean? You just got there. I thought the invitation was for one week to relax, enjoy the resort, and discuss details."

"It was." Delanie nibbled on her bottom lip and went to sit down on the plush bed.

"Then what happened? This is the chance to mix business with pleasure. I would have killed for that opportunity. I mean the owner of the resort comped your entire trip and specifically requested we send you."

Yes, and now she knew why. It wasn't just about a job and a check. She touched the pendant around her neck and exhaled heavily. It couldn't be a coincidence. It just wasn't possible. In fact, Grant had pretty much said so himself.

Admit it, Delanie. He hasn't forgotten that night any more than you have.

"Delanie? Are you still there?"

"I'm here." She sighed, hesitating whether to bring up the situation.

"Is the place just trashy or something? I mean the pictures looked great..."

"It's beautiful." She closed her eyes. "The resort itself is absolutely stunning."

"Okay. Look, whatever it is, can't you work through it? I mean they're offering to—"

"It's Grant."

Heavy silence met her statement. She could almost hear the wheels spinning in her friend's mind.

"Wait a minute, *the* Grant? The one you told me about?"

"Yes. *The* Grant. He owns Athena's Oasis."

"Well," Phoebe's voice sounded a little too bright. "That certainly makes things interesting."

"Umm, yeah, just a little."

"Does he know you took his coin?"

"I have no idea," she admitted and pushed a shaking hand through her hair. "But I have to admit I'm freaking out a bit, Phoebe."

"As well you should be. I mean if he found out and pressed charges, it could be considered a felony."

"Okay, not exactly what I wanted to hear right now," Lanie grumbled. "And besides, that's only if the coin is real..."

"Exactly. And the guy at the antique shop said it wasn't. So nothing to worry about, right?"

"Right."

"Plus, it was so long ago, he probably couldn't press charges anyway."

"Of course." There was another pause. "So what's going on? Has he been mean to you?"

Mean? No. Made her want to rip off her clothes and have sex like she was in college again? Yes.

"He hasn't been mean. I just have to question his motives for bringing me up here."

"Wait a minute, it wasn't a coincidence?"

"No. He pretty much told me that he's been searching for me for the past six years."

Silence. Then, "Okay. Well, then it's simple. Get an earlier flight home, because the man is obviously nuts."

"But, Phoebe, what about Second Chances? We—"

"Unless..." Phoebe's tone shifted, turned more thoughtful. "Unless he's just nuts *about you.* You did say you guys had this incredible connection that one night together."

"We did. But it was just one night," she protested.

Who was she trying to convince though? Her one night with Grant had emotionally linked her to him in a way she'd never been able to equal with another man.

It had taken her years to accept that fact. Her stomach clenched and she gripped the phone tighter.

"Well, maybe one night simply wasn't enough for him."

Lanie snorted, more than prepared to shoot down Phoebe's ridiculous theory. "Or maybe he knows I stole the coin."

"Maybe," Phoebe agreed mildly, though she didn't sound convinced. "But the only way you'll find out is if you stay."

Lanie sighed, shaking her head. "That's a pretty big risk."

"Okay, well forget about the whole *we screwed* bit. Think about the shelter. I mean, he's offering to donate a pretty big sum to the shelter annually. That's huge. Way more than we ever could have hoped for."

Guilt knotted in her gut. Jesus, she was a selfish witch. She closed her eyes and shoved her bangs away from her eyes. This wasn't about her. This was about Second Chances and what Grant was offering could go so far for the shelter and the women there.

"Delanie?"

Realizing she'd been quiet for too long, she cleared her throat. "I'm here. You're right, Phoebe. You're always right. Of course I'll stay. Forget I even called. I overreacted. You know me."

"Yeah, I do. And you're not the overreacting type. You're the overanalyzing type. Which is why I'm not really surprised to be having this conversation."

Delanie gave a soft laugh. "You're too good to me."

"Ditto. Oh, and by the way, Franklin called the office looking for you. Said you weren't answering your cell."

"Right," Delanie's lips twitched and some of the tension eased from her body. "Reception is terrible out here."

"I'm sure." Phoebe giggled. "That's why you're calling me right now with no trouble."

Earlier she'd turned off her phone to avoid his calls. It was another reason she'd been eager to take this trip.

She suspected he wanted their relationship to be quite a bit more serious than she did. The part she couldn't figure out was whether or not Franklin just thought she was the perfect arm candy for a senator.

As Phoebe had pointed out more than once, she was an attractive young woman from a respected family, who worked tirelessly for a battered women's shelter.

"All right. I need to unpack and get settled." She tightened her grip on the phone. "And thanks again, Phoebe."

"For?"

"For talking me down from the ledge."

"You'd do the same for me. Have a good night and keep me posted on everything. And I do mean *everything*."

"Will do. Say hi to Gabby for me."

"I will. She's been asking about you. Should I tell her you're miserable?" Phoebe teased.

"No. Tell her all is bliss. Why weigh her down with my drama." Delanie laughed. "Good night, hon."

She shut her phone and set it on the bed then leaned back against the pillow and let her head sink into the feathery softness.

She closed her eyes, hoping it would erase the image of Grant from her mind. If anything, it only heightened it.

Her fingers brushed over the faded coin around her neck. And just like every other time she touched it, the vision of that one night with Grant flickered through her mind.

A cold night, it had been snowing outside. While two hot, naked bodies joined in passion and moved together on flannel sheets.

It was a night that should never have happened.

The plan had seemed so simple. Stage an *accidental* meeting with Grant at the bar and get him to bring her back to his place. Then she'd steal the coin and sneak out.

"But being an overachiever, I just had to go for extra credit," she muttered to herself with a bittersweet smile. "I just had to go ahead and sleep with him too."

Delanie sat up on the bed and glanced outside her room to where the wind had picked up. The water beyond the resort was whipping into a frenzy of whitecaps and swells.

She lifted the coin closer to her face to stare at it. Even six years later she couldn't explain why she'd kept it for herself. That certainly hadn't been part of the plan. But when she'd untied the leather cord on the pouch and dumped the coin into her hand, the plan had gotten ditched.

The first thing she'd noticed about the coin was that it seemed old—many centuries at least. The second thing that had caught her attention was the owl on it. A weird twist of fate, since she'd just gotten an owl tattoo on her shoulder blade the week before. And maybe that's why she'd made the decision she had.

Her choices had been simple. Throw it into a lake as she'd promised the person she'd stolen it for, or keep it for herself.

The decision had been a no brainer. Not only had she kept it, but she'd had it turned into a necklace. Though she'd made sure the tiny prongs that held the coin ensured no damage would come to it.

You should've just thrown it into the lake.

She let go of the coin, the cool weight of it between her breasts calming her. No. That was another decision she wouldn't regret, no matter how much it came back to bite her in the butt.

Sliding off the bed, she reached behind her to untie the back of her halter dress. Looking over her shoulder, she caught sight of the small tattoo on her shoulder blade.

Grant's words flitted through her head again. *The last time I saw it I was taking you from behind.*

Heat spread through her body and she closed her eyes. More images assailed her. She on her hands and knees, his strong hands biting into her hips as fucked her.

She swallowed hard and shimmied out of the dress, letting it pool at her feet.

She glanced at the clock. Grant said he'd come for her at six. Two hours.

That meant she had two hours to make herself look good. Not good—great. When she pulled out all the stops with her appearance, she felt confident, ready to take on the world. She could hold her own in any situation.

Which seemed all too appropriate for the dinner she was going to attend tonight. Uneasy now, she headed to the bathroom to shower.

Chapter Two

Grant stood in his office and swirled the glass of melting ice left over from his gin and tonic.

With his gaze narrowed on the choppy waters off the island, he tilted the glass, emptying the rest of the ice into his mouth. Half made it into his mouth, the rest of it spilled down the front of his freshly pressed shirt.

He sighed and set down the glass. Of course he'd dumped half the contents on himself.

He brushed the ice off his shirt and glanced back out the window.

Thank God she was here. It had been surprisingly easy to lure Delanie Williams to Lopez Island. She hadn't even seen it coming. But then, why would she have?

She'd walked out of his life on that snowy morning six years ago and probably didn't have a clue of the chaos she'd left in her wake.

B.D.—before Delanie, he liked to call it—life had been good. The girls had loved him and he'd had no problem with his life as a serial dater. A.D.—after Delanie—he'd been lucky to make it past two dates with a woman without getting bored.

Every woman he dated, went to bed with, inevitably got compared to the one woman he'd spent less than twenty-four hours with.

It was annoying as hell, and he hated himself for doing it. Couldn't understand why he did it. He barely knew Delanie, so why should every other woman on the planet have to measure up to her?

And it wasn't just his love life that had gone kaput after that night. Things had just started to fall apart in general. His cat died, his truck got stolen, and he'd lost his job.

And those had just been the first handful of things that had gone wrong. Six years of bad luck had ensued after the coin disappeared.

He'd kept that coin in the same place day in and day out. There was no way in hell it had been misplaced. It had been taken, plain and simple. Possibly by his roommate—who'd denied ever taking it—and Grant leaned towards believing the guy. Which left only one other likely person. Delanie.

He shook his head. The idea still seemed far-fetched that she was the one who took it. What could possibly have been her motive?

The only way to find out would be to ask her face-to-face. He'd always prided himself on being able to read a person's first reaction. And tonight he'd read Delanie's.

That coin had accompanied him everywhere, it was his lucky charm. It'd been a part of him—a part of the Thompson family—for centuries.

He rubbed the back of his neck, and closed his eyes.

"This is about more than the coin," he muttered to himself. "And you'd better stop trying to convince yourself otherwise."

Seeing Delanie again was like fitting that last piece of the puzzle where it had been missing for so long.

The image of how he'd first seen her today flashed behind his closed eyes. She'd been facing away from him. Her back and shoulders bared around the thin straps of her sundress. The small tattoo of a white owl had drawn his gaze like a beacon. Then, when she'd finally turned around…

His chest tightened and he drew in an unsteady breath.

Delanie had been a pretty sorority girl, slender, with long brown hair, and brown eyes full of mischief.

But six years later she was stunning. Her slender body had softened with the curves of a woman. Her breasts were fuller, her hips more rounded, but it was her hair that had undergone the biggest transformation.

She wore it shorter now, so it just hit her shoulders. And it was lighter, almost blonde. The style made her more impish and sexy.

And he still wanted her. As much today as he had that night they'd tumbled into his bed.

Grant drew in a deep breath and winced. The smell of gin now lingered on his shirt. It was probably time for that shower.

He unfastened the buttons on his shirt and headed to the bathroom to get ready for his dinner with Delanie.

An hour later he left his room. Clean, changed, and cologned. He walked to her room, drawing in a slow breath before he lifted his hand and knocked.

His mouth twitched as he waited for her to open the door. She probably had no idea he'd had her placed in the room right next door to his.

Half a minute passed and he frowned then knocked again. Maybe she hadn't been thrilled by the idea of dinner with him, but would she deliberately avoid him? Not answer the door?

The tension eased from his shoulders when footsteps sounded inside the room. A few seconds later, the door swung open.

Grant drew in a sharp breath, letting his gaze move over her as the blood stirred in his cock.

If this was how she dressed when she didn't want to go to dinner, he'd love to see what she looked like when she did. Sweet Jesus, she looked sexy.

The black dress cut low on her breasts, showing plenty of cleavage before falling all the way down to her red-painted toenails.

He jerked his gaze back up to her face and his hand gripped the doorframe as he made a serious mental effort not to get a hard-on.

Her brown eyes appeared brighter, her expression tentative. "Sorry, I was drying my hair."

"No problem." He cleared his throat. "Are you hungry?"

She gave a quick nod, her hands twisting together in front of her. "A little. The last thing I ate was some God-awful crackers on the plane."

"God-awful crackers make for a terrible meal." He gave her a slight smile, hoping to put her more at ease.

She was nervous. Then again, he wasn't exactly Mr. Composure either after seeing her again. No matter that he'd mentally geared up for their reunion, it was still a shock.

"Ready?" He released the doorframe and stepped back, giving her room to step out.

She ran her hands over the waist of her dress and then gave a quick nod. "Yes. I'm ready." She stepped past him and closed the door behind her.

When she took those few steps past him, his gaze immediately moved over her back. The dress was cut low on the backside as well, the slinky fabric clinging to the curve of her ass.

He balled his fists against his sides and ground his teeth together. *This isn't about getting laid, buddy.* Though it would be a nice bonus.

"So, where are we going?" she called over her shoulder, not looking back as she strode down the hallway.

"I've arranged dinner in a private room on the second floor of the main house. Here."

This time she did glance sharply behind her.

"It has a great view. You'll love it," he promised and increased his stride so they walked beside each other.

He led her up the spiral staircase to the second floor. A small table had already been laid out with plates, wine glasses, and a candle burning in the middle.

Christ. He'd asked for a quiet dinner to be set up, not something you'd find on an episode of *The Bachelor*. But then, that was Roberta. The older cook was a die-hard romantic.

Delanie gasped and hurried over to the large windows that overlooked the San Juan Islands. "Look at that view!"

He smiled, thrusting his hands into his pockets. It was the reason he'd requested the dinner be held up here. The room was generally off limits. This view rarely seen by anyone, outside himself and the occasional employee.

She seemed to hesitate before moving toward the chair he pulled out for her. She sat down, her back rigid and her hands folded in her lap as she eyed the table wearily.

"Can I get you some wine?" he offered as he sat.

"I'd rather you tell me how I ended up at your resort."

Delanie bit her tongue the moment the words were out. Her stomach flipped as he lifted an eyebrow and gave a low, sexy laugh.

She hadn't planned on going straight for the attack, but seeing the tender scene he'd set up had rattled her nerves.

"Perhaps some wine first?"

He went to work filling both glasses and her gaze dropped to his hands, which were wrapped around the wine bottle.

Those hands had given her more orgasms in one night than her last two boyfriends combined.

"Here you are."

She took the glass he held out to her, annoyed to find her own hand trembling. Perhaps a little wine first would be good.

She lifted the glass to her lips and took a sip of the sweet chardonnay.

"Was I just a one night stand to you?"

His sudden question made her choke on the wine. Jeez. How the heck did she answer that question? She set the glass back down, and cleared her throat.

"How could it be anything but? Technically, we did only have sex that one night."

She lifted her gaze, not sure what she'd see. His expression was both curious and strangely intense, which unsettled her.

"That could have been remedied had you stuck around in the morning." He sighed and took a drink of his own wine.

"Look." She drew in a deep breath before plunging on. "If you brought me out here to get me into bed again, it's not going to happen."

"I didn't."

"Because I'm—you didn't?" She blinked, her stomach sinking with a disappointment she didn't want to acknowledge. *You're being an idiot, Delanie.*

He shook his head and then winced. "Well, it wasn't my initial plan. Although I admit after seeing you again…"

Something occurred to her, something she hadn't even considered. "Oh my God. Was it all a ruse? The job offer? Getting me out here with the offer to make donations to our shelter?"

"No." His mouth thinned. "Of course not, Delanie. I'm not a complete asshole."

Her smile turned a little bitchy. "But you do admit to being a partial one? I won't take it you know."

"The job?"

She nodded.

"We'll see."

107

Irritation flared at his cockiness.

A woman carrying two plates walked into the room and set them down in front of them.

"Here you are, kids. Enjoy."

Kids? Delanie's mouth twitched as she watched the older lady hurry back out of the room.

She looked down at the food before her and her mouth watered. A salmon filet rested on a bed of rice, next to it a skewer of shrimp and steamed broccoli.

"This looks amazing." She picked up her fork and speared a chunk of salmon, lifting it to her mouth. "Mmm." She chewed the bite and swallowed. "Wow. That is so much better than crackers."

He wasn't eating. When she lifted her gaze, she found him watching her, a pensive look on his face.

"What did I do to you?" he asked softly, shaking his head. "To make you get up in the morning, walk out of my house, and then basically disappear off the face of the planet?"

Her hunger diminished with the sudden question, and she set her fork down, considering her response.

"Besides call me Janie?" she asked with the only defense she had. And it was rather paltry.

"We met in a bar. It was loud when you introduced yourself to me. So I got the first letter wrong." He reached across the table and pulled her hand into his. The contact radiated warmth up her arm and throughout her body.

"I know it must have made you feel terrible. But I have a hard time believing you would throw away that night we had together over my small fuck up."

It *had* hurt. And fortunately that hurt had been the spark to ignite her into action. Meeting him that night in the bar all those years ago had never been an accidental occasion. It had been the first step in a hastily laid plan.

She'd been on a mission that night. A mission spontaneously suggested by her sorority sister. What was her name...Bridget?

Liking him was an inconvenience she couldn't have predicted. God knows what would have happened if he hadn't called her the wrong name. She might have stayed in bed all day and confessed her real reason for being there.

"Delanie." His thumb traced circles over her palm, and her breath hitched. "Did that night really mean so little to you?"

Her pulse pounded, her chest twisting tight as it grew hard to swallow.

If he only knew. That night had meant everything to her. It was why she wore the damn coin she'd stolen from him on a chain around her neck. It reminded her of the deepest connection she'd ever had with a man. The same man who'd had no qualms about breaking Bridget's heart.

She jerked her hand back from his, almost afraid he could read her thoughts. She had no illusions about what she'd done that morning. When she'd stolen his coin, she'd flat out committed a crime. A small one, but a crime nonetheless.

Being here, on this island with Grant, put everything at risk. Her status as a respected woman in her community. But even more so, her heart.

"Why did you bring me here, Grant?" She shook her head, her mouth pulled tight. "Because I'll be real honest, I'm close to catching the first ferry off this island in the morning."

He stared at her for a moment, his gaze intense on her face. "All right. You want to know why I brought you here? I'll tell you. I want it back."

The blood drained from her face. Not even trying to convince herself she didn't know what he meant, she picked up her wine glass with hands she forced to remain steady.

She might know exactly what he wanted back, but she didn't have to let him know she knew.

"I'm sorry? You want what back?"

"The coin."

Confessing she took it was way too dicey. Not to mention she'd grown awfully attached to the necklace.

She set her glass back down on the table and lifted her gaze to his. "I have no idea what you're talking about."

His nostrils flared. "The hell you don't, Lanie."

The first bit of unease settled in her gut at his unwavering accusation.

"Why would I take your coin?"

"That's what I'd like to know." His jaw hardened and he shook his head. "The only thing I do know is that I've had the worst goddamn luck since my coin disappeared."

She blinked. "Bad luck? You think that because you lost your coin you've had bad luck?"

"I did not *lose* my coin, Delanie."

She dropped her gaze, unable to handle the intensity of his stare. It was clear that he knew she took it. He just had no proof.

Thank God she'd had the sense to take off the necklace before dinner. She made a mental note to hide the thing in her luggage until she got home.

"Delanie—"

She pushed back her chair and stood up from the table. "Look, if this is any indication of how this week is going to go, I'd rather not deal with it."

"Wait." He stood, his mouth tightening. "Please, sit. I'm sorry. The last thing I want to do is have Second Chances suffer because we're having issues."

"There is no *we*."

"You know what I mean."

She stared at him for a few seconds, the blood pounding through her veins.

"I didn't take it." It was really amazing how easily the lie fell from her lips.

At first he didn't answer, then he just gave a terse jerk of his head towards the chair. "Okay. If you say you didn't take it, I won't force the issue."

Still she hesitated, torn between the burning guilt of her blatant lie and the unwillingness to sit through what was sure to be an awkward dinner.

"Please, Delanie. Roberta probably spent half the day in the kitchen prepping for this dinner."

With a brisk nod, she sank back into the chair and picked up her fork. "It's good. She's a wonderful cook."

But the food, which had looked so appetizing just moments ago, now might as well have been wood chips.

One thing he said still rang in her mind, puzzling her.

"So this bad luck," she began, lifting the shrimp skewer and pulling off a piece. "I'm sure it had nothing to do with the coin."

"I thought you didn't want to talk about it."

She bit into the shrimp and chewed it slowly. After

swallowing the seasoned bite, she licked her lips. "Okay, well certain points I'd rather not. But you've piqued my curiosity. I mean, bad luck for six years? I'm sure it's just a coincidence—"

"My cat died the day after the coin disappeared."

"Okay." She grabbed another piece of shrimp, still not convinced. "Was it old? Did it get hit by a car?"

"No. She ran across the room and jumped into a glass door."

Sounded like the result of a stupid cat to her, but she bit her tongue. "I'm sorry."

"Then my ice cream truck got stolen while I ran inside a convenience store for some nachos."

Delanie tried not to giggle, but it came out anyway. She picked up her wine. "You drove an ice cream truck?"

"It was a summer job."

"Ah. I thought it might have been your chick mobile."

"And that's another thing." He scowled and picked up his own skewer of shrimp.

"What is?"

"Women. I haven't had a relationship that lasted longer than two weeks since…" He held her gaze, his irritation obvious. "Since the coin disappeared."

"You can't expect me to believe that you haven't had sex in six years."

His gaze jerked back to hers, blue eyes alight with amusement. "I never said anything about sex."

"Of course." She rolled her eyes and turned back to the salmon. "Men never seem to have a problem with that."

"And you?"

"What about me?"

"I'm assuming you haven't exactly been abstinent since that night."

The salmon in her mouth grew heavy against her tongue. She swallowed quickly and grabbed the wine.

No, not abstinent. But damn close. The few occasions she'd taken a lover had left her so bitterly disappointed, she'd pretty much given up trying.

Franklin had been pressuring her to become intimate for months. And, truth be told, she'd been getting close to caving. As it was, she'd just hit the two-year mark without sex.

"Delanie?"

Her name sounded husky on his lips. It sent heat through her body, finally coming to rest heavily between her legs.

She closed her eyes, not wanting to admit to herself that every man who touched her ended up being compared to the man across the table.

"I've had lovers," she finally admitted.

When he didn't respond, she lifted her gaze. Surprise rippled through her. His jaw had hardened, even as his eyes burned a path over her face.

He couldn't possibly be jealous, could he? That would be...ridiculous. They'd only had one night together.

She lowered her gaze, pushing her plate away. Although, when he'd casually stated that he'd had lovers, something had clenched deep in her gut.

She sighed and glanced out over the view. The sun had only half set, casting a reddish-orange glow over the trees and water.

As if seeing Grant after six years weren't enough, now she was sitting across from him at a dinner that, for all intents and purposes, should be considered romantic.

It brought out all kinds of emotions inside her. Made her want to do stupid things and reflect on the stupider things she'd done in her past. *Get out of here before you start a repeat performance.*

"Thank you for the dinner, Grant." She set her napkin down and pushed back her chair. "Today's travel has caught up with me and I'm a little tired."

"Of course." He stood up. "Let me walk you back to your room."

"Really, there's no need," she protested. "I can find my way back."

"I'm sure. But I'd rather see you there myself." He gave a slight smile. "I was raised with good manners."

Walking back to her room she had to agree with him. Even with just that one night together, it was the first thing she'd picked up on. He'd held doors, paid for her bill at the bar...made sure she'd come five times before screwing her silly.

She bit back a groan and closed her eyes for a second. When she opened them again, they had arrived outside her room.

On impulse, she turned around to face him. He was so close, the top of her head almost brushed his chin.

Her gaze latched onto the few curls that peeked out from the neckline of his buttoned-up shirt. She breathed in deeply and could smell the mix of soap and spicy cologne.

Six years and it still seemed so fresh in her head. The way his big hands had moved over her body so knowingly. How his thumbs had strummed her nipples until she'd begged him to suck on them. The weight of his body on top of hers as he'd settled himself between her thighs. And finally, that one incredible moment when he'd thrust inside her.

Heat stirred low in her belly and her breasts ached under her dress. She wanted him to touch her again. The thought should have alarmed her more, and yet it didn't.

It was almost a relief to admit it to herself. She needed to feel his mouth on hers. It had been much too long.

She lifted her head, her tongue running over her lips.

His gaze darkened and his jaw went rigid. "Delanie..."

Without giving herself the time to reconsider, she reached up and slid her hand around his neck. Spearing her fingers upward into his soft hair, she tugged his head downward.

Chapter Three

Needing no further encouragement, his lips came down hard on hers. All the years apart melted away as his tongue pressed deep into her mouth. She was back in the bar, the taste of beer still fresh when he'd pressed his lips to hers in a first kiss.

As sweet as that kiss had been, this was sweeter. And far less innocent.

Fire raced through her blood, setting every nerve aflame as moisture gathered heavily between her legs.

He backed her hard against the door, his hands grasping her hips and squeezing her flesh. He angled his mouth and his tongue stroked deeper. His body pressed harder against her and his cock ground into her lower belly.

One of his hands moved up her hip, over her waist, and then stopped as it came along side her breast.

A tremble wracked her body and she tightened her hand in his hair, her taut nipples brushed against his chest.

His thumb stroked the swell from the side, but didn't move inward. Each brush across her flesh sent a stabbing ache straight to her pussy.

His mouth slid off hers, grazing her cheek before he caught the lobe of her ear between his teeth. A gasp ripped from her throat and her panties grew damper.

"What if someone sees us?" she whispered raggedly.

"No guests are allowed in this building. I prefer to keep some areas private. I made an exception for you." His words rode on a hot breath into her ear and she squirmed between him and the wall.

The hand at the side of her breast finally slid inward. He

slipped his palm into the neckline of her dress, cupped her fully and caught the nipple between two fingers.

"*Oh.*" She arched her back, pushing her breast harder against his palm.

His tongue flicked over her ear and then he kissed a slow trail down to the fluttering pulse in her neck. He continued to roll her nipple between skilled fingers while thrusting his hips against hers.

His cock, which had grown considerably since the kiss had started, pressed harder into her belly.

"Maybe we should take this into my room." The words barely left her mouth before she froze in shock.

She hadn't just said that. *Oh please God, don't let me have just said that.* What on earth was she thinking?

Grant lifted his head, his expression unreadable as he looked down at her. His fingers tightened around her nipple.

"We have an early morning," he murmured eventually and released her breast. He pulled his hand free from the dress and tugged the fabric back up to cover her again. "We should probably call it a night."

Humiliation and relief combined to send a flush through her body.

"Oh...of course," she stammered.

Yes, she'd regretted inviting him in the minute she'd made the offer, but the fact that he'd turned her down still kind of sucked.

This is a good thing. The last thing she wanted to do was go to bed with Grant again. Her mouth tightened. Why make the same mistake twice?

"Tomorrow we can discuss the money for the shelter when I give you a tour around the resort and island. You may even want to consider that job offer still."

The hot desire in her blood rapidly subsided at his blatant rejection. He'd become all business while she'd gone strolling down memory lane, otherwise known as Orgasm Boulevard.

"Okay." Her head bobbed up and down. That would still be a no to the job offer. She just wanted this conversation to end and for him to leave. "That sounds good."

"Can you be ready by nine?"

"Sure." She nodded again, starting to get a surreal feeling

about this whole night.

"Great. Dress comfortably." He seemed to hesitate, but then spun on his heel and walked back the way they'd come.

Delanie leaned against the door and closed her eyes with a groan. How the hell was she going to survive a week of this?

Grant shut the door to his room and lay his forehead against the wooden frame.

Was he a complete idiot? Why the hell had he turned down her invitation to continue things in her room? Especially when she'd glanced up at him with *that look* in her eyes.

The look that meant she would have allowed him to do just about anything he wanted to her at that moment. And yet he hadn't. His hand had been filled with her soft breast—the tight little nipple grazing his palm—and he'd turned her down.

"You're a fucking idiot." He tapped his forehead against the doorframe. "You could have been balls deep into her right now."

Sending her to bed alone had seemed like a good idea at the time. He'd made the split second decision not to go there with her just yet. But why?

Even though he'd told himself he hadn't brought her to Lopez Island with the intention of fucking her again, he could now acknowledge the fact he'd been delusional.

He'd originally had three purposes for bringing her out—getting the coin back, making the offer to donate to the shelter, and offering her the job as the resort's marketing director. Though the last one had been more of the dangling carrot to ensure she actually flew out. He'd known the minute she saw him she'd reject the job.

And now it appeared there would be a fourth purpose. He would have Lanie back in his bed again. But unfortunately not tonight.

Sleeping with her the first day she arrived at Athena's Oasis would have just been stupid. Pretty fucking amazing, but still, stupid as all hell.

He straightened from the door and unfastened the buttons on his shirt. Pulling it off, he dropped it on the floor then stripped down to his boxers and went to brush his teeth.

Unscrewing the lid from the toothpaste, he stilled.

What the hell was that noise?

He set down the toothpaste and stepped closer to the sink, where, on the other side of the wall, was Delanie's bathroom. The walls were paper thin—one of the reasons he never let guests stay in here.

The sound of water sloshing in the tub came again, followed by a long and high-pitched whimper.

Jesus.

Grant gripped the edge of the sink as his cock went rock hard. Again. It didn't take much imagination to realize Delanie was doing more than bathing in there.

Another long, female moan sounded and he hardened his jaw to avoid the answering groan building up in his chest.

He reached blindly for his cock, pulling it through the slit in his boxers and stroking the thick length from base to tip.

There was no way he was going to last until morning without some release. Especially after knowing Delanie was on the other side of the wall, getting herself off.

Closing his eyes, he listened to the sexy little sounds she made and pumped his erection. Envisioning her breasts covered with water as she lay in the tub fingering herself. So hot. God, what he wouldn't give to see her right now.

She'd been so hot when he'd taken her that night in college. So tight and wet. How wet was she now? Was that pretty pink pussy of hers still bare?

God, he could have spent hours going down on her. She'd been so succulent and sweet. Her cries of pleasure had rid him of the ability to think. Just to give her that pleasure, watching her face and listening to her sexy little moans.

When her cries grew more frequent on the other side of the wall, he moved his fist faster.

And then she climaxed.

"*Oh.*" Her strangled cry of release was followed by a splash, and then silence.

Grant's sac tightened and he ground his teeth together, reaching for a small towel on the counter just a second before he came.

He emptied himself over and over into the white terrycloth. Until his mind whirled back to life and he was staring at himself in the mirror.

Dragging in a ragged breath, he shook his head. Damn.

Talk about losing complete control.

The sound of the tub draining through the wall meant Delanie was finished in the tub.

He tossed the towel into the laundry bin in the corner, washed his hands and picked up the toothpaste again. His body sated from its release, his thoughts turned back to other matters.

Like the coin.

There was no doubt about it. She'd taken it. He picked up his toothbrush and shook his head, squeezing some mint toothpaste onto the brush.

The question was, did she still have it?

Twelve hours later, Grant was back outside her door. Drinking in the sight of the woman who'd kept him awake all night. The woman whose face he'd pictured while jerking himself off in the shower an hour ago.

"Good morning."

"Don't be so sure about that." Delanie yawned and stepped out of her room, shutting the door behind her.

In jeans and a faded pink T-shirt, she looked nothing like the sex kitten he'd had dinner with last night. Or a woman who had no inhibitions about masturbating in his bathtub.

Yet, in a way, he almost preferred her like this. Fresh-faced with little makeup on, casual and relaxed. It reminded him of the girl he'd met in the bar six years ago.

"So, where are we off to? I assume you're serving me breakfast first?" She lifted an eyebrow and followed him down the hall.

"Breakfast is taken care of." He winked and lifted the brown paper sack. "Roberta packed us a couple of her famous blackberry scones, and I'm having coffee brewed at this very moment."

She groaned. "Thank God. I'm going to need a little help waking up."

"Not a morning person?"

"I've gotten better over the years." She glanced over at him, her gaze suspicious. "When did you become one?"

"What do you mean?"

"I mean..." she drifted off and he was surprised to see her cheeks fill with color. "Well, after that night together. You...we..."

"Yes?" he prodded.

After all these years, that morning still seemed a bit hazy. One moment she'd been in his arms, her sweet body trembling through an orgasm. The next he'd woken to find her—and the coin—gone.

"You just didn't seem to wake up easily." She bit her lip. "I mean you did...fall back asleep."

His brows drew together. Fall back asleep? What was she...? It snapped into place and he gave a slow nod.

"Ah-ha. Yes, I guess I did fall back asleep." He gave her a closer look. "And that upset you?"

She opened her mouth and then shut it. Her cheeks turning adorably pink.

"Lanie?" She didn't even correct him when he slipped and called her by her nickname.

"Well, come on, Grant. How would you feel?" she grumbled, tucking a strand of hair behind the curve of her ear. "I mean we'd just...you'd just." She sighed. "And then I look over and you're snoring away."

"I don't snore."

She met his gaze and lifted an eyebrow. Her eyes danced with mischief, the challenge in her gaze bordered on flirting. "Oh, yes. You sure as hell do."

An honest laugh rose from his chest and he grinned. Yeah, he probably did snore a little. And how funny that she'd just called him on it—cursing while she did so.

He remembered that side of her from that night in the bar. He'd begun to wonder where that girl was, but apparently she still existed. She was just buried beneath the carefully composed woman she'd become.

"So I take it we're doing breakfast on the road then?"

"We'll eat at one of the lookouts on the island. That way I can give you a tour afterward, before coming back to see the rest of the resort."

"Sounds like a busy morning. I'm up for it." She gave a soft laugh. "Just as long as you have to-go cups for that coffee."

"I wouldn't have offered if we didn't." He led her into the

kitchen and found the travel cups full of coffee Roberta had left them.

"Cream or sugar?" he asked.

"Black."

He raised an eyebrow, but didn't comment. Just handed her the cup of steaming coffee.

"Are you ready?"

She gave a quick nod and took a sip of the coffee.

"All right. Let's go." He picked the bag of scones up again and led her out of the kitchen.

The website and pictures she'd seen of the resort hadn't done it justice. And now, though she hated to admit it, she was half in love with the resort. It didn't take much effort to imagine spending her days working up here on Lopez Island. Being close to Grant...

Delanie's feet ached from the amount of walking they'd already done today. They'd been all over the island, before returning for the grand tour of the resort.

Athena's Oasis consisted of twelve guest cabins, an indoor pool, a saltwater pool near the cliffs, a tennis court, and the main building that housed the restaurant, lounge, and a few extra rooms.

She'd been surprised when he told her that her room was one of the extras in the main building. Then again, maybe he was saving the cabins for all the tourists, with it being summer and all.

"So, where do you live?" she asked as they entered one of the empty cabins. "Do you stay on the resort somewhere, or live offsite?"

"I live at the resort." The lazy smile he gave had her stomach doing all kinds of acrobatics. "This place is my baby."

She glanced around the inside of the small wooden cabin. The décor had a simplistic feel. The double bed was decorated with a lovely quilt, while lace curtains covered the window next to it. There was also a cherry wood dresser, and small round table in the corner with a chessboard on top.

"I love this. It's so sweet and private. Do you live in one of the cabins?"

"Off and on, although I haven't been using it the past

couple of weeks."

"No? Where have you been staying?"

"In the main building." The look he gave her spoke volumes.

He was in the room next to hers. How had she not realized that until now? Heat moved through her body as the memory of last night flickered through her head.

Jeez, she'd pretty much thrown herself at him and still he'd turned her down. And yet the entire time he'd been sleeping with just a wall between them.

Yikes. He hadn't been able to hear her last night, had he? She pushed away the memory of her taking her arousal into her own hands.

She looked out over the view, inhaling the crisp salty air.

"Delanie," he said her name softly. The calloused hand that lightly touched the back of her neck sent shivers down her spine.

She turned towards him, the air locked in her lungs.

"You have a very beautiful resort, Grant."

"Thank you." The flicker of pride in his gaze was a clear indication that her words meant a lot to him.

"Are you sure about the donation? It's a lot of money—not that we aren't grateful to have it..."

"I wouldn't have offered if I didn't intend to follow through. What you ladies do for those women...it's outstanding. I want to help in any way I can." His fingers traced around to her collarbone. "I've had papers drawn up that you will need to look over and sign."

She swallowed, though it took some effort. "Thank you."

"What made you do it?"

Her stomach dropped. He was right back to questioning her about the coin.

"What made you decide to work at a shelter for abused women?"

Or not. The tension eased from her body and she gave a faint smile.

"It was never part of my plan—I actually have a degree in marketing. Which you obviously discovered somehow." She tucked a strand of hair behind her ear. "I did my last year of college back in California, and that's where I met Phoebe."

"And Phoebe is...?"

"She works with me at Second Chances. It was her idea to start working there after college. I followed her there. I..."

He gave a slight nod and brushed his thumb over the pulse in her neck.

"I didn't see it when we first met—or maybe I was just too absorbed with school, trying to get that four-point GPA." She closed her eyes, regret making her throat tight. "But for some reason I failed to notice that Phoebe was in an abusive relationship."

Grant made a soft sound of sympathy, his thumb stroking her jawline.

"Sometimes they don't want you to see it and keep it well hidden."

She nodded. "I know, and she confessed later that she'd done exactly that. By the time I suspected something wasn't right, Phoebe had left him."

"How long did she stay?"

"Two years," she said quietly. "But when she left him, she left for good. She had other friends who'd survived abusive relationships and they really helped her through it. Talked her out of ever going back to him, helped her keep a low profile and disappear from him completely."

"She was lucky."

"She was. Like I said, working for the shelter was Phoebe's idea, but once I realized her intentions and got to know the place, I had to get on board."

"That's a lot of giving you both do."

"It's gratifying. To be able to help women who've been in the same or worse situation as Phoebe." She lifted her gaze, running her tongue over her lips. "What you're offering us is unselfish. That's one heck of a donation."

"I have the money, and I've been looking into a cause like this to donate to."

Her stomach warmed, even felt a bit fluttery. The sincerity of his expression wiped away any lingering doubts about his intentions.

"You're amazing, Grant. I can't thank you enough. We can't. Everyone at the shelter has been on cloud nine since I told them about the offer. Especially Phoebe."

"I'm glad to hear it." He paused. "After the bad relationship, does she ever date anymore?"

She shook her head and sighed. "Not at all. I've tried to get her out, but she's still a bit leery."

"Understandable. She will when she's ready."

"I hope so." She licked her lips.

His gaze dropped to her mouth. "You know... I think we're done with the tour now."

"Are we?" Her pulse quickened at the sudden change of conversation and mood.

Heat flowed between them like an electrical current. His thumb swept up to her bottom lip and she sighed, moving her gaze from his mouth to the cleft in his chin.

"Yes." He lowered his head lowered, blocking out the light from the window, before his lips brushed oh-so lightly across hers.

Delanie sighed and leaned into him, ignoring the voice inside her that screamed she was not only turned on right now, but stupid.

The heat in her belly expanded to an ache between her thighs. Why was he kissing her again? When he'd turned her away last night?

Why do you care? No man had even stirred such a heated instant response like Grant.

His hand slid down her back until it came to rest on the curve of her ass. He squeezed the flesh and pulled her snug against him, grinding his cock into her belly.

She moaned, moisture gathered in between her legs and the ache intensified.

His tongue delved, passing her teeth to rub against hers and explore deeply.

He urged her backwards, not breaking the kiss as he walked her towards the bed. The back of her knees connected with the mattress just before he eased her onto it, and then the weight of his body covered hers.

Cool air brushed the bare skin of her stomach when his fingers slid under her shirt. He traced a finger around her navel, moving his knee between her legs and snug against her pussy.

She tore her mouth away to issue a strangled gasp.

"Mmm." He tugged her shirt up and off her body then lowered his head to her breast.

He nuzzled her nipple through the lace, before catching the tip between his lips and sucking. Tingles of pleasure spread to every inch of her body and she drove her fingers into his hair, holding him to her.

Grant tugged the cup of the bra down, baring her breast before he drew the nipple deep into his mouth. Sucking and flicking the tip with his tongue.

"*Oh God.*" Her hips jackknifed off the bed, but he pushed them back down, unsnapping the button on her pants.

She heard the rasp of the zipper, then his hand slipped under the waistband of her jeans. A ragged groan ripped from her throat when he worked his fingers into her panties and cupped her mound.

"God, Delanie," he muttered against her breast. "You're so hot and wet."

He slid one long finger inside her and the air rushed from her lungs, her body clenching around the sensual intrusion.

Her nipples tightened further and her pussy grew heavy with moisture. Grant grazed his teeth across the tip of her breast and she squirmed, crying out with pleasure.

"And you're so responsive. Just like I remember." He pulled his finger from her channel and moved it in a slow circle around her clitoris.

"*Mmm.*" She moved against his hand, rotating her hips in a slow dance to match what his finger was doing.

"I want you to come," he whispered, switching his mouth to her other breast. His tongue flicked over the tip.

The pleasure built higher, growing more intense with each move of his finger against her sensitive flesh.

"*Grant.*" Her nails dug into his shoulder, nearly piercing the fabric.

"Let go, baby. Just—"

"*You're so vain. You probably—*" Delanie shoved her hand into her pocket, silencing the song.

Grant lifted his head, his gaze bewildered. "What the hell was that?"

Chapter Four

"My phone," Delanie muttered, the pleasure that had been building slipping away as shock and annoyance rolled over her.

He gave a rough laugh. "Nice ringtone."

"Thanks." She shifted uneasily beneath him.

It was the ringtone she'd assigned to Franklin, simply because it fit him so well. The man had an ego the size of the state of which he was senator.

Fortunately her relationship with Franklin was still fairly casual—she'd never allowed anything more than a few heavy kisses. Otherwise, she probably would be feeling a bit guilty right now.

"*You're so vain—*"

She silenced the call again. Shoot. Franklin obviously wasn't going to give up.

"I should get this," she said huskily, and slid out from beneath Grant, tugging her bra back on.

Irritation flickered in his gaze, but she did her best not to acknowledge it.

Snatching her phone from her pocket, she flipped it open.

"Hello?"

"Delanie, darling, I've been trying to reach you since you arrived yesterday. Is everything all right?"

"Everything is fine. Yes." She watched Grant climb off the bed, casting an irritated gaze her way. She turned her back to him and pushed aside a twinge of guilt. "Was there something you needed?"

"Just making sure my girl arrived safely. I actually have a meeting up in Seattle tomorrow and was checking into the possibility of chartering a flight to Lopez Island—"

"Oh. You know, I'm not sure that's a good idea," she protested quickly, alarm sweeping through her. "In fact, I'm kind of in the middle of something. Can I call you back in a bit?"

"I suppose. Though I'm not pleased that it took you this long to even answer your phone—"

"I've been a little busy. Look, I'll call you later." And when she did, they'd probably have the *this isn't working* talk. "We have some things to discuss."

"Really?" His voice warmed. "I was actually thinking the same. I'll—"

"Look, I'm sorry, but I need to go. I'll call you later." She shut the phone, her stomach twisting. That call had already gone on about one minute longer than she'd wanted.

"Important call?"

Delanie bit her lip and forced a bright smile on her face before turning around.

"Yes, somewhat. Sorry, but I really had to take that." Her gaze drifted to the bed and disappointment clogged in her throat.

Her body still hummed from his touch, still ached to sink back onto the mattress and pull him on top of her. When she looked back at Grant, she knew that wasn't about to happen. He'd become all business—was even glancing at his watch.

"We should probably head out. We still have one more thing to do."

"We do?" His words sent another stab of sharp disappointment through her. "But haven't we toured the entire resort?"

"For the most part." His mouth curved. "There's one other place I still need to show you."

"Oh yeah?" She grabbed her shirt off the floor and pulled it back on. Glancing back at him she asked, "Will I like it?"

He closed the distance between them and traced his thumb over her bottom lip. "I think you will. I hope you will."

Her stomach fluttered again and she bit back a groan, pulling away. She fastened her jeans again, her fingers unsteady.

"Did you bring a hat? More summer-like clothes?" he asked.

"Yes." She gave him a curious glance. "Why?"

His smile widened. "You may want to wear something cooler today."

"Mmm. It sounds fun."

"It *will* be fun, I promise. We need to go pack up some more stuff before we head out."

She pushed her bangs out of her eyes, and gave a quick nod, already eager to see what he had planned.

Delanie slipped on her bikini to wear beneath her clothes, her body still buzzing from that moment in the cabin. She found her shorts and pulled them on just as her phone rang.

She glanced at it lying on the bed. Fortunately, it wasn't Franklin's ringtone.

Zipping up her shorts, she grabbed it and flipped it open. "Hello?"

"Hey, it's Gabby."

"Gabby!" Delanie gave a squeal of excitement. "Hey, how's it going?"

"Good. I only have a few minutes before Phoebe gets back from the safe house. But I wanted to check. How's that job prospect going?"

Delanie bit back a sigh. She hadn't told Phoebe about the job offer, but had confided in Gabby. Gabby had been so encouraging and had been the one to recommend holding off telling Phoebe until she'd decided whether to accept the job or not.

But where Gabby knew about the job, she didn't know about Grant. Only Phoebe had the scoop on that, and unfortunately she didn't have time to give Gabby the full scoop.

"The job prospect..." she hesitated. She had no idea if Grant had ever seriously intended to give it to her or if it was just a ruse to get her out here. She decided to be ambiguous. "I'm totally on the fence. We'll see."

"Cool. Keep me posted. Is it pretty out there?"

"Gorgeous. You would not believe it." She sighed. "Hey, how's your mom?"

"She's doing so good. Went to live with her cousin in Nevada. Hasn't spoken with my dad since she left him that night." Gabby's voice softened. "I'm so proud of her."

"That's awesome, Gabby." Delanie smiled.

And it was. Gabby's mother had been abused by her husband for years before finally leaving a few weeks ago with Gabby's help.

"Oh, hey, Justin just showed up to take me to lunch. I should go. We miss you, Delanie."

"I miss you too. Say hi to Justin for me."

"Will do. Bye, hon."

Delanie closed her phone and pulled on her tank top, then glanced around for her straw hat. Her stomach fluttered with anticipation of what Grant had planned for them next.

One thing for certain was that the next time Grant touched her, she'd ensure there were no interruptions. Reaching for the phone, she turned the ringer to silent.

Grant pushed aside the bottles of water in the cooler to make room for the sandwiches Roberta made for them.

"You are too good to me." He walked past Roberta, giving her a quick squeeze on the shoulder.

"Oh, I'm just doing my job," she scoffed, but her wrinkled cheeks went pink with delight. "Where's that young lady, anyway? You know, I have yet to get an introduction."

"You'll get your introduction," he promised and shook his head. "She's in her room packing a bag right now. We're going to take the boat out."

"Oh, wonderful. Don't forget your life vests. It gets mighty choppy out there…"

Roberta broke off and her gaze lifted to something behind him.

He turned around and found Delanie standing in the doorway. She'd changed into a pair of shorts, tank top, and had on a big, ugly, straw hat, and a massive overstuffed tote bag slung over her shoulder.

He bit back an amused chuckle. She'd certainly taken to heart the warning that they'd be in the sun the rest of the day.

"I'm set," she announced unnecessarily.

"I see that."

Knowing Roberta was itching for an introduction, and her curiosity wouldn't be appeased until she got one, he turned to the older woman.

"Roberta, this is Delanie Williams. She works for Second Chances, the battered women's shelter outside of San Francisco that we'll be donating to. Delanie, this is Roberta Smith, my chef and woman of all trades."

He went to the fridge to pick their fruit, and waited for the preening to begin.

"Oh, Ms. Williams, aren't you a lovely thing? It's so wonderful what you do for those poor women." Roberta hurried across the floor to grasp Delanie's hands. Continuing on after a quick breath. "I was just thrilled when Grant told me he was going to sponsor the shelter."

"Please, call me Delanie." Delanie gave the older woman a warm smile and then glanced over at him. "And yes, the offer Mr. Thompson has made is rather remarkable."

Their gazes locked and he winked, before slipping into the pantry to grab a couple of extra scones.

"And you're just so pretty," he heard Roberta say. "Say, are you married, Delanie?"

Delanie's responding laugh was quiet, her answer even quieter. But he still heard it. "No, just dating someone."

Grant's hand clenched around one of the scones and crumbs squeezed out the edge of the plastic wrap. She was seeing someone? His chest tightened and the sudden jealousy left a sour taste in his mouth.

"Oh, what a pity." Roberta sighed. "I was hoping—"

"Thank you again for the lunch," he interrupted, returning from the pantry. The effort it took to keep his expression placid was monstrous. "We should be back late this evening."

"The weather might take a turn tonight. They're saying possible rain, so don't head back too late," Roberta warned, wagging her finger.

Delanie laughed. "I don't mind getting a little wet."

Grant jerked his gaze towards her. Her face flamed red and she bit down on her lip. Obviously she'd just realized the double entendre in her words. "I mean, from the rain," she added in a rush.

Roberta was oblivious to any of her apparent

embarrassment and went about wiping down the counter.

"All right, well, you two kids have fun, and be careful out there."

"Thanks for the lunch, Roberta."

Grant placed a hand on Delanie's back, turning her out of the kitchen before Roberta could call her back to ask her how serious the relationship was with the man she was seeing. Then again, it was something he wouldn't have minded finding out himself.

How the hell could he have been stupid enough to assume that she was single? Though, she'd certainly acted like she was last night, and then again today in the cabin. If her phone hadn't rung, they'd probably still be in the cabin right now.

The fire that raced through his blood took on a new motive as his anger grew. How could she possibly be seeing someone else and yet let him touch her the way he had?

Delanie cleared her throat as they stepped outside and moved towards his Jeep.

"Roberta seems sweet. And...chipper."

Grant gave a tight smile. "Roberta is a gem. She's been with the resort since I took it over from my grandfather five years ago."

"Five years?" she repeated as he held open the passenger door to the Jeep and let her climb in. "Wow, you sure didn't waste time getting started after graduation."

"When I want something, I go after it." He met her gaze. "Always."

Her eyes widened. Without waiting for her to reply, he shut her door and went around to the driver's side of the Jeep.

He climbed in and started the engine.

"The resort belonged to my grandfather and he left it to me when he passed away."

"That's a pretty incredible inheritance."

"Yes. It is." He went silent again, not really in the mood for chitchat. Jealousy still burned hot in his gut.

"Roberta certainly packed us a lot of food."

He grunted in response and hit the gas, flooring the Jeep out of the resort.

Delanie's loud gasp filled the car. "Do you always drive so fast?"

Do you always fuck two men at once? His jaw clenched in an effort to avoid snarling the question at her.

"So where are we going anyway?" she asked, sounding a little more uncertain now.

"We're going on a little trip."

"A trip?" She glanced over at him. "Are we leaving the island?"

"Yes."

"Oh. But isn't the ferry the other way?"

"We're not taking the ferry."

She went silent, obviously trying to figure out what that meant. Or maybe she just picked up on the fact he wasn't in the mood to talk.

He pulled up to the private boat launch a few minutes later and parked the Jeep.

"You have your own boat?"

"It's small, but it works until I get around to buying a nicer one." He climbed down from the Jeep and opened her door.

She tried to meet his gaze, but he turned away to grab the stuff out of the back, his irritation with her still too fresh.

"Grab your bag and head on down to the dock, I'll be there in a minute."

"Okay." She hesitated a second and then walked away.

Grant closed his eyes and took a deep breath. Maybe this wasn't a good idea. The minute they got on that boat and headed to the island, they'd be stuck together for at least a couple of hours.

His initial hope that she'd come clean about the coin— maybe even return it—was dying a slow, painful death. But it wasn't even about the coin anymore. It was about Delanie.

How every time he looked at her, his chest tightened a bit. And when she gave that flirty little smirk, he just wanted to kiss her until that smile went slack with passion.

When I want something, I go after it. He'd meant the words when he'd said them, and whether or not she believed them yet, she soon would. He wanted Delanie and he sure as hell intended to have her.

He scooped up the cooler and blankets and slammed the door to his Jeep.

Delanie folded her arms across her chest and stared at Grant as he strode down the incline towards the dock. He was angry about something, but what? Things had been near perfect between them all morning. He had no right to get pissy with her.

Unless he heard that part where you said you were dating someone.

She hadn't meant to let that slip. It had just come out when Roberta had started the *are you single?* conversation. It had been a natural response, and she'd been thankful Grant had been in the other room when she'd blurted it.

He arrived on the dock, still not looking at her as he set the blankets and cooler into the boat.

"You can climb on in," he told her briskly, and went back up the hill towards the Jeep.

Delanie made a face at him and then glanced down at the boat. It was tied to the dock and rocking back and forth on the waves.

Jeez, had she ever been in a boat this little? Sure she'd traveled on ferries and spent more than a few hours on Franklin's yacht, but this...this was like all wood and probably no bigger than a bed. Not to mention it looked...old.

Go on, you nitwit. Taking a deep breath, she crouched and lowered one foot into the boat. It immediately started rocking under her weight and she went still, gripping the edge of the dock.

"Just climb in. It's safe." Grant's leather sandals slapped against the dock as he walked back towards the boat.

Not wanting to look like a complete wimp, she swung her other leg into the boat and then gripped each side. It took a second to get her sea legs and then she sat on the bench seat in the middle.

Grant stepped easily into the boat without holding onto anything. He untied them from the dock, and then walked to the back, sitting on the seat next to the motor.

"There's a life jacket under your seat, why don't you go ahead and put it on."

Not even about to argue, she reached under the bench and pulled up a black and yellow life vest.

She fumbled to put it on, trying to make sure the straps went around her body.

"Here, let me." He stepped forward and knelt beside her.

Delanie froze, closing her eyes as his warm breath feathered across her face. He adjusted the belts and then clicked them into place.

"There, you're set."

She opened her eyes and found his face just inches away from hers.

Heat flickered in his gaze, but was instantly replaced with irritation.

"Where's your life jacket?" she asked when he finally pulled away and went back to his seat.

He grunted and pulled on some cord that immediately had the motor sputtering to life. "I have a floatation cushion if I need it."

She rolled her eyes and shook her head. *He was such a guy.* And that's probably why she liked him. He was nothing like Franklin.

Franklin followed all the rules, wore two-thousand-dollar suits, and got manicures. She knew this because his nails always looked better than hers, and she'd bugged him until he'd finally confessed to getting them done. And then she'd promptly switched to his manicurist.

She lowered her gaze to Grant's hands. Large and calloused, tanned from the sun. A real man's hands. And no expensive suits or brand names on this man—though he could obviously afford them. Unless he was dressing up, like at dinner last night, Grant appeared to be a jeans and old T-shirt kind of guy. Like today, his broad shoulders filled out a plain gray shirt, the muscles bulging on his forearm.

"Okay, hang on." He twisted a lever that connected to the motor, and the boat jolted forward.

Delanie took off her hat before it could fly off her head and then gripped the seat. She glanced over her shoulder to see where they were going. She could've turned around in the seat to sit the other way, her back to Grant, but somehow the view was so much better when he was in it.

"So, where are we going?" she asked, twisting back so she stared off the back of the boat again. The shores off Lopez Island grew farther away with every passing second.

Grant didn't answer right away, but seemed to check something on the motor. "To a smaller island nearby."

"Oh. What's over there?"

"Nothing yet, really. I own it."

The air stranded in her lungs and she blinked. He *owned* an island? Was it even possible for someone to own an island?

"How do you afford all this? A nice resort? An entire island? The San Juans aren't exactly bargain realty."

His gaze met hers. "Like I said, the resort was initially owned by my grandfather. My family and I do rather well financially."

"So why did you buy...an island?"

"The island is small. It's not even on most maps. I'm building an expansion of the resort there. What will eventually become the ultimate retreat for those who come to stay at Athena's Oasis."

He twisted the handle on the motor again and the boat picked up speed.

"I see." But she didn't really. Athena's Oasis was already an impressive upscale resort as it was. People traveled from all over the world to stay there.

And yet he'd bought an entire island to extend the resort? *The ultimate retreat.* Possibilities of what that could mean filled her head.

The wooden boat slapped against the waves as they sliced through the water. The sound alone sent shivers of unease through her. She half expected the old boat to split in half each time it connected with the surface.

She gripped the edge of her seat, holding on for all she was worth. Lopez Island had become just a blur of trees and rock, they were too far out to even see the resort anymore.

"How far away is the island?"

"About another fifteen minutes. The motor's small on this boat, so it takes a little while."

She closed her eyes, letting her body move with the up and down motion. The cool salty air of the Pacific coated her lungs and filled her chest, energizing her more than any cup of coffee could.

She drew in a couple of deep breaths, feeling the tension in her body ease. The wind teased at her bangs, whipping them around her forehead.

When she opened her eyes again, Grant was watching her.

His blue eyes had darkened and she didn't miss the heat flickering in his intense gaze.

Her cheeks warmed under his scrutiny and she ran her tongue over her lips, tasting the salt from the air. With what happened between them at the cabin still fresh in her head, a heavy ache started between her legs and her nipples tightened under the thin tank top.

Maybe he was taking her out to this island for a little bit of romance. Did Grant think like that? Was he plotting this big, romantic, back-in-bed-together reunion? The idea did seem—

"So, who's the boyfriend?"

His words made her stomach drop and all her ridiculous notions evaporate. So he *had* overheard her and Roberta back at the resort.

"You don't know him," she murmured. Chances were he'd probably heard of him, but having the *my boyfriend is a senator* talk wasn't one she wanted to delve into right now.

"No, I probably don't." She wasn't deceived by his casual shrug. "But speaking as another guy, I know he wouldn't be too happy if he found out you were screwing around with someone else."

He slowed the boat and she looked over the edge to see several groups of rocks protruding under the water.

"If he found out?" she repeated, annoyance pricking. "Is that some kind of threat?"

"No." He met her gaze, his expression not so heated anymore. "The only accountability you have is to your own conscience. I have no guilt for what happened between us, though I'm not sure you can say the same."

Her nostrils flared. "What gives you the right to judge me? You have no idea what kind of relationship I have with him."

The boat jolted as he put them ashore. He stood up and killed the motor, stepping towards her.

"No. I don't. So why don't you enlighten me?"

She opened her mouth to reply, but he stepped past her. He grabbed the blankets and cooler, and climbed out of the boat.

Scrambling up from the bench seat, she put her hat back on and jumped out of the boat after him. The rocky beach crunched under her sandaled feet as she ran to catch up.

"Why don't you stick around for a second so I can?" she yelled. "Besides, it's not like we actually had sex. We just fooled around."

She winced. Now there was an illogical teenager defense if she'd ever heard one. She didn't blame Grant one bit when he turned around with a look of complete disbelief.

"I could have had you in the cabin, Lanie. You would have been getting your brains fucked out and liking it right about now if your phone hadn't rung."

Her jaw tightened. "That's a little crude, but then I guess I should've expected that coming from y—"

"Was that him?" he asked suddenly, cocking his head as he walked back towards her, his eyes lit with anger and frustration. "Was that him calling?"

She folded her arms across her chest. Why lie? "Yes."

His body went rigid and his mouth became a tight, straight line.

"You know, you seemed so damn innocent that night we met at the bar." He shook his head.

"Why do you keep bringing up that night?" she muttered and turned away, staring back out at the water.

"Because I'm trying to merge the girl I knew that night and the woman you are now. You were so genuine that night." His voice softened. "You laughed at my jokes and acted as if I were the only guy in the bar. We had so much in common. We went to the same university, had some of the same teachers..."

His voice trailed off abruptly and he didn't speak for a moment. Then, "It wasn't random, was it? You meeting me at the bar that night? You were looking for me."

She clenched her teeth, refusing to answer. Her stomach rolled with the shock that he'd put it together.

"Was it part of your plan? Flirt with me at the bar. Go to bed with me. And then steal the coin in the morning?"

She spun around and snapped harshly, "Going to bed with you was *never* part of the plan!"

Grant's head jerked back like he'd been slapped, his eyes widening.

The color drained from her face. *How easily he'd maneuvered that confession.*

"But stealing the coin was." His words were low and icy. "You were a good fuck, but you weren't that good. I want it back."

Chapter Five

She flinched. "I don't have it."

"Like hell you don't—"

"I sold it years ago," she lied. *You were a good fuck, but you weren't that good?* God that had hurt. Her gut twisted and her throat grew tight.

She heard the air leave his lungs. The anger in his gaze still remained, but now mixed with disappointment.

"You sold it. Well...to sell such a rare coin you must have really needed the money." He gave a bitter smile. "Congratulations on earning it on your back."

He turned and walked back up the beach, away from her. Her mouth gaped as she tried to blink away the tears in her eyes.

If she weren't so adverse to any form of violence, she would have slapped him. Her hand had even started to rise instinctively, before she'd realized what she was about to do and jerked it back.

Screw this. She was not going to spend another minute on this island with him, or the resort. She turned and ran back toward the boat.

It was all too clear. He'd only invited her out here, made the job offer and donations to her shelter to get the coin back.

She gave the boat a hard push off the beach so it bobbed farther out into the water, then climbed into it. Walking to the back, she tried to remember how Grant had started it.

"Lanie? Lanie!"

His voice resonated down the beach. She glanced up and saw him running back towards her.

Tears blurring her vision, she pushed the button she'd watched him push and then tugged on the cord on the motor.

The boat started to rock wildly and she glanced up to see Grant splashing out towards her.

"Lanie, what the hell are you—?"

The motor roared to life, drowning out his question. The boat jerked forward and put more distance between them.

"Jesus Christ, Lanie!" he screamed and slapped his palm against the water. "Do you know how to drive a boat?"

"I'll figure it out."

"There're huge rocks underwater that you could hit—"

Wood cracked as the boat slammed into one such rock. The blades on the motor ground against it next and the engine sputtered one last time before dying.

"That didn't sound good," Grant called from shore. "Enough already, Lanie. Start the boat and come back to shore."

"I don't know how I started it the first time," she snapped, but went to work pushing buttons and pulling on the cord.

Cool water slapped against her foot and she looked down and her stomach dropped.

Water seeped into the boat, rapidly coating the floor of the boat.

Shit. Shit. And shit!

"Lanie? Did you hit something?"

She nodded dumbly, unable to tear her gaze from incoming water.

The tone of Grant's voice changed from irritation to alarm. "Is there water in the boat?"

She nodded again, her stomach churning with the realization she was in a boat that could very well sink. And she'd brought this on herself. Why had she thought it a good idea to try to drive a boat back to the resort when she had zero experience? *Idiot.*

"Listen to me, Lanie. I need you to grab the oars and row the boat back toward shore," he said, his voice calm and coaxing, as if he were talking to a child. But then, her behavior pretty much warranted it.

"Oars?" She looked around, not quite sure what kind of oar would fit in such a small boat, but pretty sure there were none here. "I don't see any oars."

"They're the long wooden things on the floor. I..." He trailed off. "Forgot to put them in the boat, didn't I?"

"It kind of looks like it."

Water swirled around her now numb feet and the boat seemed to be lower in the water.

"*Of course I did.*" Grant cursed, pacing back and forth on shore, his fists clenched. "This damn bad luck streak will never end."

"Umm, can we deal with the bad luck part later?" she yelled, her voice shaking. "Because I'm starting to have Titanic visions here, and not the fun ones with Leonardo drawing me naked."

"Okay. How fast is the water coming in?"

"I think pretty fast. I mean there's an awful lot of water in here. It's above my ankles."

"Shit."

To say the least. Panic clawed her belly as she noticed the shoreline grow farther away with each passing second.

"Grant, what should I do?"

"Okay." Grant waded out into the water. "Lanie, I want you to jump from the boat and swim back to shore. You've still got your life jacket on."

"Swim?" she croaked.

"You can swim, can't you?"

"Yes, but—"

"The longer you wait, the farther away from the beach you're getting. You're almost in the current and then it's going to be damn hard to swim," he shouted. "I'll meet you halfway. Jump in now, Lanie!"

She dove off the boat, the fear of God instilled in her.

The icy water ripped the air from her lungs, incapacitating her as she sank an inch lower in the water. Her hat floated off her head and got swept up into the current.

Shit. It had sure looked pretty, but this was so not the same temperature as the California coast.

"Swim, for God's sake, swim, Lanie!" he yelled again.

With a shake of her head, she forced herself into a crawl stroke. Every inch of her body burned from the frigid water as she swam against the current back toward the beach.

Something began to buzz nonstop against her thigh. Her

cell phone! Oh God, her phone was in her pocket!

There are more important things than your phone, you fool, now swim for Pete's sake! She pushed harder, digging deeper with each stroke.

When she looked up toward the beach again, Grant was wading out to her. He dove under the waves and brisk strokes brought him right up to her.

He makes it look so damn easy.

Strong arms wrapped around her waist, offering support. It took all her power not to just go weak against him and let him carry all her weight.

"Almost there, baby." His voice was rough and warm against her ear. A beautiful contrast to the numbness that spread through her body.

She couldn't feel the cold water anymore. She couldn't really feel her hands either, but that was beside the point.

"You made it, Lanie." He staggered up the drop off and into the shallow water. "Come on, walk with me, baby."

Her legs wobbled right before her knees buckled.

"I gotcha." Grant scooped her up, carrying her tight against his chest.

His heart pounded in his chest; his throat raw with emotion. The panic had hit him like a truck when she'd told him the boat was filling with water. And again when she hadn't been able to start the engine and the boat had visibly sunk a few inches down into the water.

The fear had been instantaneous. Thank God he'd been able to keep a clear enough head to convince her to jump in and swim to shore.

Even soaked to the bone, she was light in his arms. Her arms wrapped around his neck as her body pressed snug against chest.

"Y-y-your boat," she muttered through chattering teeth.

Would be at the bottom of the strait in no time, but he didn't have the heart to tell her that yet. He alternated between being pissed off that she'd been so impulsive to try to steal his boat in the first place, and feeling guilty that it had been his words that had made her run.

He shook his head. "Don't think about the boat right now.

Let's just get you up to the cabin where we can get warm."

"Th-there's a c-cabin here?"

"Well, a half cabin." He adjusted her in his arms. "It's not all the way built."

He stepped into the trees, moving deeper onto the island—which, in reality, was not very big at all. It was only four acres.

The frame of the cabin lay just beyond the trees. He inwardly cursed himself, wishing like hell he'd gotten back here sooner to complete the small building.

He stepped up onto the floorboards, thankful that there were at least walls up, even if there still wasn't a roof. It would at least shield them from the wind.

"Here we go, baby. Just sit here for a second while I run back to the beach to grab the blankets and the cooler."

Lanie scooted back against the wall the minute he set her down. Her full lips had a faint blue tint to them and still shook, her expression a bit vacant.

He leaned down and gave her hand a quick squeeze. Damn. She was like ice. His body was pretty damn cold, but he hadn't been in the water nearly as long as she had.

Turning, he sprinted back toward the beach. He needed to get them under the blankets and warming up. He glanced up at the sky. The sun had disappeared between a block of gray clouds.

Roberta might have been right about that rain, though the last thing they needed was for the sky to open up on them right now.

He grabbed the blankets and the cooler, which he'd dropped on the beach when they'd first arrived.

Lord, he'd really screwed things up. If he hadn't spit out those poisonous words, she wouldn't have fled in the boat. Now it looked like they were stuck on the island together until someone figured out they were missing.

He returned to the half cabin to find Lanie clutching her cell phone. Relief spread through him. They had a way to call for help.

He dropped the items to the floor and hurried over to her. His stomach sank. Or maybe not. Water dripped from the cell phone and the screen remained black, no matter how many buttons she pushed.

"Was it in your pocket?" he asked, taking it from her cold fingers.

"Y-yes."

"It's all right. They'll find us." He gave a brisk nod and set it down on the floor. "Come on, you need to get out of those clothes."

"N-no. Too cold."

"Lanie."

She shook her head again, and he sighed, reaching for her top. He tugged it up and over her head, grateful when she didn't protest.

Don't look at her breasts. He averted his gaze from the pink bikini top and reached behind her to untie it. Once undone, he tugged the scrap from her body and tossed it aside.

This time, averting his gaze was impossible. The slope of her breasts shone with salt water, her nipples were dark pink and puckered tight from the cold.

His cock jumped against his wet jeans, but he resisted touching her. Instead he unsnapped her denim shorts and tugged down the zipper.

"Lift your hips," he ordered gruffly.

She didn't argue, just lifted her hips off the floor, her bare feet planted on the ground. She must have lost her sandals in the water.

He grasped the shorts and her bikini bottoms and tugged them off her body in one smooth pull.

Already reaching for the blanket, he tried and failed not to look down. His gaze lowered, over the slight rise of her stomach and then below. The plump mound of her sex appeared smooth and bare below a strip of light brown curls.

His chest grew tight, the blood in his body pounded toward his dick. He tucked the blanket over her body, wrapping it around her almost twice before lifting his gaze back to her face.

Her full lips were parted, now holding a healthy pink color instead of the worrisome blue they had been a few minutes ago.

Dragging his gaze higher, he stared into her eyes. The hesitant desire there was almost his undoing.

"I'm so sorry about your boat, Grant," she said, her words husky. "I should never have gotten into it. I didn't think about what I was doing. I just..." She lowered her gazes, her lips trembled. "Of course I'll pay you back."

"The boat needed to be replaced anyway. That thing was a relic." His stomach clenched with regret, and he rubbed his thumb across her bottom lip. "I'm sorry I said what I did. I didn't mean it."

She lifted her gaze again. "I kind of deserved it."

"No, you didn't." He stood up and jerked his T-shirt over his head. Cool air brushed his naked chest as he unsnapped his jeans and pushed them down and off his body. "That comment was undeserved no matter what you did."

He grabbed the second blanket and threw it around his body, holding it closed at the neck since it barely covered him.

When he sat down, he noticed Lanie's gaze locked on his crotch, her eyes round and her teeth worrying her bottom lip.

He watched the muscles work in her throat as she swallowed hard. Apparently she wasn't immune to seeing him naked any more than he was to her.

Her body still shivered visibly beneath the blanket. Just a couple of inches separated them, but all of a sudden it was too much.

His jaw clenched. Before he could analyze whether it was a good idea or not, he reached for her.

Opening his blanket, he pulled her unresisting body onto his lap and then wrapped it back around them. He adjusted her blanket to also surround them, creating a soft shield of warmth. Naked, skin to skin, their body heat merged.

"Grant." Her body curled against his and she pressed her cheek to his chest.

An unexpected surge of protectiveness rushed through him, and he tightened the arm he had around her waist, fanning his fingers across the slight curve of her stomach.

She sighed and snuggled closer, her hot breath rushed across his chest in a soft tease.

His abdomen clenched and his cock jerked against her hip. As if she'd just realized his state of arousal, she tensed, lifting her head to stare at him.

Meeting her gaze, he ran his thumb down the curve of her neck, massaging out the tension he found there.

Her breathing grew uneven and she turned in his lap, until she straddled him.

The tips of her breasts brushed against his chest, the heat of her pussy left a brand of her desire for him against his thigh. The knowledge that she wanted him, even after he'd spouted off such hateful words, sent a rush of regret and relief through him.

"Lanie..." He trailed his thumb from her neck down her back, following the trail of her spine until he reached the cleft of her ass.

Her back arched, thrusting her chest up toward his mouth. "Touch me, Grant."

He slid his hands down to grab her ass and pulled her hard against him. Her legs wrapped around his waist and a tight nipple brushed across his lips.

With a growl, he opened his mouth and drew the tip inside. Silky and textured, she tasted of woman and salt from the water.

Lanie's fingers delved into his hair, pulling at the strands when he sucked harder. He drew his teeth over the tip, her answering whimper setting his blood on fire.

So sweet and responsive to his touch. She felt so damn perfect in his arms.

He released her with a groan and buried his face between her breasts, dragging his tongue up between them. His nails dug into her ass cheeks, squeezing the soft flesh as he drew the opposite nipple into his mouth.

"*Oh God*," she gasped, squirming against him.

Her pussy brushed against his abdomen, slicker now and so damn hot. His cock rose in response, pressing against the softness of her ass.

"Kiss me," she whispered, lowering her mouth to his.

With his hands already occupied, he let her take control.

Her lips brushed his in a light caress. Once and twice, entirely too lightly. Then she pressed her mouth harder against his, and her tongue ran along the seam of his lips before plunging inside.

Dear God, the taste of her. So lush and sweet. This woman drove him mad like none had before. His tongue rubbed against hers in a slow, sensual stroke.

He rose to his knees and slid his hands up to her waist. Not breaking the kiss, he eased her onto her back, with the blanket still beneath her.

With her body now supine beneath his, he tugged the oversized blanket up to cover them, leaving them in a hot, intimate cocoon.

He angled his mouth against hers to deepen the kiss, bracing his weight with one arm. He explored every crevice of her mouth, always returning to tease her silken tongue.

Her fingers, so soft and delicate, wrapped around his cock, drawing a choked groan from him. Her hand tightened around him, up to the head of his cock in an obvious maneuver to test his length and thickness.

Her thumb stroked over the tip, catching the bit of pre-come that had escaped, before moving back down his length. Her soft sigh against his mouth indicated her approval.

She pulled her mouth away and he lifted his head. Breathing hard, she met his gaze. Her eyes took on a mischievous light, and then she lifted her thumb to her mouth and licked it clean.

Any self-control he'd maintained up until this point disappeared. With a growl, he pinned her wrists to her side and slid down to kiss her belly.

He circled his tongue around the crater of her navel, before finally dipping in.

"Mmm." She tugged at her wrists, but he tightened his grip, adjusting himself so he lay between her thighs.

The spicy scent of her arousal drifted up to tease him.

Unable to resist any longer, he moved his mouth lower. After nuzzling the small strip of curls above the juncture of her thighs, he moved the last inch and opened his mouth over the top of her mound.

He sank his tongue into the hot, moist folds of her pussy to find her swollen clit.

"*Oh.*" Her breathless cry tightened his sac and sent a rush of confidence through him.

He released her wrists to cup her ass and lift the cleft of her sex snug against his mouth. Drawing his tongue back to her entrance, he plunged inside to taste her musky sweetness.

She groaned, her ass clenching in his hands as her fingernails bit into his shoulders.

He made his tongue rigid, thrusting it inside her multiple

times, before drawing it up to flick over her clit. Faster and harder, he tormented the taut little nub, her high-pitched cries smothered in the makeshift tent of blankets.

"Please." She whimpered, her hips lifting against his mouth. "Please, Grant."

He lifted his mouth away just enough to ask, "What do you want, baby? This?" He drew her clit into his mouth and sucked hard, then released it with a popping noise. "Or maybe you want my fingers inside you?"

She whimpered, but didn't reply.

He released one ass cheek and slid his fingers around to her front. Without hesitation, he pushed two fingers into her tight, wet pussy.

She gave a choked gasp, her body clenched around his digits.

He gave a husky laugh, adjusting his body to ease the discomfort of his hard-on against the floorboards.

"Mmm, I think you like that." He captured her clit in his mouth again and alternately sucked on it and flicked it with his tongue.

She rode his mouth and fingers, her cries growing louder and more desperate.

"*Grant.*" Her thighs gripped his head, the walls of her sheath clenching around his fingers.

He followed her through the orgasm, circling her clit with his tongue while slowing the torment with his hand. Only after she went limp beneath him, her belly trembling as her breasts rose and fell, did he lift his head.

"This is why I never forgot you," she muttered, covering her forehead with her palm.

He sat up and stared down at her, taking her wrist to pull her hand away from her face.

Her eyes were still bright from the orgasm, her cheeks flushed. But beyond the obvious physical response, there was vulnerability in her gaze.

"That's not the only reason," he argued quietly and circled one of her rigid nipples with the tip of his finger.

Her chest rose with her quick indrawn breath. She made no effort to look away from his stare.

"You're right. It's not," she admitted softly.

Something in his chest twisted at her confession.

She covered his hand with her own, urging him to cup her. The softness of her breast contrasted with the hard, velvet nipple poking against his palm.

"Make love to me, Grant."

Chapter Six

He drew in a ragged breath, the disappointment almost painful in his gut.

"Lanie, I don't have a condom."

She lowered her gaze, her fingers twirling in the hair on his chest.

"I started birth control a few months ago." Her teeth nibbled on her bottom lip. "And you have nothing to worry about in the other department."

He struggled to breathe, his throat suddenly tight, shocked that she trusted him enough to give him the go ahead without a condom.

She lifted her head, her gaze uncertain. "Unless you..."

"You have nothing to worry about with me," he reassured her huskily. "Are you sure about this?"

She gave a slow nod. "I'm sure, Grant. Six years of living off a memory can leave you a little empty inside."

"Ah, sweet, Lanie." He brushed his mouth across hers. "Sweet, sweet, Lanie."

Her arms wound around his neck and he eased his body onto hers, flattening her breasts against his chest.

He traced her bottom lip with his tongue, soothing the swollenness she'd created from nibbling on it. A nervous habit he'd noticed she did often.

The soft sigh she made parted her lips enough for him to slowly sink his tongue into her mouth. Brushing past her teeth to tease hers.

Had he ever wanted a woman more? Would he ever? Since that first night together, it had always been about Lanie.

There was soft friction as their tongues rubbed together, then retreated, and then came back to meet again with more urgency.

He slid his knee between her legs, parting her thighs wide enough for him to lie between them. The warmth of her pussy nudged his cock and he groaned against her mouth.

Her tongue swept against his again, curling around and then sucking. Her hips lifted, lining his erection up perfectly with her entrance.

Poised on the edge of repeating the most emotionally intense sex of his life, he didn't even hesitate. Gripping his cock, he pushed past her swollen folds and then buried himself in her hot, wet center.

Lanie gasped, tearing her mouth away and twisting her head to the side.

He groaned, unable to even move. Oh God, she felt incredible. He remained embedded in her, overcome by the sensation of her slick warmth squeezing his dick. Jesus, she felt good.

"Too long, Lanie. It's been too damn long."

She gave an unsteady laugh that sounded more like a groan. "I know."

She lifted her hips again, driving him deeper into her core.

He closed his eyes, grinding his hips against hers until he was wedged deep against her cervix.

"Oh God," she whispered, her nails digging into his forearms and her nipples pressed tight against his chest.

He pulled out of her just a bit and then sank back in, repeating the process. Slow and steady at first, as every nerve in his body focused on the silken grip her body had on him.

She lifted her hips to meet his thrusts, rotating them every so often and causing his cock to stroke the sides of her channel.

"Christ, you feel amazing," he said through clenched teeth.

He lowered his head, licking one of her tight nipples. She let out a mewl of pleasure and he buried his cock deep into her again. Moving faster now. Deeper.

She matched the increased pace he set, wrapping her legs around his waist as her cries grew louder by the second.

His sac tightened and he drew in a ragged breath. He reached between them and skimmed his thumb across her clit, making sure she went over the edge with him.

Her scream of pleasure mingled with his hoarse groan. He thrust to the hilt, finding his release deep inside her.

His mind went to mush. It was all he could do to remember to breathe.

"Mmmpph."

Grant blinked, his vision returning to normal as he looked down at Lanie.

Her eyes were shut and her body lay limp beneath him.

"You okay, baby?"

"Mmmph."

"Is that a yes?"

Her eyes flickered open, capturing him with a languid brown stare.

"That's most definitely a yes." She stretched beneath him, moving all the right parts against his body. Her foot moved up and down his calf.

He bit back a groan, feeling himself hardening again.

"Grant, that was..." she trailed off and sighed. "I needed that. You have no idea how much."

He pushed a damp strand of hair off her forehead, his mouth curving downward a bit. She needed that? But she was in a relationship with another guy. Shouldn't that mean her sex life was active? Hell, she was on birth control.

The thought of her with another man left an acidic taste in his mouth. Curdled the jealousy in his gut.

She dropped a kiss on his shoulder, her gaze still heated. It was clear that the last thing on her mind was another man.

Their makeshift tent had grown darker; a sure sign the sun had set.

"I think we're going to end up spending the night," he said quietly. "Roberta's so damn romantic, she'll probably assume we just spent the night before she gets worried."

"Well," she looked up at him through lowered lashes "I'm not so sure I'm going to complain about that. In fact, I kind of like the idea."

"Oh, yeah?"

"Yeah." She moved her foot up to his ass and pressed down.

Still inside her, his cock grew rock hard again.

"Well then." He smiled and grasped her hips, rolling onto his back and setting her astride him. "Why don't you show me how much you like it?"

Lanie stared down at him, her heart pounding in her chest and desire flowing heavy through her veins. He shifted, sending his cock deeper inside her.

"Oh wow," she whispered, her eyes closing.

With her on top of him, the blanket lifted, letting in a cool breeze and amplifying the sound of waves on the beach.

His hands settled on her hips, lightly holding her, but it was clear he'd given her the reins.

She lifted herself up just a bit and then sank back down. The friction and depth of the stroke made the breath lock in her throat.

Her nipples tightened as she rocked down on him again. She leaned forward, placing her hands on his chest and rotating her hips. Lifting herself up and pressing back down onto him.

"You're going to kill me, Lanie," he said hoarsely.

She gave a soft laugh, the power of the position giving her more confidence.

"You like that?" she murmured and leaned forward, smoothing her fingers up to rub his nipples.

"Hell, yeah." He slid his hand from her hip to the middle of her back, pulling her forward until her breasts dangled above his mouth. "I also like this."

He captured one puckered tip between strong lips. Sucking and licking it until she writhed on his cock.

She moved faster and harder, the air escaping her lungs in choked gasps.

He switched his mouth to her other breast, thrusting up into her as she rode him.

When he reached between them to rub her clit, she exploded. Lights flashed behind her closed lids, her body clamped around him and milked his cock as he came inside her a moment later.

She collapsed on top of him, falling forward and burying her face against his neck. She kissed his rapidly-beating pulse, savoring the salty male taste of him.

"Lanie," he sighed, moving his hand up and down her back. "I don't think I'll be able to walk anytime soon."

"You don't need to," she murmured drowsily and slid off him. She moved to lie next to him, snuggling against his side.

Grant slipped an arm around her back with one hand, and urged her head to his chest with another. His lips grazed across her forehead.

"You're amazing," he said.

Her mouth curved into a smile and her eyes drifted shut. "I try."

His chest rose and fell beneath her cheek, gradually slowing until she knew he'd fallen asleep.

Tonight had changed everything. The realization was just a passing thought in her over-stimulated mind.

Closing off all analytical thoughts, she breathed in the scent of him and let herself fall asleep.

Waves smashed onto the beach and the wind lifted the blanket around them.

Lanie stirred, snuggling closer to Grant with a sigh. She didn't know how early it was, but there was a hint of daylight peeking through the edges of the blanket.

"Are you awake?" His chest rumbled under her cheek with the question.

Her mouth curved into a half smile. "No."

"Liar." He stroked a hand down her back. "You know what woke me?"

"Hmm."

"Your stomach growling."

"It did not." She nudged him in the ribs with her elbow.

"All right, I was already awake, but your stomach did growl a couple times in the past half hour."

"You've been awake that long? Why didn't you wake me?"

"Because I enjoyed having you asleep in my arms." He brushed a kiss across her forehead.

Her stomach flipped and warmth spread through her body. She bit her lip, knowing her cheeks were turning pink with pleasure. God, she was so easy.

"Do you have any idea what time it is?" she asked to change the subject.

"Mmm. A little after six, I'd guess."

"Ouch. That's pretty early."

"Yes, it is." He sat up and the blanket lifted off them, letting in a rush of cool air.

"Cold!" she yelped and tugged the blanket off him and wrapped it around herself, leaving Grant sitting up naked.

"Did you say you brought extra clothes?" he asked glancing toward the beach. "Or are they—?"

"In the boat."

"Right." He gave a nod. "I figured. Tell you what, just use one of the blankets toga style until the wet stuff dries."

"Not a problem."

"I'm going to run down to the beach and grab that cooler. At least we have some food." He leaned over and rubbed his thumb across her lower lip. "I'll be back in a few."

She nipped at his thumb and then gave him an impish grin. "Okay."

Delanie watched him wrap one of the blankets around his waist and then walk back down to the beach.

She stood up and stretched, easing out all the newly acquired aches in her body. Was this the part where she was supposed to regret what had just happened between them last night? Because she didn't. Not in the least.

It had felt right. All of it. Making love to Grant and being held in his arms. In fact she kind of had the itch to do it again. Soon.

She pulled the blanket around her, fastening it in true toga fashion before walking down the trail after him.

He stood on the beach, collecting the few items he'd brought out of the boat earlier.

"I don't suppose *you* have a cell phone?" she called out. "You know, since I went swimming with mine and all."

He turned around, his amused gaze running over her. "I don't. Mine was in the boat under my seat."

She winced, guilt making her stomach twist. "Right. I'm sorry."

He waved his hand and shook his head. "Stop apologizing. I can easily buy a new one. I'm just glad you're okay." He closed the distance between them and touched the curve of her breast peeking out of the blanket. "So, you've done this toga thing before, huh?"

"Hey, I was in a sorority." She grinned and glanced down at herself and the fleece blanket. "I went to my share of toga parties."

"I bet. You look beautiful, like a Greek goddess."

"Thank you." She lowered her gaze, her smile widening.

It couldn't get much better than being called a goddess. Speaking of Goddesses, where had the name of the resort come from? Athena's Oasis.

She glanced out at the water, looking for any sign of a passing boat in the early morning light. Nothing.

"They'll find us," he assured her, obviously having read her thoughts. "And we've got plenty of food to get us through another night if we need to."

She knew she could trust him to keep her safe. And, ultimately, get her off this island, even if he had to cut down a tree and make a canoe. Not that it would ever come to that.

She bit her cheek to avoid grinning. She cleared her throat. "So why did your grandfather name the resort what he did?"

"Athena's Oasis?" He looked at her for a moment, his gaze clouding a bit, and then sat down on the beach. "It all goes back to the coin."

"The coin?" she repeated, her stomach sinking. Of course. It always went back to the coin.

He gave a slow nod. "Well, as you know, the coin was a silver tetradrachm of Athens, minted in 454-415 BC."

Minted in 454-415 BC? Her mind spun. *Shit. Oh dear God in heaven. The coin was real!*

"On one side is the Athens owl and on the other the Goddess Athena."

What the hell kind of crackhead antique dealer had she spoken to that day? A knock-off. He'd told her it was a *knock-off.* The jerk had offered her two hundred dollars for it, which he'd assured her was a great deal for a fake. Fortunately, she'd turned him down because of the emotional attachment she'd developed to the coin.

Sweat broke out on her brow. No wonder Grant had tracked her down. Good lord. A coin that was thousands of years old.

"...was passed down through my family."

"Wait what?" she shook her head to pull herself back to the conversation.

He gave her a strange look, probably wondering why she had a total look of horror on her face.

"The coin was a family heirloom passed down to the first son of each generation of my family." He shrugged and tossed a rock into the water. "Like I said, it was also my good-luck charm. That's why I'm not really surprised the boat sank," he admitted with a wry grin. "It's all part of the bad luck."

She blinked, her jaw half open in amazement. Why hadn't Grant called the police? Or, heck, just hired a hit man to come after her?

The magnitude of what she'd taken from him that morning hit her hard. Her hands shook as she grabbed a rock and mimicked him, tossing it into the water. Had she known what she was stealing that morning, she never would've agreed to Bridget's plan.

She drew in an unsteady breath, wrapping her fingers around another rock. There was no doubt in her mind what she had to do. Return the coin to him when they got back to the resort and hope he forgave her for taking it. And for lying about selling it.

Thinking about his reaction when he saw it eased some of the tension that had weaved through her muscles.

"One thing I just hope you'll eventually tell me, Lanie," he said quietly, "is why you took it in the first place."

Chapter Seven

She closed her eyes. Wasn't that the question of the decade? The least she could give him right now was an honest answer.

"Bridget Hanson."

Her confession was met with silence. She opened her eyes, looking at him hesitantly.

His brows were drawn together in confusion, his head tilted to one side.

"Do you mean Brittney Hanson?"

Her cheeks filled with color. Jeez. She hadn't even remembered the girl's name right.

"Oh. Yes, I guess her name was Brittney. Wasn't it?"

His scowl grew even more intense. "What does she have to do with anything?"

"Umm." She licked her lips, her hands clammy. "I sort of...umm...okay, I'm not defending what I did. It was a bad idea I just didn't think through—"

"*Lanie.*"

"Right. Sorry. Brittney was my sorority sister. I guess you two had dated for a while—"

"Two weeks."

She blinked. "What?"

"We were together for two weeks."

"I, umm..." She cleared her throat. Oh God. Please don't let Brittney have been some kind of nutbag pathological liar. "She'd said two months in college."

"She lied." He held her gaze. "But go on."

Her pulse quickened. Okay. One little lie. Brittney probably had her reasons.

"Okay. When she had that whole pregnancy scare, she said you were unsupportive."

"Excuse me?" Grant stood up, his gaze narrowed now. "Pregnancy scare?"

"Yes. She said you told her you weren't ready to be a dad and she should just have an abortion. And then you dumped her."

"If that little brat had a pregnancy scare..." his words dripped ice, "...it was with another man. I never touched her."

"Never touched her?" she repeated dumbly. "You mean you guys..."

"I kissed her once. Once, Lanie. And it was a complete turn off." He shoved a hand through his hair. "We grew up in the same town and ended up at the same college. I'd never had any interest in her, and yet for some stupid reason I took her up on an offer to see a movie one day. Two weeks together. One kiss."

Her stomach rolled and she suddenly felt a bit lightheaded. "You never had sex?"

"Let's put it this way. I'm probably the only guy on campus who *didn't* sleep with her. Brittney was pretty liberal with her lovers."

Lanie stood up, walking the opposite way down the beach.

"Where are you going?" he called after her.

"I think I'm going to be sick."

"Hey, hold on a second." He ran after her. "You haven't told me why you stole the coin and what Brittney has to do with it."

"You don't want to know," she muttered. "Trust me."

He grabbed her elbow, swinging her back around. "Lanie. I want to know."

"No, you don't." She shook her head and moaned. "It's absolutely horrible."

"Tell me." He didn't release her, his mouth tightening. "What did Brittney have to do with this?"

She closed her eyes and took a slow breath in. "We were in the bar together the night I met you. We'd had a few drinks. When she spotted you, she told me what you'd done to her."

"What I'd allegedly done. She lied," he ground out. "Go on."

Opening her eyes again, she tried to gauge how he'd react to her next words.

"I got pretty upset with what she told me, partly because I'd been drinking. She told me about this coin you loved, and how funny it would be if someone took it from you."

"Yeah. Real funny. She'd had her eye on the coin since I brought it to show-and-tell in second grade," he said tersely. "And she convinced you to steal it?"

"Yes," she whispered. "It was just another challenge for me. I was never one to back down from a dare, and I think she knew it. That's why she picked me."

There was an audible click as his teeth snapped together. He released her arm and fisted his hands.

"I'm sorry."

"It never occurred to you she might have been lying?"

"She was my sorority sister. I gave her the benefit of the doubt."

His jaw tightened. "And yet you couldn't even remember her name."

"I made a bad decision that night, Grant." Guilt brought another heated flush to her face. "I'm not going to deny it."

"It'd be kind of hard to," he replied with a bitter laugh. "And then you rolled out of bed with me and sold the coin for a couple grand."

Nausea rolled through her as she stared at the myriad of emotions flashing across his face. Anger, frustration, disgust. Not even a hint of the tenderness or caring he'd shown her last night.

"Grant," she drew in a deep breath, ready to tell him the truth about the coin. "I didn't se—"

The whine of a motor cut off her words, and they both turned toward the water to see a Coast Guard boat approaching the island.

"Looks like we've been found," he said wearily. "I'll go grab the rest of the stuff back at the cabin."

She started after him. "Wait, Grant—"

He lifted his hand and shook his head. "Later. Let's just get back to the resort first."

Disappointment stabbed deep. The need to tell him she'd kept the coin had been so profound.

Maybe it would be better just to hand it to him anyway. With a heavy sigh, she turned back to wave down the boat.

After the Coast Guard dropped them off on Lopez Island, Grant drove them back to the resort.

"We were lucky Roberta called the Coast Guard," Lanie murmured, looking over at him.

He grunted in response, not trusting himself to speak, with his emotions all over the map.

He'd known all along she'd taken the coin—had even come to a point where he'd forgiven her. Then she'd told him the reason why she'd taken it, and he'd lost it. All the goddamn warm and fuzzies had flown out the window. Her motivation had been so absurd and selfish.

Six years ago. It's in the past. The voice of reason argued in his head. After that amazing night they'd had, could he really justify throwing it all away? He drew in a long breath, already knowing the answer.

Turning down the road to the resort, his eyebrows shot up at the three media vans outside.

"What the hell?" he scowled and parked the Jeep.

He glanced over at Lanie, who'd gone quiet, and saw the look of trepidation on her face. She didn't seem the least bit surprised by their presence.

He barely had time to ponder the thought before all hell broke loose. A wall of noise hit them as reporters burst through the doors of the resort, shoving microphones and cameras in their faces.

Grant climbed out of the car, trying to squeeze past the crowd to open Lanie's door. He arrived at the other side of the Jeep to find someone else had done it for him.

At first he figured the older man to be her father. Tall, graying hair and distinguished-looking. But then, right after he pulled her from the vehicle, he dropped a very un-fatherly kiss on her mouth.

Grant pressed his hand against the Jeep, his jaw clenching as his stomach threatened to toss up the apple he'd eaten on the boat ride back.

The reporters clapped and gave cheers of approval, barely waiting for the couple to pull apart, before thrusting a microphone in the man's face.

"Senator Adams, how does it feel knowing your fiancée is safe?"

Senator? He was a fucking senator? And had they just said fiancée?

"Wonderful." He slipped his arm around Lanie's waist. "The moment I learned Delanie had gone missing, I cancelled all re-election appearances to come help in the search. Which I'm sure the voters of California will understand."

"Ms. Williams, do you plan on suing the resort for putting your life at risk with such a dangerous boat?"

Grant's teeth snapped together. That was it. He would not stick around and listen to this bullshit for one second longer. He spun on his heel, pushing past the crowd to stride back inside the resort.

Roberta stood inside the doorway, her eyes filled with tears.

"We were so worried. When you didn't come back or answer your cell phones, and then we found Delanie's hat floating in the strait, we assumed the worst. I—"

"Don't let any of those reporters back into the main building. And tell Ms. Williams to sign the sponsorship papers and then I'll have copies overnighted to her in a few days."

"But, what about—"

"I don't want to see her again." He spun around, the pain of knowing she'd lied again shredding him apart inside. "I'm going away for a couple of days. And I want her gone before I return."

Roberta didn't even ask to whom he referred. Compassion and understanding flickered in her gaze. She gave a quick nod and bit her lip.

"I'm so sorry, Grant."

Her soft words further twisted the knot in his gut. He went to the kitchen window and looked outside, just in time to see Lanie leading the senator into one of the cabins. She yelled something at the bodyguard who tried to follow them. The man scowled, but with obvious reluctance, let them go inside alone.

Grant closed his eyes, not even wanting to consider what they were doing in there. Pain and rage mixed a potent combination in his blood. He clenched his fists and struggled to breathe. He needed to get the hell away from there. Before he did something stupid—like beat the shit out of a senator.

"Hold down the fort for a bit, Roberta, and I'll give you an extra week's vacation time." He forced a smile. "I'll see you in a few days."

The blood pounded in Lanie's veins. She pried Franklin's arm from around her waist and stood on her tiptoes, trying to see where Grant had run off to.

Oh God, he must surely be thinking the worst right now. And after their conversation on the island... Jeez.

"Excuse me," she raised her voice above the flurry of questions being hurled at them. "I need a moment with the senator."

Not waiting for a response, she grabbed his arm and dragged him away. Somewhere they could talk—or where she could rip him a new one to be exact—and not be photographed and recorded.

Spotting the cabin Grant had taken her into yesterday, she tugged him into it. His bodyguard made to follow them in and she glared at him.

"Don't even try it. I need a moment alone."

Franklin sighed and then gave the guard a quick nod. "We'll be fine."

The moment he stepped inside, she swung the door shut.

"How dare you?" she snarled. "How dare you turn this into a P.R. event?"

Franklin sighed and gave her a wary look. "Delanie, I apologize. Of course I was worried about you, and, as I mentioned, I was already in Seattle. But with the upcoming elections, it just seemed—"

"And you told them I was your fiancée. What the heck were you thinking? We're not engaged."

He waved his hand. "A technicality. I brought the ring with me and had hoped to discuss it with you."

"Discuss it with me?" her voice rose. "Discuss it with me? You are so...argh! I don't have time for this. I don't. You can just march your ass back out there and tell those reporters the engagement is off. Or hell, try honesty for once and admit there never was one."

"Delanie—"

"Either you do it, or I will." She met his gaze and then swung open the door to the cabin, running back to the resort.

The reporters seemed pre-occupied with something else now. Her stomach dropped as she realized what was happening. She broke into a run.

"Grant!"

But the Jeep peeled out of the driveway, past the reporters and away from the resort.

"Oh God." She wrapped her arms around her waist, her eyes filling with tears.

"Miss Williams. There is speculation that this might be a campaign stunt, and that you were never on a boat that sank. Would you care to comment on that?"

The reporters swarmed toward her again, hurling questions left and right.

"No comment." She shook her head, lifting her hand to cover her face and hurried back into the resort.

Roberta ushered her in and shut the door behind her, locking it immediately.

"Are you all right, dear?"

She shook her head, struggling to swallow against the lump in her throat.

"Where did he go?"

Roberta sighed. "He left, said he'd be gone for a few days. He was terribly upset."

"Oh jeez," she whispered. "What a mess."

"It certainly is." Roberta clucked her tongue and sighed. Her face grew red. "I'm so sorry...but he left instructions for you to leave the resort immediately and that he'd overnight the paperwork to you."

Lanie flinched as if she'd been hit, her stomach rolling hard. "That final, huh?"

"I'm afraid so. Perhaps you could stay at a nearby hotel and try to work things out when he returns?" she suggested hopefully.

She shook her head, forcing a smile. Wondering if she might get sick. "I'll go pack my things."

Roberta's expression fell and she heaved a sigh. "All right. I'll arrange transportation to the ferry. Unless you're leaving with the senator."

"No. I won't be leaving with the senator."

She glanced out the window and watched Franklin try to

win over the reporters again. She didn't believe for a second he'd tell them they weren't engaged. Which was fine, she'd make an official statement when she returned to San Francisco.

"Thank you, Roberta." She turned back to the older woman and touched her shoulder. "For everything."

Seeing the disappointment in the other woman's gaze was almost her undoing. Before she started crying like an idiot, she turned and went to her room to pack.

Chapter Eight

Grant pulled the Jeep up to the resort and put it in park. He leaned back against the headrest and sighed, staring at the main house. He reached up and ran his hand over the three-day growth on his chin. Damn, he needed to shave. Either that or, at this rate, just grow it out into a beard.

Regret rested heavy in his gut; despondency had hung thick over him the past few days. All because he knew she was gone.

With a sigh, he climbed out of the car and walked up the steps to the front door. A couple a few feet away were dragging luggage out of a cabin, obviously checking out.

It was second nature to give a friendly wave, and the couple responded with an enthusiastic wave of their own.

He turned to open the front door and found it already open.

Roberta stood in the doorway, flour on her apron and a relieved smile on her face. "You're back."

"Of course." He smiled and stepped through the door, giving her shoulder a squeeze. "You knew I'd be back."

His gaze drifted around the interior of the building.

"She's gone, Grant."

Tension coiled in his muscles and he gave a stiff nod. "I assumed as much."

Hell, he'd ordered her gone. Of course, there was that part of him that wanted her to ignore his request, to stubbornly stick around and explain to him that it had all been a mistake.

"How have things been?" he asked.

"Business as usual." Roberta paused. "She left you a letter."

He turned abruptly to face her, his pulse quickening. "Did she now?"

"Mmm-hmm."

"Maybe it's a letter saying she wants to sue us."

Roberta clucked her tongue at him. "I somehow doubt that."

"Did you read it?"

She waved a towel at him and scowled. "I'm nosey, Grant. But really, I have my limits."

"It's sealed, huh?"

She laughed softly. "Yes. And I just don't trust that steaming it open trick."

"Thanks. I'll go look it over in a few."

He turned down the hall to his room. The hell with a few, he wanted to rip it open now.

Grabbing the handle to his door, he twisted it and pushed into the room.

The letter lay on his bed like the day of reckoning put inside an envelope. He sat down on the edge of the mattress, eyeing the plain white rectangle with apprehension. Almost afraid to open it and see what she'd written inside.

He finally reached over and picked it up. It was heavier than he expected, with a lump on one side.

His brows came together as he drew his index finger beneath the seam and tugged open the seal. Turning the envelope upside down, he shook it until a necklace fell out into his palm.

The blood pounded through his veins and his mouth fell open. Not just any necklace.

He lifted the chain until the pendant swung in front of his face. The silver tetradrachm of Athens was held by tiny prongs that secured it into a pendant.

He brushed his thumb over the raised owl, the hairs on the back of his neck lifting. Was he actually holding *his* coin? Or was it a replica?

Reaching for the envelope, he tugged out the letter.

Grant,

I wish you hadn't left so suddenly, without giving me the chance to explain. I know that in your eyes I'm probably just a liar and a thief, and in reality, I guess I am.

I never intended to keep the coin. I promised Brittney I'd throw it into the lake, but I couldn't do it. And neither did I sell it. The coin was the only reminder I had of the best night of my life. The night where I screwed up and gave both my body and my heart to the man I'd gone to steal from. I know there is no defense for my selfish actions. I don't expect you to understand or forgive me, but I thought you deserved to know my motives.

With the return of this coin, I hope your good luck returns and you find all the happiness you deserve in life.

With love,
Lanie

Grant reread the letter for the third time, his head spinning and his mouth going dry.

She hadn't sold the coin, that realization alone was mind boggling enough. But the coin became the secondary focus. One line in her letter spun wildly inside his head. *The night where I screwed up and gave both my body and my heart to the man I'd gone to steal from.*

Her heart. Was she saying...? Was it possible...? His chest tightened and he dropped the letter, picking up the coin again.

How long had he wanted this back? Had he blamed all his bad luck on its disappearance?

The pendant lay heavy in his hand, a tangible reminder of all he'd thought was important to him. And yet, even with the return of the coin, he'd been dealt the biggest stroke of bad luck yet.

He'd just lost Lanie for the second time.

"You need to stop freaking out," Phoebe said, handing her a brownie on a paper plate. "I'm sure he'll send the paperwork like he promised. It's only been four days since you left."

"I know he will," Delanie said softly. "I'm not worried about that."

"Oh yeah? Then what's this about?" Phoebe lifted an eyebrow and tossed her black curls over her shoulder.

Delanie scooted over on the couch in their office, making room for Phoebe to sit down.

"I don't know." She tore off a piece of brownie and sighed. "I guess I just expected to hear *something.*"

"Huh? Oh." Phoebe's eyebrows rose and she gave a slow nod. "*Oh,* I see. This is about that letter you left him, huh?"

Delanie popped the bite of brownie in her mouth and nodded, not lifting her gaze. The rich chocolate treat melted against her tongue and she sighed.

"This is excellent," she said after swallowing the bite. "Who made it?"

"Gabby baked them and brought them in."

"She's fabulous. How are things with her and Justin?"

"They're ridiculously happy. You should have seen them this week when—" Her eyes narrowed. "Hey, you changed the subject. We were discussing Grant."

Delanie winced at his name, and the fact that Phoebe was so quick to go back to the subject of him.

"Look, I thought you said you were glad to be off the island," Phoebe pointed out, nibbling at the edge of her own brownie.

"I was. I am," she corrected herself. "It's just—"

"Well, thank God you're out of the denial stage." Phoebe nodded. "I mean, I could tell the minute you stepped off the plane."

"You could tell what?" Delanie touched her neck. Had he left some kind of giant-sized hickie or something?

"That you're completely in love with the man."

Delanie's eyes widened, her mouth flapping as she tried to form a response.

"It's true, don't even deny it." Phoebe gave her a sidelong

look while polishing off her brownie.

"Deny what?"

Gabby strode into the room, looking extra young with her strawberry-blonde braids peeking out from beneath a San Francisco Giant's baseball cap.

At twenty-four, she was already considered the baby employee at the Second Chances office. But, despite her young age, she worked her butt off and there wasn't a thing she wouldn't do for the shelter.

"Nothing. I'm denying nothing," Delanie muttered. "These are fabulous by the way." She lifted the small bit of brownie she had left and then popped it into her mouth.

"Glad you like them." She turned to Phoebe. "So what's she denying?"

"That she's in love."

"I'm not in love."

"You're in love?" Gabby squealed and leaned forward to pat her leg. "That's so great! Who's the man?"

"I'm not in—"

"The owner of Athena's Oasis," Phoebe went on. "They met six years ago and apparently he never forgot her. And she shows up at the resort and they end up having mind-blowing sex all week. Well, until she left early."

"Oh. My. God. It was just a fling." Delanie threw up her hands, biting back a scream of frustration. "When did my life become a movie on some women's network? This is completely—"

"Romantic. That's what it is. I'm so glad I'm not the only one getting hit by Cupid's freaking arrow." Gabby sighed and twisted the end of her braid around a finger. "So when are you going to see him again?"

Never. The question was the final straw. Her eyes flooded with tears and her throat grew tight.

"Oh, no. Oh God. I'm sorry, I totally said the wrong thing," Gabby said quickly. "I was just teasing you. I mean, flings are great. I used to have them before Justin and I got together." She broke off, her cheeks bright pink. "So not what you wanted to hear... Umm, you know, I think I hear someone buzzing at that door. I'll go check that out."

She shot out of the room before Phoebe had even handed

Delanie the box of tissues.

"Sorry, we probably overdid it a bit," Phoebe said quietly.

Delanie grabbed a tissue and dabbed her eyes, shaking her head. "It doesn't matter. I mean, it never would have worked between me and Grant anyway."

"Why not?"

"Well, for one, I committed a felony against him."

"Hush. If he was going to press charges he would have done so by now." Phoebe stood up and folded her arms across her chest. "You're going to have to do better than that."

"Okay..." Delanie swallowed against the lump in her throat. "Then there's the biggest problem. He lives in Washington State."

Phoebe stared at her for a moment and then shrugged. "And?"

Delanie blinked. Didn't her friend see the problem here? "And I live in California."

"What, you don't want to move to Washington?"

"Move to..." she trailed off, her stomach in knots over the tempting idea. "Even if I wanted to, I couldn't. I have my life here. We helped this shelter get where it is today—"

"Delanie, sweetie, you know I love you. But let's be real." Phoebe sighed. "Working for an abused women's shelter was my dream, and sometimes I feel like I suckered you into it. You helped me get up the nerve to get so involved and for that I'll always be grateful."

"But I love Second Chances, Phoebe," Delanie protested, surprised at her friend's words.

"I know you do. And I've selfishly kept you here for years." Phoebe hesitated. "What I'm trying to say is that if you wanted to move to Washington for a guy you're in love with, the shelter would be fine. Besides, didn't you just tell me yesterday he'd offered you that job as marketing director for Athena's Oasis?"

Just the idea of it sent a spark of excitement through her. The spark was quickly snuffed out with guilt. "I don't know if he'd still give it to me. Besides, I'd hate leaving you here alone. Especially since you keep thinking you're seeing your ex all over the place."

"Completely my imagination. It's nothing, I'm sure. Besides, I wouldn't be alone," Phoebe replied softly. "I have lots of friends here at Second Chances, and with Gabby getting promoted last month I've been spending more time with her."

Delanie dropped her gaze, knowing her friend was right. She closed her eyes. Not that it mattered. There was still one part of the equation that made it impossible.

"You should go, Delanie."

"Phoebe, I left him that letter. I made my feelings for him clear..."

"He loves you too."

"Really?" The ache in her chest increased. Her lips twisted downward in disappointment. "If that's so true, why didn't he call me? Or come after me? He got everything he wanted from me, and that was the coin."

"I don't care about the coin."

The blood drained from her head and she gripped the armrest of the couch. When she opened her eyes Grant stood in the doorway, his gaze locked on her.

"Okay. Wow," Phoebe said. "That was weird. You must be Grant. Hi, I'm Phoebe, I work here at Second Chances with Delanie. I just have to say thank you for all you've done for us, and now I'm going to walk out the door and leave you two alone."

Grant stepped to the side, letting Phoebe scoot past him through the door. Before she left, she turned around and grinned, giving a big thumbs up.

He shut the door the minute Phoebe disappeared down the hall.

Lanie blinked, half convinced she was dreaming. Her heart pounded in her chest and her hands began to tremble.

"Did you mean it?"

"Did I mean what?" Her pulse doubled.

"What you said in the letter." He reached the couch and sat down beside her, his gaze searching her face.

She knew to which part he was referring. The part where she'd said she'd given him her heart.

"Look, you have your coin back." Emotion became a heavy lump in her throat and she stood up. "Your good luck charm—"

"I don't care about the damn coin." He caught her wrist, halting her from walking away. "And I'll keep saying it until you believe me."

She stared down at him, heat spreading through her body where his fingers touched. "Grant..."

"If I had been honest with myself in the first place, I could have admitted the truth."

"And what's that?"

"That my searching for you for six years had nothing to do with the coin, and everything to do with you." He held her gaze and his thumb brushed over the inside of her wrist.

"What are you saying?" she whispered, her breath catching as hope flared in her heart.

"I'm saying that losing you six years ago hurt," he said with naked vulnerability in his eyes. "But losing you now would kill me."

Relief raged through her, weakening her knees. She bit her lip, which began to tremble.

"Lanie." He slid his arms around her waist and pulled her close, pressing his cheek just under her breasts. "You're the only woman for me. I suspected it back then, and I sure as hell know it now."

Delanie closed her eyes against the tears of relief and joy. She threaded her fingers into his hair and tugged his head against her breasts.

"Oh, Grant..."

"I love you." He sighed. "And I shouldn't have taken off for three days the minute I saw that jackass senator show up at the resort."

"He was out of line," she agreed, toying with a strand of his hair. "It was all just P.R. to him. I gave my official response to the media when I got home."

"I saw that." He pulled her down onto his lap. "So, how do I persuade you to move up to Lopez Island and become my wife?"

Delanie's pulse skipped, her future aligning quite nicely in her head.

"You could add a slash to it."

"Slash?"

"I'm kind of holding out for wife slash marketing director of the resort."

"Done. You know I wanted you to have that job." He reached into his pocket and pulled out a chain, the coin pendant following. "I didn't have a chance to grab a ring, but I brought this. I want you to have it."

Her mouth parted, her started gaze locking on his. "But I just gave it back to you. It's your good-luck coin."

He fastened the chain around her neck and let the pendant drop against her breasts.

He touched her cheek. "If ever I had a good-luck charm in my life, you were it. And I don't intend to let you go."

Her stomach flipped and her knees weakened. "Good, because I'm head over heels for you, buddy. I love you."

"I love you too," His mouth curved into a mischievous smile. "Janie."

Her eyes widened. Had he just called her—? She squealed as his hands shot out to tickle her sides.

"Gotcha," he whispered and then his mouth closed over hers.

Protecting Phoebe

Dedication

Thank you to Melissa at DAWN for your help and information on domestic violence. Thanks to Craig, the waiter I met on my birthday, who wanted me to name a character after him. Thanks to my family and friends for your continued support, and thank you to my editor Laurie for making my books shine!

Chapter One

The thick fog that hung over the San Francisco morning made a perfect backdrop to the fear residing thick in her gut. People became indistinguishable in the reduced line of sight. All kinds of evil could hide in the thick shadows.

And she was worried about one in particular.

Phoebe tightened her grip on the stack of books in her arm and increased her pace to her car.

How many times had she promised herself she'd never be afraid again? How many daily affirmations had she done to prevent the body-trembling fear from taking over?

She reached her car, her throat dry and her hands shaking. Jamming the key into the lock, she managed to wrench it open and stumble inside. Her fist slammed down on the lock and she drew in a long, shuddering breath.

Still think you're seeing things, Phoebe? a bitter voice taunted in her head.

Her hands continued to shake as she stuck the key into the ignition. The engine roared to life, screaming loudly as her foot pressed the gas peddle to the floor. Shit. Fumbling for the brake, she dropped it and put the Civic in reverse.

Her tires squealed as she pulled out of the parking spot. She scanned the empty lot, her pulse pounding and her tongue thick against the roof of her mouth.

A couple of rows down in the parking lot she could see the figure of the man she'd seen earlier. Even in the dense fog, she got a good impression of his physique—tall and on the skinny side. Unfortunately, his features weren't as clear.

She hit the gas and rounded the corner in the opposite direction, tearing her gaze from the man.

It could be anybody.

An unsteady laugh spilled from her throat and her fingers clenched around the steering wheel. Okay. Maybe she'd convinced herself *it could be anybody* a few weeks ago, when she'd had the first sighting at the sushi restaurant, but this was too much of a coincidence.

A short while later, she turned the car onto the highway, casting one more glance into her rearview mirror. *There's nobody there. Calm your ass down, silly.*

She flipped on her stereo and willed her nerves to settle. The fear in her gut began to subside slowly. In its place began the slow simmer of anger.

"You're late." Gabby greeted her the minute she walked in the door of Second Chances, the women's shelter where they worked. Gabby's smile faded as they walked back to their office. "What's wrong? You look awful."

"Nothing's wrong," Phoebe muttered and strode briskly to her desk. Jeez, could her friend really read her that well?

"Bull and shit. Something is totally wrong." Gabby followed her, folding her arms across her chest. "Seriously, Phoebe, you're like beyond pale and you're already the whitest chick I know."

The urge to confess what had happened this morning flirted with the tip of her tongue. But Gabby didn't need that kind of emotional dump. Not with everything in her own life going so right at the moment.

Gabby had been all aglow for weeks now. Ever since she'd fallen in love with her old roommate and moved back in with him. Phoebe made sure to check everyday to see if a ring had popped up on her friend's finger.

"Tell me." Gabby sat down on the edge of her desk. "I'm not budging—or sharing the box of chocolate Justin gave me this morning—until you tell me what the heck is going on."

Phoebe shoved a hand through her black curls and bit back a groan. Gabby knew her weakness for chocolate, but even for the promise of Ghirardelli's, she couldn't talk about this morning.

"Okay, since you're obviously clamming up like a virgin on prom night, I'm going to take a wild guess."

178

Phoebe looked up, waiting for her to continue. Apparently Gabby had been holding off until they made eye contact. Her expression gentled and she sighed.

"Did you see him?"

Phoebe drew in a sharp breath, surprised again at Gabby's perceptiveness.

"Shit." Gabby shook her head, her expression switching from sympathy to fury. "That settles it. There's an officer in the other room right now. He's taking Jenny's—the new girl who checked into the shelter last night—statement. Once he's done, you need to talk to him."

Phoebe glanced out the window of her office, trying to see between the cracks in the blinds in the other room. There was an officer here? Was it *him*?

Her stomach flipped and she scowled, cursing herself for having such a ridiculous juvenile reaction to the thought of the officer who sent her pulsing pounding every time he showed up.

"Why bother? It's not like he can do anything," she said quietly after a moment. "I don't have a restraining order against Rick. I never filed any charges against him in the past, so there's no record of abuse."

Gabby drummed her nails on the desk, nibbling her lip. "Okay, well, has Rick approached you? What's going on?"

"Nothing yet. I don't even know if it's him," Phoebe confessed. "I could just be paranoid—" *yeah right* "—it could be absolutely nothing."

"One too many coincidences. I think we both know that." Gabby shook her head. "I'm worried about you, Phoebe. And Delanie is worried about you too. Before she moved up to Washington, she made me promise I'd keep an eye on you. And I have to say, this has stalker written all over it."

A light tap on the door had them both glancing up.

Phoebe's throat went dry and warmth spread through parts of her body that had been cold with fear for the last hour.

It *was* him. Officer Craig Redmond.

His presence filled the doorframe. He was probably just under six feet, but broad-shouldered and built. His hair was short, with closely cropped black curls. His skin a soft mocha, with expressive, coffee-brown eyes that were now focused intently on her. He had great eyes.

179

God in heaven, the man was sexy. She swallowed hard and averted her gaze. And *young*. The officer was probably just barely out of college.

"Good morning, ladies." His voice, deep and smooth, sent a shiver down her spine. "I just finished taking Ms. Leman's statement." He paused. "Thought I'd check in and make sure there've been no problems lately?"

Phoebe could feel his gaze heavy on her—as she could every other time he'd come to the office when the police were called—and her breath hitched. With dismay, she felt her nipples tighten under his close scrutiny.

She cleared her throat. "Things are pretty quiet lately—"

"Actually, Phoebe could probably use some advice from you," Gabby interrupted. "That is, if you have a moment."

Phoebe's eyes rounded and her mouth gaped. She lowered her gaze to the desk and inwardly cursed. Gabby had *not* just said that.

"Is that so?" The officer's tone warmed. "Something I can help you with, Ms. Jeffries?"

"Actually, she's a Miss," Gabby went on perkily. "She's not married. She's single and very much available—"

"Gabby!" Phoebe sputtered and lifted her head to glare at her friend.

"Right. You know? I'm going to put on a pot of coffee and give you two a moment to chat." Gabby grinned and slid off the Phoebe's desk. She paused in the doorway, her whisper anything but, "Ask her about the ex-boyfriend."

Craig Redmond stepped into the office and a moment later the door swung shut.

Phoebe's pulse quickened and she ran her tongue over her lips. The sudden silence in the room emphasized by the heavy ticking of the clock on the wall.

"So I'm supposed to ask about your ex-boyfriend?" he finally said softly.

She winced. "Yeah, I heard."

He gave a quiet laugh and crossed the room, pulling out Gabby's chair and bringing it over to Phoebe's desk.

She watched him sit down next to her, his uniform tightening across his broad shoulders, and another wave of awareness swept through her.

Too young, Phoebe. Not to mention the fact you've given up dating.

Despite her declaration, her body still reacted when she met his dark, sensitive gaze. What was wrong with her? For years she'd avoided developing even the smidgen of interest in a man. Why was this guy so different?

"What's going on, Ms. Jeffries?"

"Call me Phoebe. Please."

Ms. Jeffries made her feel about a decade older than him. Which, actually, probably wasn't too off base.

"Okay. Phoebe." His full lips twitched into a slight smile. "What is the situation with your ex?"

She leaned back in her chair and crossed one leg over another, drawing in a deep breath. His gaze seemed to follow the movement.

"It's nothing really," she muttered. "I'm probably wasting your time, Officer."

"It's not a problem. Really. Especially if there's anyway I can help." He cleared his throat. "Or the San Francisco P.D. in general."

"Of course. Well, let's see. Back in my last couple years of college, I dated a man..."

"How long ago was this?"

The question was perfectly normal coming from a cop, but Phoebe pursed her lips. Well, might as well put her age on the table. Get it out there.

"Seven years ago. I was twenty-two the last time I saw him and just finishing up college." She watched his face, looking for surprise or disappointment. There was neither. Maybe she'd read him wrong, maybe there was no interest on his side.

"Okay. Go on."

She closed her eyes, not wanting to see the reaction on Craig's face when she told him the next bit. And, with her eyes shut, it also helped her go back to that moment in time. To those last few days with Rick.

"The two years I was with him, he was physically abusive. I didn't want to leave him, though. I was convinced that I loved him. He said we were soul mates and there was no other woman he would ever love more than me." She grimaced, wondering how she could ever have bought such bullshit. "I was young and naïve. Told myself that what was happening was normal or that I'd just pushed him too hard the days he knocked me around..."

Images flickered behind her closed lids. Of Rick holding her in his arms, kissing her cheek in the same spot his fist had connected with moments before. He'd beg for her forgiveness, crying and confessing he didn't know what had come over him.

"You stayed with him for two years?"

Officer Redmond's gentle question prodded her from the disturbing memory.

"Yes," she admitted huskily. "I did. And then I left him." Or had tried to. "I finally managed to cut him out of my life completely. Changed my number and last name. Moved." She shrugged and opened her eyes. "After a while he seemed to get the point, and moved on. Last I heard, he'd relocated to New Jersey."

There was a pause, before he asked, "Have you seen him at any point in the past seven years?"

"No, I haven't. I did everything in my power to make sure he couldn't find me. And then...the last few weeks, I keep thinking I see him. Various places."

Craig sat up straighter in the chair, his eyes narrowing. "Has he approached you? Threatened you?"

"No, he hasn't approached me. Which makes me wonder if it's him."

"It sounds like you managed to start a new life," Craig said. "Disappeared from his line of sight. How do you think he could have found you again?"

Phoebe hesitated and felt some of the blood drain from her head. "A few months ago, I received an award for the work I do here at the shelter. At the ceremony, a reporter took my picture and there was a write up in one of the smaller papers." She paused and nibbled her lip. "I honestly didn't think he'd see it or even be looking for me anymore."

Craig's gaze softened. "You never know with some of these nuts. Your co-worker seemed to think there was a possibility he was stalking you. Is that a concern of yours?"

Her mouth hung open as she tried to figure out how to respond to that. "Maybe if I could be sure it was him I was seeing. But I'm not. If I'm just being paranoid..."

"Have you been paranoid like this in the last seven years?

Thought you'd seen him before?"

"No, I haven't."

He stared at her, and the concern in his gaze surprised her. It seemed a little more personal than just an officer's businesslike concern.

"And I realize there's really nothing you can do." Her laugh came out awkwardly.

"Not until he makes a move, unfortunately. Stay vigilant." He shook his head and set something on the desk. "I'm going to give you a card with a number to call. If he approaches you or threatens you, contact us again."

Phoebe palmed the card, curling her fingers over it and feeling like a complete idiot.

"Thank you for your time, Officer."

"No problem." He hesitated and stood. "I wish there were more I could do. But until—"

She lifted her hand to stop him and grimaced. "I know. Trust me, I know how this works. Gabby was just worried about me."

"She a good friend outside work?"

"Yeah."

"Good. She'll keep an eye out for you. Stick close to you."

"No doubt." Her mouth twitched. "She's actually convinced me to go out with her and her guy tonight. There's a funk band playing down at The Retro, you ever been there?"

He gave a soft laugh. "Once or twice."

"Was it worth the cover charge?"

"Might be. The only times I was there I was working undercover."

Her mouth rounded. "Oh. I see."

His gaze turned considering before he stood and gave curt nod. "You ladies take care and give us a call if there's any trouble."

"Will do." She watched him turn and leave the office, her gaze shifting downward to his ass in the tight pants. *Yum.*

The door closed behind him and she pressed a hand to her warm cheek.

Gabby was right. She really did need to start dating again. Or at least get her sex life back on track.

Though she still had no clue where she'd gotten the gonads

to tell the officer about her plans tonight. It wasn't like he'd show. Why would he?

She was likely just part of the business he took care of during the workday. He probably went home, cracked a beer, and forgot about anything that had to do with his day job. Maybe had some hot little girlfriend waiting for him back home too.

Gabby rushed in, her gaze bright. "How'd it go?"

Phoebe scowled and swerved her chair back to her computer. "I just made a complete idiot of myself. You are so on my shit list, missy."

Chapter Two

After five minutes of shimmying his Hyundai into the tiny parking spot, Craig climbed out and clicked on the alarm.

He smoothed his hands down the crisp designer shirt and wondered for the tenth time since he'd left his house what the hell he was doing.

Jogging across the street when there was a break in traffic, he drew in a deep breath and shook his head. The line outside The Retro had dwindled to only a few people.

The man who stood outside, checking IDs and taking money, glanced up and spotted Craig. His bored expression morphed into a scowl of dismay.

"What the hell, you'd think they'd send someone else undercover this time. I promise, man, I'm not letting any minors in."

Craig grinned and lifted his hands. "I'm off duty tonight. I swear."

The bouncer lifted an eyebrow and held out his hand. "ID and ten dollars."

Craig fished his wallet out of his jeans and drew out his license and the money.

The bouncer glanced down at the license and took the money. "Twenty-five? Hell, you're older than you look." He handed back the ID. "Don't know why you're shitting in the same place you eat, bro, but go on in."

"Thanks." Craig slipped the license back into his wallet and stepped through the doors of the bar.

The snap of the bass greeted him, driving the beat of the laidback seventies funk song the band played.

Shelli Stevens

He wove through the crowd, scanning the group of people for *her*. Though it was possible she hadn't even come. She sure hadn't seemed all that excited when she'd told him of her plans tonight.

But she *had* told him. The blood rushed through his body, tightening his dick and making him draw in an unsteady breath. Damn.

He'd been called out to the Second Chances office many times in the past few months. And each time he'd noticed her.

Phoebe Jeffries. She was confident, friendly, and sexy as hell. And up until today, he hadn't let himself think for one moment that she held even a spark of attraction toward him.

But today, when they'd been closed in her office together, discussing her past...

His fists clenched at his side and his jaw tightened. He'd never have imagined her having been an abuse victim. She was too strong. Didn't put up with shit.

But maybe that's what happened to someone when they overcame that type of horror.

As if his internal sensor knew she was near, his gaze swung to a table in the corner of the bar.

Phoebe sat on the outside edge, nursing a beer between her palms and looking uncomfortable.

His blood pounded a little harder as his gaze ran over her. Damn.

Her black curls hung loose around her face, instead of being pulled back in a clip like she usually wore it. And he hadn't thought it possible, but she was even sexier outside of work than she was in the skirts she wore to the office.

He thought about the thigh she'd inadvertently flashed him earlier today, when she'd crossed her legs during their conversation. They'd been so smooth and pale, and the sight of her soft-looking skin had almost given him an erection on the spot.

There was no skirt on her tonight—her denim-clad legs under the table gave that fact away, but the light blue blouse was cut low and he knew when he saw her up close it would be a near match to her eyes.

Her gaze lifted toward where he stood, almost as if she'd known he was there. He saw her eyes widen and her mouth part slightly.

186

She leaned over to whisper something to Gabby. A second later, Phoebe slid out of the booth and crossed the crowded floor toward him.

"Hi." Flipping a curl off her shoulder, she gave him a hesitant smile. "I'm surprised to see you here, Officer. Are you working tonight?"

The light caught her face, her gaze sparkling up at him. He was right, her shirt was an almost-exact match for her eyes. They were the prettiest blue.

"You can call me Craig. And, no, I'm off duty." He moved his gaze over her face before letting it drop for just a moment to her cleavage. "You mentioned this place earlier and I thought I'd drop by."

He lifted his head again to watch her expression, wondering how she'd react to his blunt reply. Though the fact that he'd shown up at all should be a clear sign of his interest in her.

She didn't look at all uncomfortable, if anything her smile grew.

"I'm glad. You should join us."

"You sure your friends are cool with that?"

Phoebe lifted an eyebrow. "Did you forget that part where Gabby practically threw me at you earlier?"

He gave a soft laugh. "No, I didn't forget." Unable to stop himself, he reached out and wrapped one glossy black curl around his finger. "Why do you think I really showed up tonight?"

She swallowed visibly and ran her tongue over her lips. "Well. In that case, can I buy you a beer?"

"I was about to make the same offer."

"You can get the next one." She stepped back and smoothed her hands down her thighs. "What do you drink?"

"IPA."

"Okay. I'll be back in a second."

As she moved past him, he swung his gaze to watch her advance on the bar. His gaze lowered to her ass, snugly cupped in the dark blue denim.

Damn, she was hot. And that confidence he'd noticed earlier carried over outside the office. No giggling, or silly games. She'd known exactly what she was doing by mentioning her plans to him for tonight, and when he'd taken the bait, she'd clearly been pleased.

She leaned over the counter, talking to the bartender, and the jeans tightened even more over her backside. He tore his gaze from her, willing his blood not to rush to his dick.

He took the moment to check out the band on stage and some of the people dancing on the small dance floor.

Someone moved to step past him and his shoulder slammed into Craig's.

Craig stepped back, his brows drawing together in irritation, as the taller man didn't even bother to apologize.

The man just gave him a hard stare, before scooting by him and out the door of the club.

His gut prickled with a warning that something wasn't right. A feeling he'd gotten all too used to with his job.

"Your beer."

He turned at the soft statement and found Phoebe with a pint in her hand.

"Thanks." He accepted the drink with a slight smile, still thinking about the hardness on the other guy's face.

"Sure you're up for hanging with Gabby and Justin? They're fun. I promise."

"I'm up for it." His mind shifted back to the woman in front of him and his thoughts hit the gutter. "I'm up for a lot of things."

"I'll just bet you are." Her laugh was throaty, her amusement genuine. "Come on, then."

Craig followed her to the table, not at all surprised to see Gabby grinning from ear to ear as she noted his approach. She whispered something to the man beside her and he glanced over, his gaze narrowed.

Maybe a little overprotective? Now that he knew Phoebe's past, he wouldn't be surprised to face that from her friends.

"Hey, look who I found." Phoebe slid into the booth and then scooted over, making room for him.

Craig sat down on the plastic cushion of the booth, his thigh brushing up against Phoebe's. His cock strained against his jeans and he drew in a slow breath.

"Well, hey there, Officer Redmond." Gabby drawled and nudged her man in the ribs. "This here is my guy, Justin."

"Craig. I'm off duty." Craig reached across the table to

shake Justin's hand. "Hey, what's up, man?"

"Not a lot." Justin shook his hand, but his expression clearly indicated he was still withholding judgment on Craig.

"Phoebe mentioned earlier that this band might be worth seeing, so I dropped by."

Phoebe made a quiet harrumph.

Justin laughed. "Not so much. These guys are sucking up the place big time."

"Yeah, you so owe me." Gabby scowled and took another swig of beer. "I gave up watching the game on TV tonight for this."

"You guys Giants fans?" Craig asked, lifting his IPA.

"Hell, yeah, we are," Justin replied. "Season tickets."

"That's cool. Yeah, I try to make at least a game a month."

Phoebe cleared her throat. "We should go to one together sometime. I've never been."

He glanced at Phoebe, surprised by her statement. He found her gaze on his lips. She jerked her head up, as if realizing she'd been staring. Her cheeks filled with color.

Desire built low inside him, rushing through his blood. He drew in an unsteady breath. Had she been thinking about what it would be like to kiss him? Because he sure as hell had been having similar thoughts. For a few months now, really.

Damn but if he didn't want to just cup her face and run his thumbs over the cheeks, before taking her lips in a hard kiss.

What would she taste like? What kinds of sweet sounds would she make when he sank his tongue deep into her mouth?

Phoebe shifted next to him, as if sensing his sensual thoughts. Her thigh scratched against his.

A hint of desire flashed in her eyes, pushing his primitive side further to the surface.

Wanting to test her limits, he gave a slight smile, still holding her gaze, and let his right hand rest on her knee.

A small, visible tremble ran through her and he heard the shift in her breathing.

Never mind if the band sucked, the idea of getting her on the dance floor and pressing those sweet female curves against his body held entirely too much appeal.

"Dance with me?" His words were soft, and though he'd meant it to be a question, it sounded far more like a command.

He half expected her to turn him down, instead she tilted her head and gave a slight nod.

"Why not?"

Setting his beer on the table, he slid out of the booth and held out his hand to her.

She took it and he curled his fingers around hers, tugging her to her feet and onto the dance floor.

Finding a space in the crowd of dancers, Craig slipped his hand low on her hip and pulled her close.

God, she was so completely in over her head. Phoebe swallowed hard, but didn't protest when he pulled her body snug against his.

Their bodies ground together, moving to the snapping bass of the funk song. She felt the thick curl of his cock—which had to be semi-erect—just above her pelvis.

He moved his hand behind her hip, almost cupping her ass cheek, his other hand on her upper back, pressing her close.

She bit back a groan as moisture gathered heavily between her legs, her nipples tightening under her shirt.

The way they danced wasn't particularly dirty, almost every couple on the floor danced in a similar fashion. But the way he moved against her had to be a promise of what he'd be like in bed.

And she wanted him there. All too much. This was crazy. She closed her eyes when he nuzzled her ear. Absolute insanity.

She wrapped her arms around his neck and pressed her body closer to him, grinding her hips against his.

His breathing grew heavier and his cock stirred against her, grew harder.

He caught her chin with firm fingers, lifting her head. He gave her no warning before his mouth slanted softly across hers.

Heat exploded in her belly at the first light caress. The second pass of his mouth over hers came firmer, his tongue sliding easily between her lips to flick against hers.

Phoebe's head swam, the room tilted and she had to tighten her grip on him to stay grounded.

He lifted his head with a groan and pressed her head back against his shoulder.

"Sorry," he muttered.

"Don't you dare apologize."

He laughed and the hot rush of air from his mouth against her ear almost made her legs weak.

"Okay. Then I won't."

His tongue slid along the curve of her ear and she stumbled with a gasp.

He gave a husky laugh and she flushed. He knew exactly what he'd done to her with that little tongue trick.

"Easy, baby," he murmured and then lifted his head a bit.

Disappointment stabbed that he'd put another inch between them. Just when things were getting good.

She was at the point where she didn't care. She'd gone far too long without a man, and here was Craig, ready to make her feel like a woman again. Make her feel alive.

Maybe it was because he was a cop, and it made her more inclined to trust him. That he wouldn't hurt her and he'd never be the type to abuse a woman—even as her logical side knew that theory was crap. Statistics had long proven that police officers had a high rate of abusive behavior. But somehow, on a gut level, she knew she had nothing to worry about with Craig.

She trusted him. Even if she had no reason to, she did. And it scared the hell out of her. But at the same time, she wanted him. Wanted to do spontaneous, crazy things she'd never done in her life. Had been afraid to do after Rick.

Or maybe it had something to do with the fact that Craig was younger. He was sexy, confident, and endearing. Plain and simple, he made all the bells and whistles in her body come to life. So why the hell *shouldn't* she take this step? It didn't have to be serious. It didn't even have to be a relationship. It could just be one night of sex if she wanted. And right now? She wanted.

She lifted her head from the curve of his neck and leaned back a bit, meeting his heated gaze.

"Come home with me tonight."

Surprise flickered in his eyes before they burned even hotter and his nostrils flared.

"You sure you know what you're asking, Phoebe?"

"I know damn well what I'm asking," she fired back and gave him a slow smile. "Do you know what your answer will be?"

191

His gaze lowered to her mouth. "My answer would be...whose place is closer?"

Tension threatened to weave through their sensual discussion, but she pushed it aside and tried to make light of her reply.

"Doesn't matter. I'd rather you come to my place." Going home with him meant she'd be in unfamiliar territory. Gave her the handicap.

Understanding flickered in his gaze and he moved his hand over her back in a gesture that could only be described as reassuring.

"Your place it is." The song ended a moment later and he moved back from her. "Do you want to go back to the table and have another drink with your friends first?"

"No." She licked her lips. "I'd rather go. Now."

"My car or yours? Or separate?"

"Separate." She gave a slight smile. He was catching on quick.

They moved back to the table to grab her purse. Gabby and Justin watched, looking intrigued.

"Hey, guys. We were just going to order some nachos. You want some? We can get a full order."

"We're actually going to head out," Phoebe said and felt her face burn red. "Thanks for inviting me, guys. I'll catch up with you on Monday."

"Nice meeting you," Craig said and reached over to shake both of their hands again.

Phoebe cleared her throat and shot Gabby a quick look. "I'm going to run to the bathroom real quick. I'll meet you near the entrance outside, all right, Craig?"

He gave her a slow smile and nodded. "Sounds good."

Biting her lip, Phoebe spun and hurried across the club, knowing Gabby probably thought she'd lost her mind. Which is why she'd called the last-minute bathroom meeting with her.

Sure enough, she'd only been in the neon-lit restroom for about ten seconds when the door swung open again and Gabby strode inside.

"What the hell?"

Chapter Three

"Hey." Phoebe braced her hands on the sink and met her friend's stunned look in the mirror.

"Hey? That's all you can say? Hey?"

"Are you looking for something in particular?"

"Yeah, like maybe...Hi, Gabby, let me explain why I've decided to give up seven years of celibacy to go screw a cop I barely know."

Phoebe bit her lip to avoid laughing. "Who says I'm going to screw him?"

Gabby folded her arms across her chest and lifted an eyebrow in response.

"Fine. I'm going to go have hot monkey sex with a younger man who happens to melt my panties." Phoebe turned around, the first sense of doubt sweeping through her. She sighed and admitted apprehensively, "And I just need to you tell me that I'm not stupid for doing it."

Gabby stared at her for a moment and then strode forward, wrapping her arms around her.

"Ah, hon, of course you're not stupid. You're just horny." Gabby let out a soft laugh and pulled away and gave her a stern look. "If you're really, really sure about this, then use a condom and be careful."

A condom. Hopefully Craig was thinking that far ahead, because she sure as heck didn't have one. Worst-case scenario, he could hit a gas station.

"Thanks...I will."

"I like Craig. I mean, I don't know him that well, but he seems like a good guy." Gabby hesitated. "You sure you want to do this?"

"Yes." Phoebe nodded and shoved a few curls back over her head. "I think it would be better if I just dove right into the sex, without tiptoeing in over weeks and endless dates. If I do that, I'll chicken out."

"Okay then. So do it."

"And, Gabby... I just," Phoebe bit her lip again. Damn, was she really going to admit this? "He just *really* turns me on. I can't think of anything else when he's close to me. I want him like I've never wanted another guy before. I can see how good we'd be together in my head."

"The way you two looked, I'm not surprised." Gabby squeezed her hand. "Delanie would be so proud of you. You'll have to call her tomorrow and let her know you broke the abstinence streak."

Phoebe rolled her eyes. "Please, she's too busy planning the wedding to care. And it's not that big of a deal."

"*Seven years.* Who goes seven years without sex?"

Another woman who'd entered the bathroom strode past them to a stall, muttering, "I sure as hell wouldn't."

Gabby and Phoebe broke into a fit of laughter.

"Okay," Gabby said between giggles and stepped forward. She arranged Phoebe's curls, undid another button on her shirt, and then handed her a tube of lip-gloss. "Put this on and then go. Now. Before he thinks you've changed your mind and drives home."

Phoebe's stomach sank and her eyes widened, even as she swiped on a layer of the fruity gloss. "Oh God, do you think he would?"

"No. You're way too hot. He'd wait at least another ten minutes."

"Thanks, Gabby. You're too good to me." Phoebe made her way out of the bathroom, with her friend close on her heels.

"I'm not," Gabby muttered. "If I was too good, I'd encourage you to go on a second date before sleeping with him. But I've always been an advocate for a healthy sex life."

"Don't I know it." At the door to the bar, Phoebe spun around again and gave her friend another quick hug. "Say goodbye to Justin for me. I'll call you tomorrow."

"I want details."

"What, like *he inserted tab A into slot B and I screamed until I lost my voice*? Later, sweetie." Phoebe winked and turned, pushing the door to the club open and striding outside.

The air was significantly cooler than when they'd gone in, even though it was early summer.

She shivered, looking around the parking lot and wishing she'd grabbed her jacket.

"I was starting to think you'd changed your mind."

Her heart slammed against her ribs at his soft statement, and she swung around to find him standing by the corner of the building.

"Not on your life." She smiled, her pulse sliding into overdrive as she closed the distance between them. "Question for you. Do you have condoms?"

He opened his mouth and then shut it, cursing. "No. I didn't want to come across as too..."

She laughed and fingered one of the buttons on his shirt. "Don't worry about it. Why don't you just stop at a store and grab some, then come to my place?"

"I can do that." His heated gaze moved from her mouth to the V of her neck.

Her breasts swelled under his perusal, and she thanked God that she'd worn a cute lingerie set tonight. Maybe she'd subconsciously known he'd show. Then again, she'd let the information slip about where she'd be tonight hoping he would.

"If I'm going to meet you at your place," he murmured, drawing a finger over her collarbone and sending heat through her blood. "I'll need your address. Are you comfortable with that?"

"Yeah," she whispered as the ache between her legs grew and her panties dampened. "I'll write it down for you."

Before she lost it completely and slammed him against the wall of the brick building to kiss him again, she stepped around him to the bouncer.

"Excuse me. Do you have a pen I could borrow?"

The bouncer looked beyond her to Craig and scowled, but grabbed a pen from the metal table he sat behind.

She pulled an old receipt from her purse and leaned over the table, scrawling her address on the paper. The heat lamp above warmed her cold fingers.

"Okay." She set the pen down and spun back to Craig. "Here you go."

His fingers brushed hers when he took the slip of paper from her. "Thanks. I'll walk you to your car."

She gave a nod, a little relieved and a lot pleased by the gesture. At her car, she turned and gave him a small smile.

"Meet you back at my place?"

"I may just beat you there," he promised quietly. "You want me to pick up anything else?"

"Surprise me." Feeling all too brazen, she leaned forward and brushed her mouth against his. "See you in a few."

With a wink, she slid into her car. Craig waited until she'd locked the doors and started the engine, before jogging across the street to climb into his car.

Phoebe started to pull out of her spot, following Craig as he pulled into the street. Then she slowed and glanced in the mirror back at the bar, giving a soft curse.

Shoot. She hadn't closed out her tab.

She glanced back out her windshield and watched Craig's taillights disappear from view.

He had to stop at the store anyway, so she had a few minutes. Reversing, she eased her car back into the parking spot and ran back into the bar to settle her bill.

A few minutes later she was back outside, waving goodnight to the bouncer and heading to her car.

She unlocked the door, slid inside, and then started to shut the door, but a long hand grabbed the frame, wrenching it back open.

Phoebe screamed and gripped her key in her hand like a weapon.

"Hang on, I just want to talk."

The blood rushed from her head and her stomach dropped. Fear sent her pulse pounding even as she couldn't tear her eyes from him.

Rick crouched by her car, a goofy smile on his face.

"I thought that was you, Phoebe. I haven't seen you in years."

Oh God. This had to be a nightmare. Rick wasn't sitting right beside her car, talking calmly to her as if they were long-lost friends.

She *hadn't* been paranoid. He had been following her. The beer she'd drank earlier surged in her stomach as panic assailed her.

"What have you been up to lately?" He reached a hand forward to touch her face. "I've missed you so much."

Phoebe gave sharp growl and slapped his hand away. "Don't touch me. Ever."

His brows drew together and he leaned in again. "Phoebe, sweetheart—"

"I said get the hell away from me!" Her shrill words resonated in the parking lot.

His demeanor changed in the blink of an eye. In the light of the street lamp, she watched his ears turn red with anger, a sign she'd grown to recognize as a warning that he was about to lose it.

"I just want to talk," he said through clenched teeth.

Move past the fear, Phoebe. You have to. She drew an unsteady breath and hardened her gaze.

"You're going to be talking to that bouncer over there if you don't back off." She attempted to close the door, but his hands tightened on the frame. "I made it clear seven years ago what I thought of you—that hasn't changed."

His knuckles turned white, he gripped the door so hard. Her mouth went dry and her stomach did back flips.

"You had no right to leave me like that. We're soul mates—"

"Excuse me, sir," she screamed, trying to catch the bouncer's attention.

The bouncer glanced up and then began to make his way toward them.

Rick let go of the door, his eyes glittering with rage.

"This isn't over, Phoebe."

"Is that a threat?" Anger slowly replaced fear now that she knew the bouncer was aware of her situation. "Because I hope you do threaten me, Rick. I'll slap a restraining order on your ass so fast your head will spin."

She jerked the door shut, elbowing the lock down. Her hands were amazingly steady as she stuck the keys into the ignition and started the car.

Looking in her rearview mirror, she watched the bouncer confront Rick. She slammed the car into reverse and hit the gas, hoping to God she didn't get sick on the way home.

Craig drummed his fingers on the steering wheel and glanced around the complex parking lot. Why hadn't he gotten her phone number? What if he'd read the address wrong?

Anticipation had his blood pounding and his cock still rock hard from that kiss she'd pressed against his mouth outside the club.

God, he wanted her so bad it literally hurt. His balls ached and his jeans may as well have been iron, they were so damn tight.

Headlights bounced off the side of the building as a car turned into the parking lot. The speed of the car caught his attention and held it as it whipped into a spot without signaling.

Hell, was that her? He got out of the car, scowling as he adjusted the bag in his arms that held wine, condoms, and food. If that was how she drove, maybe she was late because she'd gotten pulled over.

He bit his tongue as he approached her car, not wanting to blow the night by lecturing about her driving.

The driver's side door swung open and she stumbled out. She didn't even look his way, just began hurrying toward the building.

"Phoebe?"

She gave a sharp scream and spun around, her keys thrust out in front of her like a sword. A very small sword.

Her eyes were wide with panic, streaks of black mascara marking her face.

Shit. His gut clenched and he drew in a swift breath, closing the distance between them.

He slid an arm around her waist and her eyes widened, almost as if she were surprised to see him.

"Easy, baby," he pulled her into the curve of his body and pushed a bunch of curls off her forehead. "Are you okay? Can you tell me what happened?"

"I saw him," she said, her voice unsteady. "I saw Rick. It's him. He *has* been following me."

His chest swelled with anger and his arm tightened

protectively around her.

"Where did you see him?"

"At the club."

He flinched, rearing back in surprise. "How? I watched you drive away."

"I turned back because I forgot to close out my tab."

"Damn, Phoebe. You shouldn't have gone back in alone. You should've waved me down. Or—"

"I was hardly alone." She shook her head and her curls bounced. Her lower lip trembled and tears stained her cheek. "I mean I parked right outside the club."

It didn't matter. The bastard had still gotten to her. His jaw hardened and he slid his other arm around her, pulling her into his arms.

"Did he touch you? Threaten you?"

"I...God it's all a blur right now. I can only remember how I felt at the time. The panic. The fear. And then the anger. It just—" She broke off and blinked, leaning back to glance into the grocery bag he held. "Oh. I am *really* going to need this."

She grabbed the bottle of wine from the sack and turned away, moving toward the front door of the condominium building.

"Come on up," she hollered shakily over her shoulder, the bottle clutched in her grasp.

Craig bit back a curse, knowing wine was probably the last thing she needed. He glanced around the parking lot, not putting it past her ex to have followed her here.

No other cars had entered the complex after hers, however, and the night was quiet.

"Are you coming?"

At her hesitant question, he turned on his heels and jogged over to the door where she stood.

She typed in the code that opened the door, and after a second there was a click, signaling the lock had popped.

He followed her across the floor to the elevators. They stood together, waiting for the doors to open.

"How long have you lived here?" he asked gruffly.

"Six years. I like the security."

The doors slid open and they stepped inside.

"God, what I wouldn't give for a corkscrew right now," she

muttered. "Or is this one of those corks that just pop off? If so, I could just pop it in here."

Craig drew in a slow breath and debated how to handle this.

"Baby, I'm thinking we should hold off on the wine."

"Oh, trust me. I'm going to need the wine." Her laugh was harsh. "I'm not a big drinker, I promise. But right now, I need...something."

He closed the small distance between them.

"Let me take care of you. I'll get you a glass when we get inside your place. Make you something to eat," he promised.

She lifted her gaze to his and the frustration and misery in her eyes sucker-punched him in the gut. He lifted a hand and trailed his fingers lightly across her cheek.

His stomach clenched and the breath locked in his throat. How the hell could anyone ever hurt this woman? Right now, everything inside him just wanted to protect her. Make sure she never had to be afraid again.

The elevator dinged and the doors slid open. She blinked and lowered her gaze, stepping around him and out into the hall.

"I'm down on the end," she said.

He adjusted his grip on the grocery sack and followed her down to her place.

She unlocked the door and pushed it open, leaving it wide so he could follow her in.

He shut it behind him and reached for the lock. Or locks. Jesus. Scanning the door, he counted four. Though, it really didn't surprise him.

After securing each lock, he turned and found her in the kitchen, searching the drawers. Likely for a corkscrew.

"Make yourself at home," she called out. "I'm just looking for...where the hell is it, I know it's here. I used it at New Year's."

Craig crossed the living room to look out the window. The building had a partial view of the bay, if you turned your head just so. They were high up in the building though, the twentieth floor according to the button she'd pressed.

"Nice view."

"It's not bad. If you look to the left you can see the bay..."

Pop. The sound of the cork flying free from the bottle signaled she'd located the corkscrew.

He turned from the window and joined her in the kitchen, reaching into the bag to pull out the food he'd bought.

"When did you last eat?"

She shrugged and tilted the bottle to her mouth, taking a hard swig.

"I'm on a liquid diet tonight."

His mouth twitched and with a gentle hand, he reached out and plucked the bottle from her hand.

"You don't want to waste a good bottle of wine that way." He turned and opened the nearest cupboard and luckily found exactly what he was looking for. "Let's at least use a glass."

"Whatever floats your boat. Just fill it up to the top, please." She glanced down at the counter and her lips parted and she made a little noise of surprise. "Oh my gosh, you bought chocolate?"

"Yeah. And strawberries, meat and cheese." He grinned and glanced at her after filling up her glass. "I'll get hungry soon."

Of course, he'd planned on the bulk of the food for after they got down and dirty. And even though he knew that part of the night was off the agenda, it didn't bother him.

His biggest concern was focusing on what had happened to her after leaving the club. Even now, he fought the urge to just pick her up and carry her to the couch and pull her onto his lap. Somehow he knew she'd fight him on it. She was too independent. Too proud.

He watched her unwrap the chocolate bar and break off a square. Popping it into her mouth, she groaned and closed her eyes. A moment later, she took another long drink of the wine.

She opened her eyes again. Her face turned a slow red as she whispered, "I'm sorry. You must think I'm a complete lush."

Craig leaned against the counter and reached out to rub a flake of chocolate from the corner of her mouth.

"I think you've had a pretty awful night. And I know a lot of people would probably do the same damn thing."

"It wasn't all awful," she murmured, her gaze heating a bit. "There were a few parts I liked. Quite a bit, actually."

Chapter Four

"Were there now?"

Craig ran his thumb over her bottom lip and her mouth parted on a soft sigh, her pupils dilating.

The blood in his veins stirred and the breath in his chest hitched. Christ, he wanted her. Wanted to back her up against the counter and stand between her thighs, while taking that sensual mouth with his.

And how much of an asshole does that make you? Her emotional state alternated between panic and flirting. There was no way he could take advantage of her tonight.

"Why don't you go sit down on the couch," he said, his voice gruffer than he intended. "I'll bring us some food and then we can talk."

The panic flared in her eyes again, before she narrowed them and took another drink of wine. "I'm not sure I want to talk."

"Phoebe..."

"Fine." Her nose wrinkled as she moved past him into the living room. She stumbled over a pile of books on the floor before plopping down onto the couch.

Hmm. Looked like the wine was already hitting her. He glanced at the bottle and noticed she'd already taken out a quarter. Apparently she was a lightweight.

He found the cork and closed up the bottle again, setting the white wine into the fridge. He scanned the contents inside then grabbed himself a can of soda.

Next, he cut the strawberries and arranged them on a plate with the cheese and salami, before walking to the couch to join her.

"How you holding up?" he asked, setting the plate on the coffee table.

"I'm fine. Just fine. Why wouldn't I be?" she said a little too brightly, reaching for a strawberry. "Look at you, Craig. You really know how to impress a girl."

He laughed softly and smiled. That may have been his initial purpose, but now it was just something to offset his appetite and her alcohol consumption.

Grabbing a slice of salami, he stacked it on a slice of cheddar and took a bite.

"Don't you want any wine?" she asked when he popped the tab to his soda.

"I'm good, thanks."

She stared at him hard for a moment.

"Oh jeez, you've changed your mind, haven't you?" she asked, her eyes widening. "You don't want to sleep with me anymore."

"Phoebe, listen to me," he reached out and caught her hand.

She tried to jerk away, but he held tight. Anger flashed in her gaze, her temper no doubt encouraged by the wine.

"Listen to me," he repeated again. "We need to talk about your ex."

"There's nothing to talk about."

"Bullshit. What if he comes after you again? It sure as hell sounds like he's planning on it."

"So then let him." Her jaw hardened. "Yes, I was hoping he'd never find me again. That he'd stay the hell out of my life. But you know what? I'm ready this time. I'm a second degree black belt in Tae Kwon Do and if he even *tries* to touch me, he's toast."

His eyebrows rose, her admission surprising him. And though, at the same time, not so much. It fit with the woman who was beginning to reveal herself layer by layer to him.

He watched the anger, pride, and determination in her gaze. It was obvious she meant every word she said. That she wouldn't hesitate to fight him if it came to it. Even though he was new to his job, he'd seen enough to know that sometimes you didn't always get a fair fight.

Softly, he asked, "And what if he has a gun and shoots you

from six feet away?"

She blinked, looking stunned as the glass of wine wobbled in her other hand.

He took it from her and set it on the coffee table.

"Listen to me, Phoebe. Stalkers don't play by the rules. It's great that you can defend yourself, but you need to know that there's a real good possibility you're not going to get a fair fight with him." He ran his thumb over the palm of her hand, holding her gaze intently.

Frustration and a hint of fear flickered in her gaze before she lowered it.

"Phoebe, I want you to file a temporary restraining order against him."

A temporary restraining order? Phoebe frowned, though the idea wasn't new. From the moment she'd first suspected that Rick had found her again, she'd considered the idea of one, but the fact that she hadn't been able to prove it was him had slowed her down. Until tonight. Tonight he'd shown his hand.

Her head swirled with the idea and the fears. All the legal tape that meant. She dealt with this on a daily basis. She knew what kind of step this would be.

"I know I should," she hedged.

"Of course you should. He has a history of violence with you, and now there's reason to believe he's stalking you." Craig paused. "Can you remember anything he said to you tonight?"

She swallowed hard and frowned, trying to remember exactly what he'd said. The wine she'd guzzled, in combination with Craig's thumb making soft rotations on her palm, made it hard to focus.

Warm tingles moved through her body and her breathing slowed.

"Phoebe?"

"I think he said something about us being soul mates. And something like...*this isn't over.*"

His grip tightened on her hand, but he didn't say anything.

"I hate this," she whispered raggedly. "I *hate* him. I changed my number and kept it unlisted, I changed my name, I moved to another city... I thought he was gone from my life. I should have never accepted that award in person."

Craig gave a soft curse and reached for her, pulling her onto his lap.

"The world is full of way too many assholes like him," he muttered, smoothing a curl back from her face. "I'm sorry. We'll file the TRO in the morning."

She lowered her gaze to the collar of his shirt. The top couple of buttons were undone, showing a hint of his solid upper chest. Her pulse fluttered and desire stirred low in her belly.

"Are you going to leave me tonight?" she asked huskily.

His body tensed. "Do you want to be alone?"

"No." She wiggled a finger under the collar of his shirt, running her short nail over his light brown skin. "I don't want to be alone."

His chest rose against her cheek and stayed risen as he held in the breath. A few seconds passed before he exhaled unsteadily.

"I can sleep on the couch if you'd like," he offered carefully.

A soft laugh escaped her throat and she lifted her head from his chest to meet his gaze.

"If you stay, you will *not* sleep on my couch. You'll sleep in my bed." She quirked an eyebrow. "I just explained that I can defend myself, Craig. I'm not asking you to sleep over for protection."

Heat flared in his gaze and she felt the unmistakable hardening of his cock against her thigh.

Obviously torn, he muttered, "Phoebe, you've had a big shock tonight. You've been drinking. This may not be the time—"

"Look. I'm not a little girl. I'm a grown-ass woman." She curled her fingers around a button on his shirt and pushed it through the hole. "I'm asking you to stay and make love to me tonight. I need you to hold me." Her confidence slipped on that last confession. "I *have* had a shock. And forgive me for coming on strong, but this is how I want to deal with it."

He glanced down to where she'd undone another two buttons, baring his chest.

"By sleeping with me."

"Well, that was the plan when we left the club anyway." She gave him an impish grin and, because his chest looked so damn enticing, leaned forward to brush a kiss across it. "I haven't changed my mind. And unless you have..."

"No." The word came from between clenched teeth. "Hell, no. You win."

He slipped his hand between them, fumbling with the buttons on her shirt as his mouth covered hers.

Her moan was a mixture of relief and pleasure. His tongue eased past her lips to stroke against hers, while his fingers delved into the cup of her bra to stroke her nipple.

Pleasure spiked through her and she let out a ragged whimper. Amazing how fast she could lose control with him. How he could make her brain turn to mush.

Cool air on her shoulders indicated he'd won the race for who could get the other's shirt off first. Her fingers went lax the moment he touched her breast.

She bit her lip and then resumed her task, managing another button even as he unfastened her bra and tossed it to the floor.

"Beautiful," Craig whispered.

His large hands cupped her breasts, squeezing the flesh and tugging the nipples into harder points. Oh God, it felt so good.

With a frustrated groan, she tore her mouth from his to rapidly undo the rest of the buttons on his shirt. She was so out of practice.

A moment later his shirt hung open, showing the defined muscles of his chest and abdomen. Her mouth dried at the sight. So sexy. So male.

The last thought sent a tiny wave of unease through her. She hadn't been with a man in seven years. Hadn't let herself trust one enough to become physical with him. There'd been too much bitterness covering the small layer of fear.

And yet, here she was, throwing it all to the wind. Ready to jump between the sheets with a man she barely knew.

"You sure about this?" His question indicated he sensed her inner turmoil. She lifted her gaze to meet his, searching his eyes for any sign that he'd hurt her or excessive dominance.

His expression only held desire and a surprising amount of tenderness.

"Yes," she murmured and pushed his shirt off his

shoulders. "I'm sure." Leaning forward, she flicked her tongue over one dark nipple. "But thank you, Craig, for checking."

The air hissed from between his teeth and his fingers delved into her hair.

So he liked that, did he? She smiled and gave the other nipple the same treatment.

His groan encouraged her and she shifted on his lap, letting her nails drag down his chest as her tongue teased him.

His hands slid down to her ass, squeezing the flesh through her jeans.

Hot moisture gathered between her legs and her inner muscles clenched, seeking release.

"Come here." He eased her off his lap and stood them both. "Let's go to the bedroom."

Part of her wanted to dig her heels into the rug and declare the couch a fine and dandy place to do what they were about to do. But when he caught her hand and urged her down the hall, she knew she'd want the bed for what happened afterward. The real question would be if he'd really hold her like she'd said she needed.

It doesn't mater, she told herself firmly. Nothing mattered except this moment with him. It wasn't permanent and there certainly weren't strings. Even if, by some crazy chance, he wanted them, she wasn't sure she was ready for that.

Once inside her bedroom, he shut the door firmly behind them and reached for his belt buckle.

Tension coiled through her and she couldn't move as she watched him undress. The jeans fell heavily to the floor, leaving him naked except for his briefs.

His thighs were solid and muscular, but she only briefly noted them before her gaze locked on the thick coil of his erection beneath the cotton.

She swallowed hard, her pulse fluttering and her panties growing damper.

Her gaze dropped to the gun that was strapped around his ankle. Her pulse jumped, but not with arousal this time.

"Sorry." He noted her widened eyes and removed the gun, laying it on her dresser. "I know it's a shock."

"I understand."

He stepped toward her, sliding one hand around her waist

and the other into her hair. His mouth brushed across hers again. Once, twice, until her knees began to shake.

She turned him, backing him up to the bed until he sat down. Bolder now, she straddled him, her knees on each side of his hips.

Her breasts swung free in front of his face, and he made a strangled groan before reaching for them. His lips closed over one nipple, drawing it deep into his mouth.

The air rushed from her lungs and she tangled her fingers into his hair, arching her back.

He cupped her ass, squeezing the flesh while he teased and sucked on the tips of her breasts.

"Craig." His name left her lips on a ragged plea.

"What do you want, baby?" His head lifted from her chest and he gazed up at her.

"I want to come." Humiliation almost bloomed in her belly, but she shoved it aside. She wouldn't be embarrassed for taking control of her sexual pleasure.

Relief filtered through her when he just smiled. Apparently he wasn't shocked or offended by her declaration.

"I want you to come too." He reached for the button on her jeans and slid it through the hole.

His hands closed around her ribcage and he lifted her to her feet on the bed, so she stood in front of him.

He eased her zipper down and then hooked two fingers in each side of her jeans. Tugging the denim down, he also caught her panties, dispensing both to her ankles.

She kicked them free, the cool air washing over her naked body. A tremble racked through her when she watched his eyes darken as he drank her in.

"Damn, baby, look at you," he muttered and placed his hands on her outer thighs. With skilled thumbs, he parted her labia and stroked an index finger down her cleft.

A ragged gasp rushed from her throat and a rush of moisture flooded her pussy.

"You're all warm and wet for me." The male appreciation in his voice only heightened the intensity of her arousal. "How do you feel inside?"

She bit her lip, watching as he pushed his index finger deep into her. The invasion was a sweet and thorough pressure.

Her body clenched around him, her mouth forming a silent O.

"Tight. Jesus, you're tight." His heated gaze flicked up to hers. "I hope you can handle me."

He accompanied the statement by adding another finger inside her.

Her legs shook and her mind spun. The image of his cock flashed in her head. Could she handle him? Darn good question. But she'd sure as hell try.

"Yes," she whispered raggedly.

He pulled his fingers from her and she almost cried out in disappointment. Then he brought his fingers to his mouth and sucked them dry.

His nostrils flared and he closed his eyes. "Tight and you taste good."

"Oh God..." Her body quaked.

Craig's mouth curled into a slow sexy smile. "You're going to scream when I eat your pussy, baby."

His words turned her muscles to jelly, the visions so blunt and intoxicating, she forgot to breathe.

He gripped her thighs, urging her forward as he lay down on his back on the mattress. With his silent ministration, she straddled his face, her pussy just above his mouth.

His tongue delved into the slit of her sex, his strong hands still gripping her thighs.

"*Oh.*"

The sensation was so intense she blindly reached out for something to hold, finding the headboard and gripping it.

His tongue thrust deep into her this time, moving in and out, fucking her. His thumb found her clit, rubbing it in slow circles.

The position was so new to her, so erotic, it brought her quickly to the edge of an orgasm.

Her knuckles turned white, she gripped the headboard so hard. Her body rose and fell against his face. Responding and following the movement of his tongue.

He switched his technique, thrusting three fingers deep inside her, while flicking her clit with his tongue.

Phoebe's head spun, sweat broke out on her body and her breathy pants turned into guttural moans.

His lips closed over her swollen nub, drawing it deep into

his mouth and sucking.

True to his promise, a sharp scream fled her throat as her pleasure peaked. Her thighs tightened around his head and her entire body tensed.

Lights flashed behind her closed eyes and she gasped in air like it was a novelty. Her nails dug so hard into the headboard, she felt a few break.

After the trembling slowed and her mind returned from the orgasm cloud, she still felt the wet licks of Craig's tongue against her clit.

His fingers no longer gripped her thighs, but moved softly over them. As if comforting her through the aftereffects.

She released the headboard and blinked, stunned by the intensity of her climax.

Craig's mouth left her and he placed a kiss on each thigh.

Her gaze drifted down to him as his head returned to the mattress. His eyes glittered up at her with desire, his mouth still wet from her juices.

"I..." Her lips trembled. How could she put into words the emotions rushing through her? Would it even be wise to try?

He gave a lazy smile and, still lying back, reached up to massage her clit.

"Wanna go for two?"

He quirked an eyebrow and licked the traces of her off his mouth.

Phoebe groaned raggedly and shook her head. "I don't think I can handle it. Yet."

She moved off him and glanced down at his bulging erection. *Wow.* It had grown even more since he'd first undressed.

Gulping, she reached out and ran her hand over it though his briefs.

"I think I'm ready for you now."

His cock twitched against her fingers, as if begging to be released.

She licked her lips and grasped the waistband of his briefs, tugging them downward.

His erection sprang free. Dark, thick, with a swollen, fat head. A drop of moisture gathered on the tip and her mouth watered at the sight.

"Phoebe," he rasped. "Grab the condom. It's on the corner of the bed."

"In a minute." She lifted her gaze from his cock to give him a coy smile. "I like to play fair."

Leaning forward, she nuzzled his erection before sliding her tongue out to catch the drop of arousal from the tip.

The air hissed from his throat in response and his hips jerked against her.

"Oh. Obviously I did something right." Her smile widened and she wrapped her hands around his cock to feel his girth.

He was long, but more so thick. Her fingers couldn't quite close around him. The urge came on strong to take him in her mouth, to see if she could make him squirm the way he'd made her.

A wave of doubt washed over her. What if she was terrible at it, though? She hadn't given a blowjob in years...since Rick. The thought sent a wave of ice down her spine, but she brushed it off.

This night was about Craig.

"Phoebe." He reached out and touched her arm. "Baby, you don't have to do anything you don't want to do."

"I *want* to. I'm just afraid I might suck."

"Isn't that kind of the point?" He gave a soft laugh and she watched the muscles in his lower abdomen bounce.

Some of the doubt eased from her mind and she relaxed a bit, moving her hand up and down his length. "You know what I mean."

"Baby." His voice came out husky now. "I promise that if your mouth is on my cock, it's not going to feel bad."

"Unless I was to, say, bite down really hard or something?"

"You're a sadist."

"Kidding." She laughed softly and leaned down again. Her curls fell against his thigh and she nuzzled his length.

His cock twitched against her lips and she watched his stomach clench.

A good sign that she was pleasing him. Her tongue flicked out over the base of him, before she slid it up his length to circle the head.

He exhaled harshly and his thighs tightened. Her confidence bloomed, the slightly salty taste of his flesh made her blood pound.

She parted her lips against the head of his cock, hesitated a moment, and then slid her mouth down over him.

Her initial reaction that he was thick was reiterated when her lips stretched wider to bring him deep.

"Jesus," he gasped, his hips jerking against her.

Instinct kicked in and she closed her eyes, savoring the feel and taste of him while she moved her mouth up and down his cock.

Slipping her hand low, she cupped his sac and squeezed lightly.

"I need you. Now," he rasped harshly, sitting up and plucking her off him like she weighed nothing. He traced her mouth with his thumb. "Otherwise I'll end up coming some place other than the condom."

His not-so-subtle implication that he'd come in her mouth increased the ache between her legs. The idea was so seductive. But the urge to have him inside her—hard and full—was even more so.

"Okay," she whispered, still grasping his cock gently. "I want to ride you though."

Chapter Five

Craig groaned, her words making his dick twitch and grow even harder—which he hadn't thought was possible.

"Get the condom."

She released him and scurried across the bed to grab it and rip it open.

Despite her awkward fumbling, she had it on him in half a minute. He wondered, and not for the first time tonight, how long it had been since she'd been with a man.

She sat back on her heels, biting her lip and obviously out of breath. Nerves?

He touched her knee gently. "You're sure about this?"

She relaxed a bit and rolled her eyes with a soft laugh. "You're still asking me that? Yes. I'm sure."

He arched an eyebrow, relieved. "Then what are you waiting for?"

"Not a damn thing." She laid her palms against his chest and pushed him flat on his back.

He hit the mattress and stared up at her, catching the breath she'd just knocked out of him.

She swung her leg across his hips and straddled him. His cock, tight and aching, nudged the soft, wet heat between her legs.

The urge to thrust up into her was primal. But knowing she wanted to be in control, he ground his teeth together and chanted in his head the word *patience*.

Only she didn't ease down onto him, just rubbed her pussy back and forth against the head of his cock.

Unable to avoid touching her, he reached up and curled his

fingers around her hips and guided her downward just a bit. The tip of him nudged just between the folds of her sex, stroking her lush, wet channel.

"Ride me," he commanded softly, barely holding onto the thread of control. "Ride me like you said you wanted to."

Desire flashed in her eyes. With a cross between a growl and a moan, she pressed herself downward.

His cock eased steadily up into her, stretching her. Her sweet body hugged his cock so tightly, it increased the waves of pleasure rolling through him.

Her mouth parted and her lower lip trembled.

"Jesus," he choked out. "You're tiny. Can you take me deeper?"

He was only halfway inside her. She gave a shaky nod, drawing in quick breaths as she lowered herself another tiny bit onto him.

"Oh God, Phoebe." The air hissed from between his teeth and his control snapped. "I can't—" he gripped her hips tighter and lifted his hips, thrusting upward and completely into her, "—wait."

A gasp ripped from her throat and her body convulsed around him.

"*Craig.*" Her nails dug into his chest, the walls of her pussy squeezing him until his eyes crossed. "Oh God."

"I'm sorry, baby." He stayed buried inside her, giving her a few seconds to adjust to him.

He knew he was thick and, judging by the mix of pleasure and pain on her face, she was struggling.

"I'm okay," she croaked. "I am. I promise. Just...give me a second. You feel...really, really good. Really, really big, but really good."

"Yeah?" A wave of masculine triumph rushed through him. He moved his hand to where their bodies connected, and then slid a finger upward to find her swollen clit. "How about this? If I rub your clit does it feel really good?"

"Ah, *oh.* Mmm." Her eyes closed on a sigh. "Good's an understatement."

He massaged the hot nub until her muscles relaxed around him. Until she grew wetter and moved against him.

She began to ride him, lifting up a little and then sliding

back down.

She leaned forward, her palms flat on his chest, as she increased her pace. Her breasts bounced, the hard nipples jiggling so close to his mouth.

He lifted his head, caught one tip with a growl and sucked it for a moment, before releasing it with a pop.

She cried out and let go of his chest, leaning back now as she rode him. Bringing him deeper with the new angle.

Blindly, he found her clit again, rubbing faster as his own climax approached.

"Craig. Oh my—" She threw her head back and gasped, her muscles squeezing him mercilessly.

Seeing her complete abandon while she came thrust him over the edge. He gripped her hips and plunged to the hilt, groaning loudly as he was blinded by his own orgasm.

They trembled together, gasping and shuddering. A few minutes passed before his body went slack, his cock empty from its release.

Phoebe whimpered and slid off him, rolling to the side and onto her stomach on the bed.

He pinched the condom off and slid out of bed. "Be back in a second."

The muffled grunt—since her face was buried in the pillow—was the only response he got.

After disposing of the rubber and cleaning himself up in the bathroom, he walked back to her bed.

She hadn't moved, just lay on her stomach, the pale curves of her ass waving like a second invitation to his gaze.

"Can I get you anything?" he offered. "Water?"

With a soft laugh, she rolled over onto her back and stared up at him.

"You." She patted the mattress. "I just want you."

Needing no further encouragement, he climbed back into bed and pulled her into his arms, drawing the blanket over them.

She snuggled against him, burying her face against his chest.

Tenderness stabbed at him and he ran a gentle hand down her back, holding her tighter.

"Try to sleep, baby." He brushed a kiss against her

forehead.

"Mmm."

Her lazy murmur was followed shortly by even breathing.

Damn, that sure hadn't taken her long. His lips twitched and he closed his eyes, his own pulse slowing as a yawn popped his jaw.

It had been a long day. Passing out sounded good. Passing out with Phoebe in his arms sounded even better.

A few minutes later he fell asleep.

He woke to the sound of a car alarm going off in the parking lot. Lifting his head, he glanced at the clock radio on her bedside table.

Almost seven in the morning.

"Hey."

He jerked his gaze to the left and found Phoebe snuggled against his side, watching him. Wide awake.

"Is that your car alarm?" he asked, already on alert for the possibility of more danger.

"No. I don't have an alarm on my car. Probably my neighbor's, it's always going off." She sighed and rolled her eyes. "If I leave my window open at night I can hear it, even way up here."

He grunted. "How long have you been awake?"

"Twenty minutes or so. I didn't want to wake you," she confessed.

"Why so early?" He reached for her, pulling her half on top of him. "It's Saturday morning."

Her lashes drifted down to her cheek, but he'd seen the flash of embarrassment in her gaze.

"I've slept alone for a long time. This is almost...new to me again."

"Has it been a while?" he asked softly, stroking her hair. "Since you went to bed with a guy?"

She tensed and started to lift her head from his chest, but he urged her cheek back down.

"Why?" She paused. "Was I terrible?"

"God no." He laughed and kissed her forehead. "I only asked because you kept dropping hints." And God, when he'd first slid inside her... "And you were pretty damn tight. Not that

I'm complaining by any means."

She groaned and slapped his chest playfully. "Ever consider that maybe you're just built like a frickin' bratwurst?"

"Thank you," he replied and laughed at her snort of disbelief.

"*Any*way. Yes. It has been awhile. Honestly... God, I can't believe I'm about to admit this to you, but Rick was the last guy I was with."

He did the math in his head and then blinked in shock. "You went seven years without sex?"

"Sheez, you make it sound as if I said I'd joined a convent."

"You may as well have."

"Look, I realize seven years is a long time to be abstinent."

An insane amount of time for a woman. And she'd broken it for him. He moved his hand over her back, and a sliver of possessiveness rushed through him.

"I'm glad you chose me."

"Are you now?" She lifted her head, her gaze twinkling with mischief.

"Hell, yeah." He caught her chin between his forefinger and thumb and glanced at her swollen mouth. "And let me tell you that you had nothing to worry about with the oral stuff."

"Oh. Right. That." She bit her lip and averted her gaze. "I...had some issues... Rick would pressure me in that department and then would tell me how terrible I was at it."

Tension coiled through him at her deceptively casual words.

"Pressure you?" he repeated, trying to keep his voice calm. The steel crept into his tone regardless.

"I didn't really want—" she began awkwardly. "I mean, the whole relationship was unhealthy." She sighed and tried pull away from him, but he drew her closer instead. "You know what? I shouldn't have said anything. This is way too much baggage I'm throwing out for a one-night stand."

The air locked in his lungs and he blinked in shock. "Who the hell said this was a one-night stand?"

Her eyes widened, before she lowered her lashes abruptly. "Well, what else would it be?"

Now there was a damn good question. He hadn't thought past anything besides going home with her last night. Holding her in his arms, and discovering the sweet sounds she'd made in bed.

He sure as hell hadn't set out thinking long-term, but the idea of short-term rocked him to his core. Just one night with Phoebe? Hell, no.

"Craig," she began hesitantly. "I can't get involved with anyone."

Annoyance pricked deep and he bit out a terse, "Why not?"

"Because I just can't. I gave up dating. I don't trust—"

"Any man?" he finished, his jaw clenching.

"That's not it."

"We're not all like him. Your ex."

She lifted her gaze, her eyes flashing. "Of course I know that."

"Give me a chance, Phoebe. I don't want this to be a one-night thing." He caught her hand, stroking the inside of her wrist.

She licked her lips and he felt her pulse quicken under his fingertips.

"Well," she hedged. "Maybe it doesn't have to be a one-time thing. Obviously we work well in the bedroom."

"We could work well out of the bedroom too." His irritation grew.

She was stonewalling him on any attempt to make this about more than sex.

"I'm not sure I'm ready for that."

He lifted her wrist and placed a kiss on the rapidly beating pulse.

"Give yourself a chance. Give *us* a chance."

Panic mixed with desire in her eyes before her lashes fluttered down to hide her expression.

"Craig, please don't rush me," she begged, her voice husky. She shook her head. "I've already taken a huge step with what happened last night. But as to more than sex...I—I need to think about it. I'm sorry."

"Right." His jaw flexed. She was brushing him off. Last night had been nothing but getting laid for her. "Well, since we've already fucked, maybe I should just leave now."

He'd said it sarcastically, but she bit her lip and then looked up at him again, regret in her gaze.

"Maybe that's for the best."

Shock ripped through him, but like hell would he let her see it. His pride took over. With a feigned casual shrug, he slid off the mattress and went in search of his clothes.

Once dressed, he glanced back at the bed, a little more than surprised that she was still so quiet. She was sitting up, knees drawn to her chest with her arms wrapped around them.

Her gaze remained on the bedspread, her sensual mouth now drawn into a taut line. Everything about her demeanor screamed *back off.*

And so he did. He turned, and without a backward glance, left her room and then her apartment.

Chapter Six

The slamming of her apartment door seemed to compound the slamming of the door to her heart.

Phoebe closed her eyes, willing away the despondency that churned her stomach. It was better this way. It was.

She drew in a deep breath and fell back against the pillows. With every second that passed, she visualized Craig getting farther away from her apartment.

By now he'd be in the elevator going down to the lobby. In a few minutes he'd be crossing the parking lot. Each step he took led him farther away from her. Which is exactly what she'd requested.

So why did she feel like she'd just taken ten giant steps down into the emotional dumps?

Despite the mental low, physically she felt incredible. She kicked her legs free of the sheets, unable to ignore the pleasant soreness between her legs. Her thighs had a slight ache from being extra stretched out and every part of her body tingled with life.

She traced her fingers over her stomach, reliving the sensation of Craig's mouth on her. Heat gathered between her legs and her breathing quickened.

With a curse, she swung her legs off the bed and groaned. Maybe having sex with Craig hadn't been the best idea. It had broken the seal on her abstinence. He'd reminded her exactly what she was missing out on.

But more than the sex, the moments after they'd been intimate were what really gave her butterflies. How wonderful it had been just to be held by a man. But not just any man. Craig. He was such a nice guy. A man who wouldn't hurt her. Who she knew would actually go to lengths to make sure she was protected.

Protected. Shit! Her eyes widened and she rushed out of the bedroom toward her front door.

She'd forgotten all about Rick for a few moments. Forgotten all the normal steps she took to keep herself safe.

When she was just feet from the unlocked front door, it began to open.

No. Oh God, *no.*

With a scream, she dove toward it, trying to slam it shut before he could get inside.

He pushed back, forcing it open until she stumbled backward.

Phoebe let out a shriek and reached for the baseball bat she kept in the closet.

"*Stop.* Phoebe, *stop.*"

The bat—firmly gripped in her hands—wavered as she finally realized who was inside her apartment.

Not Rick.

Craig shut the door with a quiet click and slid the locks into place.

"Easy, girl. Are you okay?"

She nodded dumbly, her heart pounding a mile a minute in her chest. How could she have been so stupid not to lock the door after he left? She was never that careless.

She lowered the bat and returned it to the closet. Shaken by her own foolishness. "Why did you come back?"

Craig didn't reply and she glanced up, sensing it wasn't just because he refused to take no for an answer.

"What? What is it?"

"I think your ex figured out where you live," he finally said quietly. "When I got down to the parking lot, there was a crowd of people gathered around your car."

Her stomach sank and she gripped the counter. "What's wrong with my car?"

"The windows were smashed in. A note was left under the windshield wiper."

She closed her eyes, nausea sweeping through her. "And what did the note say?"

"Phoebe…"

"Please, just tell me, I'm going to figure it out the minute I go down there."

"It said *whore.*"

"Of course it did." A manic giggle spilled past her lips and she shook her head. "That was always his favorite word for me. Which was ridiculous since he was the only man I'd ever fucked…until you, I mean."

She winced, realizing she probably shouldn't have been that forthcoming. Especially when she saw Craig blink in surprise, his mouth falling open a bit.

Great. Now she looked like a woman who could barely get laid. So help him if he even made a comment…

Fortunately, he just cleared his throat and sighed. "I've called the station. They're sending someone over to file a report."

Her fingers clenched around the counter. "I don't want to involve the police."

Craig closed the distance between them and took her hand, giving it a light squeeze.

"Yes, you do, Phoebe. You need to. And this will only help your case in getting a restraining order."

"Craig, please. Just let me deal with this—"

"Alone? Hell, Phoebe, it sounds like you've been dealing with things alone for too long now." He pulled her into his arms, not releasing her even when she pressed her hands flat against his chest. "I know you're not ready for a relationship. You made that clear. But last night you trusted me enough to bring me into your bed. Trust me enough now to help you through this."

Her body trembled. A combination of frustration, fear, and desire making every nerve come to life.

It was just so unfair. She shouldn't have to deal with this. Rick shouldn't have come back into her life, turning her world upside down and threatening everything she'd built for herself. Made her live in this edgy state of *what's going to happen next?*

"Well?" Craig prodded gently.

"Craig—"

"Please, Phoebe. You shouldn't have to go through this alone." He pushed a curl behind her ear. "And I don't want to hand you off to someone else. Let *me* be the one to stand beside you."

She closed her eyes. It was so hard to let go. To give that kind of trust to a man. Especially when facing the biggest obstacle and fear of her life. Rick.

But Craig's words had claws. They reached deep inside her and refused to let go. Twisted everything around until the idea of going through this without him seemed more terrifying than giving over that kind of trust.

He cupped the back of her head, urging her cheek to his chest. She didn't resist. She slid her arms around his waist with a ragged breath and went limp against him.

"Okay," she whispered. "Okay."

His chest rose high against her cheek as he drew in a deep breath.

"Thank you," he muttered, stroking her back, "for trusting me, baby."

She did trust him. Whether it was smart to or not, it didn't matter. It was instinctive and right now she needed him.

The pounding of his heart, each stroke of his hand down her back drew the fear and tension from her body. Removing them like the toxins that they were.

"You'd better get dressed." He eased her away gently. "The police will be here any minute now." His gaze slipped over her and heat flickered in his eyes. "I like you naked and all, but would rather keep those sweet curves between us—and not the guys down at the station."

"Not good at sharing, hmm?" Phoebe gave a weak smile and nodded. "I'll throw on some clothes."

"I share lots of things," he leaned down to brush a slow kiss across her mouth. "Just not my woman."

My woman. Her pulse quickened. Did he consider her his woman?

A sharp rap sounded at the door and he drew back.

"Go, put on those clothes. I'll let them in and get things going."

"Okay." She slipped all the way from his grasp and headed back to the bedroom.

She hit the underwear drawer and grabbed a pair of stripped cotton panties. The bra she chose didn't match, but worked well under the T-shirt she pulled on over her favorite jeans.

Sliding her feet into flip-flops, she re-entered the living room, where Craig was talking with two uniformed officers.

They turned to look at her, straightened and gave a polite nod.

A flush worked its way into her cheeks as she thought about how it must look to them. Surely they had to know that Craig had spent the night. And that she and Craig were probably lovers.

Whore. The memory of what Rick had scrawled on the note ran through her head.

Her stomach clenched as a wave of doubt swept through her, planting the tiny seeds of shame. *Maybe he was right? You did go to bed with Craig on basically your first date. If you can even call it that.*

"No," she whispered, her lips barely moving and the word inaudible to anyone but her.

She knew better. She'd been through therapy and had helped reassure countless women at the shelter they were not to blame. That they were not whores, or liars, or deserving of someone's fists.

And damn Rick for making her doubt herself—even for a second.

She lifted her chin and folded her arms across her chest, turning her focus to the officers.

"Hi," she said softly. "Thanks for coming out."

"No problem." One of the officers gestured toward her kitchen table. "If you want to take a seat, we'll go ahead and get started."

"Of course."

Craig brought a clenched fist up to his mouth and tapped it against his lips. It helped—just a little—restrain the anger building inside him.

As he listened to Phoebe's description of her ex, his stomach clenched. It was the man in the bar last night—the tall one who'd smashed into him and then run off with a dirty look.

Had her ex realized Craig had been with Phoebe that night? Had the encounter been deliberate? Shit, he should've listened to his instincts more.

He paced to the window then glanced out over the city and

partial view of the bay.

Whatever it took, he'd make sure that asshole didn't get within three feet of Phoebe again. Even if he had to move her in with him.

Blinking, he tilted his head and gave her a considering look. Hey. Now there was an idea....

He waited until the officers left and they were finishing breakfast before bringing up the suggestion to her.

"It's a bad idea." Phoebe shook her head and dumped out the rest of her coffee.

Watching her, Craig folded his arms across his chest and wondered how he could convince her to stay with him.

"It's not a bad idea. It's a damn good idea. I don't like the idea of you being here alone."

"You don't have to like it."

Craig caught her arm as she went to walk past him. He turned her around to face him, slipping an arm around her waist and pulling her snug into his embrace.

"I know I don't have to like it. And I know I can't force you to stay with me." He lowered his head and brushed his lips across hers. "But you'd be safe." He kissed her again. "And you'd be with me."

She hesitated, but made no move to pull from his arms. "I don't know if he'd really hurt me. I think he's just trying to make my life miserable now that he's found me again and I turned him away."

Craig thought about the rock sitting on the driver's seat in her car. And the note on the windshield. It sure as hell didn't seem like her ex was just trying to be an annoyance. It sounded like an unhealthy obsession.

"Just a few days, Phoebe. We can get the temporary restraining order set up and give Rick a bit of time to show himself. Because he will." He touched her cheek, a tightness in his chest. "He will, baby. You have to know that."

She bit her lip and then nodded. "You're probably right. I guess I'm still a bit in denial. It's been so many years—"

Her home phone rang and they both glanced at it. Craig pursed his lips, suspicious already of who might be calling.

"I'm unlisted," Phoebe murmured with a shake of her head and pulled free from his arms.

"Good."

"In fact, it's probably the video store. I'm a week late with the latest Jason Bourne movie." She grimaced, lifting the receiver to say hello.

Her face drained of color and her fingers clenched around the phone.

Craig wrenched the phone from her hand just before her body began to tremble.

"This is the San Francisco P.D.," he said tersely. "Who is this?"

"Ah, you must be Phoebe's newest bed buddy." The male on the phone used a soft-spoken voice. "Does she like it when you kiss her ear? I know she always enjoyed that with me."

"You're a sick man."

"You know, I thought all the police officers had left—I didn't realize you were one as well."

Fuck. He was watching her apartment. Craig's gaze swept to the window and the buildings beyond, before focusing on Phoebe.

She stood gripping the counter, watching him, her mouth tight and eyes wide.

Anger exploded in his gut. Made his vision blur and the phone shake in his grip. Damn it, he wished the man had the balls to show up in person. Then they'd see who the hell was terrorized.

"This conversation is being recorded, Rick."

"She told you my name? I suppose I shouldn't be surprised." He sighed. "And I think we both know that you're not recording this conversation. Perhaps next time you'll be more prepared."

Craig's jaw hardened. "I'm taking her down to get a restraining order this afternoon."

"Smart move...of course you'll have to serve it to me and sadly, I'm between residences at this time."

The amused laugh from the other man had Craig biting back a curse.

"It doesn't matter, you'll be arrested if you approach her and informed of the order."

"Look, I'm just going to be honest with you, Officer," Rick went on smoothly. "I've only just found Phoebe again after all these years, and she means quite a bit to me. We were each other's first, you know. Completely in love. Soul mates. And I don't intend to let her slip through my fingers again."

"Keep talking, asshole. Your threats just build our case against you."

"Oh, it's not a threat. I'm sure once Phoebe and I have some alone time, she can be...persuaded to give our relationship a chance."

Craig snapped. "Touch her and I *will* kill you."

He slammed the receiver down and closed his eyes. Damn it. The guy dug himself under the skin and just needled.

"I'm unlisted," Phoebe said softly from behind him, her tone full of disbelief. "I don't understand how he could've gotten my number."

Craig turned to face her. "What did he say to you when you answered the phone?"

He hadn't thought she could get any paler, but she blanched and proved him wrong.

She straightened her spine and looked away. "It doesn't matter."

Craig closed the distance between them and touched her cheek lightly. "It does matter, Phoebe. Please."

"He said..." Her throat worked as she swallowed hard. "He said, 'Hello, sugar, I've been thinking about our last night together'."

Craig drew in a slow breath, all kinds of possibilities flickering through his head.

"Will you tell me what happened?" he asked gently. "You don't have to if you're not ready."

She didn't answer right away. He watched her eyes kind of glaze over, as she went to another place in her head.

"The night he's talking about is the day after I called things off with him," she finally said tonelessly. "I left him, but didn't think to go into hiding. I was home alone—my roommate had gone out of town. He forced his way inside my apartment...and then on me."

Craig pulled her fully into his embrace, trying to keep his grip on her light, even as every muscle in his body went taut with rage. The bastard. He wouldn't trust himself an inch if he ever came face to face with her ex.

227

Phoebe pressed her cheek against his shoulder and he heard her unsteady indrawn breath.

"I left town for good the next day. Went into hiding with relatives and friends, until I could lose myself in another city. I even changed my last name."

"I'm sorry, Phoebe. God, I'm so sorry, baby."

"Thank you. It's still not easy for me to talk about, but I've come to terms. Lots of therapy." She gave a humorless laugh. "And then being involved with the shelter helps. It certainly reminds me that I'm not alone with my experience."

Craig just held her, brushing kisses across her forehead. What could he say? Words held little weight to something so horrible.

"I hate that he found me again. Hate it."

"He'll fuck up. Fast. And then his ass will be in jail."

After a few moments she pulled back and gave a tepid smile. "Thank you, Craig. And I think I will take you up on that offer to crash at your place." She bit her lip, her lashes fluttering down. "It'd be stupid to stay here alone now that he knows where I live."

Relief surged through him, but he forced a casual nod. "Good. Why don't you throw some things together and we can head out. We can take care of the restraining order on the way."

"Okay. Let me grab a quick shower too?"

He watched her leave the room to go pack. Unease mingled with the relief. Serving Rick that restraining order would never happen. The man had pretty much told him that. And even knowing it was coming, Rick had insinuated that it wouldn't keep him away from Phoebe.

Craig folded his arms across his chest and went to look out over the city again. If Rick was so determined to get to Phoebe again, it left them only one option—to get to him before he got to her.

Chapter Seven

"You keep checking the rearview mirror. Are you afraid he's following us?"

Settled against the soft leather seats of Craig's Hyundai, Phoebe turned her head to read his reaction.

Except for the slight tightening of his mouth, there was none. He offered a casual shrug, his gaze once again drifting to the mirror.

"Just being cautious."

"I appreciate it." She tucked a strand of hair behind her ear and glanced out the window.

And jeez, she really *did* appreciate it. Everything Craig had done for her thus far.

She kind of liked that Craig had called her bluff. Had returned to her apartment, even if her trashed car had been part of the reason. That he'd been so concerned about her safety, he'd pushed her to come home with him. Actually, no kind of about it. She liked it.

The realization that he was working himself into her life and into her heart was still a bit terrifying. And she had been bluffing this morning when she'd pushed him away emotionally—had tried to discourage him from anything serious. She still wasn't clear on whether she'd been lying to Craig or to herself, but one thing she knew now was that she was done running from whatever they had. It was just too good. Too...right. Normal.

But her reason for going home with him now wasn't as cut and dry as she'd implied. No, things were a little more complex.

No way in hell would she be a sitting duck for Rick. Waiting for him to approach her again—on his terms—when he knew she'd be vulnerable.

He was watching her. All the time now. She was one-hundred-percent certain on that. Well, she'd just use that to her advantage to draw him out into the open. If he wanted her back to the point of displaying stalker tendencies, seeing her shacking up with Craig would surely get his boxers in a twist.

He'd get careless and screw up. Come out of hiding at inopportune times. And she'd be ready. This time, she'd be ready.

"You're so quiet," Craig interrupted her thoughts. "How are you doing?"

"I'm doing all right."

Her lips twitched. He probably thought she was shaking in her boots. Terrified. And for a while, she had been. But now...now she just wanted to deal with this. Finish it. Deal with Rick—whom she'd thought gone from her life for good—permanently this time. Instead of running and hiding from her fears, she'd face them.

She glanced down at a nail, resisting the urge to bite it. It was a bad habit she turned to in times of stress.

"I'm a little bummed to find out he was calling from a pay phone."

"I wasn't surprised."

"Me neither, really." Fisting her hands, she glanced at Craig. "But I am surprised that the restraining order process was so quick. I thought these things took forever."

"Time is of the essence for someone trying to keep a person away from them." He gave her a pointed glance. "Sometimes a restraining order means nothing. It's just a piece of paper that the victim hopes will keep her safe."

"Wow, that's a positive way of thinking." Her mouth tightened.

"It's a realistic way of thinking."

He was right though. Years of working at the shelter had taught her that. If someone wanted to hurt you enough, a piece of paper meant shit to them.

Craig turned his car into an apartment complex and pulled into a numbered spot.

Twisting in her seat, Phoebe watched for any other cars to follow them into the parking lot. None did, but a few passed by the entrance. One seemed to slow just a bit, before it was gone from sight.

Her pulse quickened and she drew in a slow breath. Was it him?

"This is it." Craig gave her a quick smile before turning off the engine and opening his door.

Phoebe followed him out, stretching and feigning a casual ease. Every nerve in her body was alert, her mind churning with the idea that Rick might have followed them here.

Craig moved to grab her stuff out of the trunk and she approached him, placing a hand on his shoulder.

"Thank you," she murmured, and tucked herself against him, cupping his face. She brushed her lips over his in a soft caress. "For everything."

Surprise flickered in his gaze, before he dropped her duffle bag and slipped his arms around her, covering her mouth again with his.

The possessive kiss sent a thrill through her. It took a minute to shake her mind free from the fog of desire that threatened. But she managed. Barely.

Teasing her tongue out to stroke against Craig's, she hoped like hell that Rick was watching.

Craig groaned and pulled back with a curse. "We should get inside."

"I like the way you think."

Amusement danced in his eyes. "Man, you've gotten frisky."

"Yeah, go as long without sex as I did and you'll understand." She winked and went to pick up her bag.

"I can get that for you—"

"I've got it. You keep your eye out for the fucktard and your hand near your gun."

He reared back in surprise.

"Yes, I just called him a fucktard. And trust me, I've called him far worse."

His smile spread slowly across his face. "I like you, Phoebe. A hell of a lot actually."

"Do you now?" She arched an eyebrow, her stomach fluttering as they made their way to his apartment. From all his gestures, she'd gotten that impression, but to hear him confess it just made it all that much better.

"Yeah. Does that still bother you?"

Hesitating, she tried to answer the question to herself first. Surprised by the answer, she murmured, "Not as much as it did earlier. You're growing on me, Officer Redmond."

He caught her hand as they began to ascend the stairs. His thumb brushed over the inside of her palm. "Thank you for trusting me."

"Well, you make it surprisingly easy to do."

Pleasure flickered in his gaze. "So does this mean you're okay with this being more than just a one or two night thing?"

Phoebe felt the familiar panic rise inside her but pushed it aside. She took a moment and really thought about how she'd feel if, after this was over, Craig just walked back out of her life and she went on as usual.

There was no other choice.

Softly, she murmured, "I don't want just a couple nights with you, Craig."

Relief flashed in his eyes and his grip on her hand tightened.

"Good." Giving a small smile, he turned and led them up the rest of the stairs. "You hungry? We've barely had anything to eat all day since we forgot to get lunch after getting the restraining order. We could do an early dinner."

"Starving, actually," she acknowledged with a grimace. "I didn't want to be a burden though and make you stop for food."

"Asking to grab something to eat isn't a burden, Phoebe."

"It wasn't just that. I had a lot on my mind."

"I bet." Craig gave a small nod while unlocking the door to his apartment. "Would you eat a hamburger if I grilled a couple?"

"Oh, yeah. Got potato chips?"

"Barbeque flavored."

"I'm all over that." She grinned and followed him into the apartment.

"I'd rather you be all over me," he murmured, closing the door and locking it. "But we can save that for later."

"I suppose I walked right into that one." She grinned and let her gaze wander around the apartment.

Bachelor pad for sure. Mismatched furniture, retro movie posters on the wall, and a sink half full of dishes.

"You live alone?" she asked.

Strong arms slipped around her waist, while his warm lips moved over the back of her neck.

"Yeah." He moved his hand lower on her body so that his fingers almost grazed the swell of her pussy.

Warmth slid from her belly to the juncture of her thighs and she bit her lip.

"I want you again," he confessed.

"So I see. Or should I say feel?" She pushed her bottom back against him, rubbing against his cock.

He choked on a gasp. "I thought you wanted to eat."

"I do." She turned around in his arms and then sank to her knees in front of him. "And I think I just found the perfect appetizer."

His hiss of arousal coincided with the slide of the zipper on his jeans as she tugged it down.

She kept her gaze locked on his while pulling his erection from his boxers. Heat burned in his narrowed eyes and his breathing grew heavier.

A thrill chased through her at the spontaneity of the moment—the eroticism of it all. And most of all, how wonderful it felt to have Craig watch her with such need and barely controlled restraint.

She kissed the tip of her finger and then tapped it against the fat tip of his shaft.

"Phoebe." Her name was a growl of warning as his hips thrust forward, grazing his cock across her lips.

Heart pounding, she wrapped her fingers around his shaft and then parted her lips, guiding the head into her mouth.

She flicked her tongue over the satiny-steel flesh and then closed her eyes with a moan at the slightly salty taste of him.

It was so different giving Craig head than it had been before with her ex. There was no fear or reluctance this time. If anything, the desire to please him turned her on as much as him. And the taste of him was so sensual and addictive.

Opening her mouth wider, she drew him further inside, moving her lips over the head of his cock and then back up, while pumping his shaft with her fingers.

"God, Phoebe, don't stop, baby."

Stop? God, she was going to continue until she'd drunk

every last pulse of his climax. Until she watched him lose that thread of control and gave himself to her completely. She wanted it. She wanted him.

She lifted her gaze to watch his tight, pleasure-drugged expression and moved her mouth faster on him.

His lips barely moved as he chanted her name, his hips thrust to bury his cock deeper into her mouth.

Pleasure spun deeper inside her, where the taste and feel of him filled her every thought and movement.

When his hands dove into her hair, cradling her scalp as he slid deep to the back of her throat, she didn't resist. Instead, she relaxed and savored the first taste of him when he came.

She moved her hand down to his sac, cradling him and squeezing gently, encouraging him to release it all, taking everything he gave.

"Jesus," he muttered after a long gasp. "Phoebe, baby...wow. That was..."

"Mmm." Her mouth around him still, she hummed her reply as her lips curled into a smile.

He moved back, sliding out past her lips and tucking himself back into his jeans. Then, leaning down, he slipped his hands around her ribcage and lifted her gently to her feet.

"Amazing," he said, nuzzling her neck. "You're so damn amazing."

A thrill raced through her at his words and the touch of his lips against her skin. "You're not so bad yourself."

"What can I do for you, baby?" He slid his hands to her ass, lifting her off the ground and carrying her to the counter, where he set her on the edge. "Let me return the favor."

"Mmm. Tempting," she replied. And, oh God, wasn't it. Especially when his hand moved to rub over the apex of her jeans. "But I may just have to ask you hold that thought until after dinner."

He arched an eyebrow and his lips quirked. "Seriously?"

She squeezed his shoulders and laughed softly. "Seriously. I want my dinner now."

Craig winced and grasped his chest. "Denied for a hamburger."

Smothering a giggle, and with a surprising lightness in her heart, Phoebe watched him turn away and move into the kitchen. She slid off the counter and moved on to one of the bar stools, watching him pluck ground beef from the fridge.

"Not even the frozen ones? Wow, I'm getting the good stuff too. I should have you cook for me more often."

"Yeah, you should."

Her cell phone rang and she glanced at her purse on the counter. Craig stilled and followed her gaze.

"Check who it is."

She nodded and pulled her phone free, her palms suddenly damp. Could Rick have gotten her cell number? He'd gotten her address and home—

Relief eased the tension from her body. It was Delanie.

"It's just a friend. Mind if I take this on your balcony?"

"Go for it. I'll be out in a few to barbeque."

"Thanks." She flipped open her phone and headed for the back door. "Hey, girl, it's about time I heard from you."

Craig finished seasoning and forming the beef into patties and then walked out to the balcony where the barbeque was.

Hoping he'd given her enough privacy for a moment, he noted with relief they seemed to be talking about small things. His body still hummed from the impulsive blowjob she'd given him. God, how did he get so lucky?

Phoebe glanced up at him and winked, still cradling the phone against her ear.

"Well, I'm so glad you called, Delanie. I miss you." She nodded. "Okay...yeah. I'll keep that in mind." She held his gaze. "We'll see, it's a possibility. I can't promise he'll want to though, it's a long drive."

He raised an eyebrow while sidestepping her to fire up the grill.

Why did he get the impression she'd been talking about him?

"Of course I'll be careful. Hey, you've got enough on your plate with the wedding details, stop worrying about me." She sighed. "I will. I promise... Okay, miss you too, hon. See you soon."

Out of the corner of his eye, he watched her hang up the phone.

"Sorry about that," she apologized, coming to stand next to

him. "That was Delanie, she used to work at Second Chances until a few weeks ago. Tall, blonde chick?"

"I think I remember her." He nodded. "I've been coming to the shelter since I started working for San Francisco P.D. six months ago."

"What were you doing before that?"

"School. Got a degree in Criminal Justice. It took a while since I was working full time."

"You're young."

"Twenty-five." He turned to set the two beef patties on the grill and shrugged. "Not that young. Does it bother you?"

"No." She moved behind him to slip her hands into the back pockets of his jeans. "Not at all."

When her lips nuzzled the back of his neck, his cock twitched in response.

Pressing the spatula down on the beef, he closed his eyes and listened to the sizzle of juices dripping.

She grazed her teeth over his skin and he jumped slightly, resulting in her soft laugh.

He cleared his throat, determined to at least get some dinner in them before he carried her back to his bedroom. Or hell, even the couch. The counter. It didn't matter.

"Not to pry," he began, fighting to keep his voice steady, "but when you were talking to your friend, you mentioned something about a long drive? You going somewhere?"

"Yeah." She pulled away and he immediately missed the warmth of her body as she went to sit down in one of the chairs on the balcony. "Delanie's getting married next week, kind of a low-key, last-minute thing. It's up on one of the San Juan Islands in Washington State."

"Nice." He flipped the burgers and tried to recall what he knew about the Islands. "So you're driving?"

"Yeah. Gabby, Justin and I." She paused. "Delanie wants me to bring a date. Well...not really any random date, she wants me to bring you."

Craig glanced over his shoulder, his eyebrows high with surprise. "Me?"

"Yeah." Her cheeks went pink. "Delanie's a bit like a dog with a bone. Once she figured out that I was...um, seeing someone, she decided that it was her duty to meet him.

Or...you."

Pleasure raced through him, stroking his pride and ego just a bit. "So you told her about me?"

Her gaze lowered. "No. Gabby did. I mean, I would have. I meant to call her..."

"Ah."

Disappointment slowly replaced the pleasure, and he turned back to the grill. Of course. What had he been expecting? He'd barely gotten her to admit that she might be okay agreeing this was more than just a one-night stand. She'd hardly go off chatting to all her friends about him.

"You know...if you wanted," she began and he could hear she was nervous by her tone, "...you could come. To Athena's Oasis."

"To what?"

"Sorry. It's the resort where they're getting married. Her fiancé owns it."

"Sounds nice."

"It is. At least, I hear it is. I've never been... Anyway, if you wanted to come, I'd love you to."

He scooped the burgers off the grill and deposited them onto a plate, glad his back was to her. So she couldn't see the look of pure dismay on his face. Did she really want him to go? Or was it more of an *I need a date* situation. Of course, a road trip through three states was one helluva date.

But as he thought about it, he didn't care. He liked the idea of going with her, of having the time to convince her that he wanted more than just a short-term relationship.

"I'll see if I can get the time off. Just let me know the dates."

"Really?" She stood up and followed him back into the apartment. "Are you sure?"

He glanced at her and shook his head. "You second guess things too much. Do me a favor and grab some condiments out of the fridge?"

"Sure. And later? I'll just grab the condoms." She winked and hurried past him and his gaze immediately honed in on that cute ass of hers.

Damn. He'd better be able to convince her, because letting her go wasn't even about to be an option.

Chapter Eight

Phoebe's gaze stroked the corners of Craig's bedroom. Taking in the queen-sized bed covered with a black comforter. There were more movie posters on the wall—*Scarface* and *Platoon* this time. She made a quiet harrumph. Maybe he was actually some kind of movie buff.

She sat down on the edge of the bed, barely paying attention to the television show Craig had turned on before leaving.

He'd left her with the softest, most arousing kiss and then the firm instructions to be ready for bed when he returned. And she had no doubt as to what he meant by ready for bed.

She reclined against the pillow, letting her hand drift over her bare stomach as warmth stirred in her lower belly. She'd stripped down to nothing, challenged by his instructions and feeling bold.

Her gaze drifted to the doorway. How much longer would he be?

He hadn't gone far—really just outside on the balcony to make a few personal phone calls. Or, at least, that's what he'd told her, though she had no reason not to trust him.

Footsteps sounded outside the bedroom and then a moment later Craig loomed in the doorway.

He went rigid, gripping the doorframe. "Damn, woman."

"Hey." She rolled onto her side to look at him. "Everything taken care of?"

"Not everything," he muttered and crossed the room toward her.

Before he even reached the bed, his shirt was off and on the floor. His jeans came next, followed by his boxers.

He sat down on the edge of the bed and trailed a finger over her collarbone. The breath hitched in her throat when he moved it over the slope of her breast to swirl around her nipple.

"I could get used to this."

"What?" Her voice came out husky.

"Having you in my bed."

Heat, wet and heavy, gathered in her pussy and she bit her lip, watching him watch her. He kept making little remarks about long term, and with each one it became not nearly as intimidating hearing them. In fact, the idea of being in his bed on a more permanent basis sounded all too tempting.

His gaze moved over her body lingering between her legs. "Were you thinking about me while I was gone?"

"You and that *Scarface* poster on your wall."

"Love that movie." He gave a soft laugh. "Al Pacino is the man."

"Mmm-hmm."

His mouth twitched and then he grabbed his cock and waved it at her. "Say hello to my little friend."

Phoebe couldn't bite back a snort. She giggled and rolled her eyes.

"There is *nothing* little about that guy."

His grin widened as he slid his hand over the dip between her ribcage and hip, before skimming up over the curvy swell.

"I love your body. I could stare at it...touch it...kiss it all day."

Phoebe's stomach clenched and her smile grew a little tight. *Okay, he was probably going a bit over the top there.* "You flatter me."

His gaze jerked to hers as if he sensed her insecurity. "I don't feed women bullshit, Phoebe. You're a sexy woman. I wouldn't say it if I didn't think it."

"Thank you." Her cheeks warmed further and she lowered her gaze, hating the moment of uncertainty she'd had.

And the strange thing was she didn't have body issues. She was comfortable in her skin. Maybe it was because Craig was the first man she'd taken into her bed since...*don't even go there.*

The wave of ice and rage almost diminished her arousal, but she shoved it violently into an emotional closet.

Grabbing Craig's hand, she slid it over her hip and between her legs.

"Touch me," she whispered. "Please."

He held her gaze, his palm cupping the mound of her pussy while he toyed with the slick folds.

"You don't need to beg, baby. I can't keep my hands off you."

He slid a finger deep inside her and her body clenched around him.

"Yeah, you were thinking of me." His smile widened. "Did you think of my mouth on you?"

She closed her eyes on a sigh. "Well, you were really good at that part."

"Well, you've got a pussy made for eating." He gently pushed on her hip and rolled her onto her back. "And on that note, why don't you just get yourself comfortable."

Her pulse kicked up as he grabbed a pillow and nestled it under her ass.

With her lower body raised again, she was completely exposed and vulnerable to him.

She watched him lie on the bed between her legs, sliding his big hands over her thighs as he studied her body.

"So sweet." His breath feathered across her mound. "So soft."

His lips brushed her inner thigh and a tremble racked through her body.

"Relax, baby. You're so tense."

"Because you're being an awful tease, Officer Redmond," she muttered.

Her hips lifted on a gasp as he placed a kiss on her pussy.

"How's that for teasing?" he asked, before he tongued his way into her slit.

The only response she could manage was a strangled groan, her fingers tangled into the bedspread.

He parted her swollen lips with steady fingers and then dropped a kiss on her clit.

"There it is. That sweet little thing." He kissed it again, flicking his tongue over the sensitive nub.

"Craig..." Her eyelids fluttered shut and she surrendered to the exquisite torment of his mouth.

He continued to kiss and lick at her flesh, teasing her pussy until she rode his mouth like he was the damn roller coaster at the fair.

And he was relentless, bringing her closer and closer to that bright orgasmic peak. Until she finally tumbled over the edge, her body clenching and shaking against him.

It took a moment to regain her senses and, once she did, Craig was sheathing his cock with a condom.

"I need you, baby, now." He moved up next to her and began to lift her on top of him.

"Wait—" She pressed her palms against his chest and licked her lips. "This time I want you...to be on top of me."

His gaze flicked to hers. "Are you sure?"

"Yes." She nodded. There was no fear now. No hesitation even. She just wanted—no needed—the weight of his body on top of hers. To feel his hips spreading her thighs wide. There was complete trust and the knowledge that Craig would never hurt her.

He watched her for another moment, before giving a slow nod. Easing her back against the mattress, he positioned himself between her spread legs.

The tip of his cock nudged her swollen folds.

She held her breath, digging her nails into his shoulders and giving a slow nod.

He lowered himself onto her, inch by inch. His cock sank deeper into her body while the weight of him pinned her against the mattress.

"Damn, you feel so good." His face pinched tight as he obviously tried to go slowly.

"So do you," she admitted on a choked laugh. "Please, just take me, Craig. You won't hurt me, I promise."

With a groan of helpless regret, he plunged deep and she answered with a hiss of pleasure.

"Thank you," she whispered.

"No problem." He stayed buried for a moment, locking them together, before he pulled out of her slightly and then slid back in again.

She followed his rhythm, each thrust he made into her body sending a warm ache of tenderness and desire through her. She kissed his shoulder, crazy thoughts running through

Shelli Stevens

her head.

Thoughts like *I don't ever want another man besides Craig in my body again.* It was as if he was meant for her. His body designed for her, to please her, because they sure fit well together.

Their sweat mingled, making it easier for their bodies to slide together as their movements grew quicker—more harried.

Phoebe lifted her legs to wrap around his waist, clasping her ankles together and letting him hit even deeper into her.

"Baby," he choked out. "I'm going to come."

"*Yes.*"

And she wanted him to. Have him fly over that same edge he'd pushed her over earlier.

The pleasure already coursing through her spiked suddenly. His finger had found her clit and rubbed it steadily as his thrusts became harder.

One of them groaned. She didn't know if it was her or him, she was so gone with the intoxicating sensation.

"*Phoebe,*" he screamed, pushing deep again and staying there.

She could feel him swelling inside her as he came—and even then his finger didn't stop tormenting her clit. And then she was there with him. Hurling over that cliff of pleasure.

Her heart rate finally settled to somewhat normal and she became aware of Craig's lips nuzzling her neck. The delicious weight of his hard body above hers.

Tracing her nails over his back, she sighed and enjoyed the moment, not wanting to move in the slightest from the position.

All too soon he lifted himself off her, though, dropping a kiss on her damp shoulder.

"Be right back."

Disappointment in her stomach, she watched him walk naked from the room—presumably to the bathroom—and admired his solid backside.

How could she have gone so many years as she had without this? Without sex? She stretched, loving the subtle aches in her body, though they weren't nearly as prominent as they had been when she'd woken up this morning after making love for the first time the night before.

Made love…

242

"Hmm." She pursed her lips and nodded. Maybe it was odd, but it fit.

"Are you tired?"

She glanced up to see Craig re-enter the room.

"A little, we got up kind of early and have been on the go all day." His question sparked a yawn. "What time is it anyway?"

"Just after seven, it's still early." He crawled into bed and touched her cheek. "Want to watch a movie or just sleep?"

"Both." She turned her head and pressed a kiss into the palm of his hand. "Let's put a movie on and if I pass out even better."

"Deal." He slipped an arm around her, pulling her close, and then reached for the remote.

"I got that info you asked about."

About to get in his squad car, Craig looked up to see his friend and fellow officer crossing the parking lot.

Craig took the printout Evan handed him and scanned it. His blood rushed through his veins and his thumb pierced through the top of the paper he gripped it so hard.

"Shit." The word came out on a low growl.

"Yeah, it doesn't look good, bro. You better tell your girlfriend to watch her back."

Craig nodded and clenched the paper into his fist, then tossed it into the car.

"Thanks, Evan. I knew it was bad, but not this bad." He sat down in the squad car and jerked his head at his friend. "And hey, I think I'm going to have to bail on the club this weekend."

"Yeah?" Even raised an eyebrow and grinned. "Taking the girl—uh—work home with you?"

Craig gave a short laugh, but at this rate it was hard to find anything to be amused about.

"Something like that. Later, man."

Pulling away from the station, Craig headed straight for the offices of Second Chances and hoped it was a slow morning.

What had started as concern and the mild urge to protect her had just combusted into full-out fear for her life.

It was different when he'd thought Rick Conrad was nothing more than a pathetic loser who liked to beat up defenseless women...but seeing what was on that printout scared the shit out of him.

And all that fear centered on what could happen to Phoebe.

Hell, he shouldn't have let her go to work today. Should have begged her to stay at his place until they could locate Rick.

With a curse, he grabbed his cell phone and dialed her number. She answered on the second ring.

"Craig? Is everything okay?" Her voice was hesitant. "I thought you were at work?"

"I am," he said tersely and ran the cruiser through a yellow light. "I'm on my way over to your office."

"Now? Gabby and I were just going to run to lunch—"

"Don't go. Stay in the office until I get there. We need to talk. Please, Phoebe. I wouldn't ask if it weren't important."

There was a short pause, then a wary, "Okay. Okay, I trust you. I'll stay inside."

"You promise?"

"I promise."

"I'm about fifteen minutes away. If you see any sign of Rick, you call 911."

Another pause. "Craig, you're kind of scaring me."

Good. Being scared meant she'd be more careful. More alert. "I'll be there soon."

"Who was on the phone?"

Phoebe set her cell down on the desk and thrust a hand through her curls.

"Craig. He's on his way over. He wants me to hold off on lunch. I think something's up with Rick." She grimaced and glanced up at her friend with apology. "I'm sorry, Gabby. You can go without me if you want."

"No way. I'll just tell Sherice we'll pass today."

Gabby lifted the receiver on her desk and punched in a few numbers, then spoke quietly to their coworker on the other end.

Phoebe glanced out the window and tried to push aside the nervous flutters in her belly.

What was going on? Craig hadn't sounded good at all. He'd sounded grim. Worried. Whatever it was, it couldn't be good.

And of course it centered around Rick. The nervous flips in

her tummy faded as anger replaced it. He had no right. No right to reenter her life and turn it into a state of panicked chaos. To threaten everything she'd worked so hard for.

"Tell you what. Why don't I run out and grab us something? Do you want burritos?"

Phoebe bit her lip and gave her friend a narrowed glance. "I don't know. Maybe we should stick around."

"Craig asked you to stick around, hon, not me." Gabby sat up from her desk and walked over to hers. "And I'm hungry."

"We could have food delivered."

"The place I'm craving doesn't deliver."

"Craving?" Phoebe rolled her eyes and gave a soft laugh, some of the tension easing from her body. "What are you, pregnant?"

"Yeah, I think I am, actually."

Pregnant? Phoebe's mouth flapped as she stared at her friend. "Have you taken a test? What did Justin say?"

"I haven't told him," Gabby muttered, looking a bit pale now. "And no, I haven't taken a test. I'm a few weeks late though...and my boobs hurt."

"They hurt?"

"Well, they're sore." Gabby tugged at the end of one reddish braid, biting her lip and shifting her weight from one foot to the other. "We forgot to use a condom a while back. I wanted to pick up a test while we're out. That's another reason I suggested lunch."

Head spinning with the knowledge that her friend might be pregnant, and a little excited for her at the same time, Phoebe gave a quick nod and gentle smile.

"Okay. Go grab burritos and a pregnancy test. And when you get back, I'll hold your hand while we wait for the lines to appear."

"Ah, now that's a good friend." Gabby's expression shifted into a bit of relief. Her lips curled upward and she nodded, and scooped up her purse. "Be back in like fifteen."

"Okay. Chicken burrito—no salsa," she hollered after her friend as she made her way towards the door.

Gabby gave her the thumbs up sign and slipped outside, the door humming with the electronic lock as it clicked shut behind her.

With a sigh, Phoebe glanced back at her desk and began running over the details of the latest woman who'd come into the Second Chances house.

The shrill of her cell phone jerked her from her work a few minutes later, and she picked it up and answered.

"Hey," she murmured, recognizing Craig's number.

"Hi. You okay?"

"I'm fine." The front door buzzed. "Is that you?"

"Is what me?" his voice sharpened. "I'm about five minutes away."

"Oh, hang on someone's at the door," she told him, heading toward the front. "I thought it was you."

"It's not. Phoebe, get someone else to answer the door."

"Easy, Craig, what's got you on edge?" The door came into focus and she sighed. "It's just Gabby. Maybe she forgot her key card."

"Does she normally forget her card?"

"I don't know. She—"

Her pulse jerked and sweat broke out all over her body. Rick. He stood right behind Gabby with a gun pointed at her back.

"He's here."

Chapter Nine

"*Fuck*. Do *not* open the door."

"He's got Gabby at gunpoint," she choked, her gaze connected with the wide eyes of her friend.

"I'm calling for backup. Don't let him in, Phoebe. The man's dangerous. It's what I was coming to tell you. The last woman he dated disappeared without a trace and he's under investigation for suspected murder. Do *not* go outside."

Gabby's face was void of color, the stark terror blatant in her expression.

Suspected murder. Her head spun with the info. And looking into Rick's steely gaze, she could very well believe it.

Her focus shifted to Gabby and the obvious terror her friend was trying to keep under control.

"Open the door, Phoebe. I just want talk." Rick's voice came clear and chilly through the glass.

Gabby mouthed 'no'—warning her, like Craig had, not to be so foolish.

"Phoebe, what are you doing?" Craig demanded. "You aren't opening the door are you?

"Craig, I have to." She thought of the baby that her friend may or may not be carrying. Thought of the love Gabby and Justin had just found for each other. Her head moved back and forth. "I *have* to, Craig."

"*No*."

"I can take him." Anger and resolution had her repeat more confidently, "I can take him," before closing her phone.

She reached for the handle on the door again and Gabby shook her head fiercely, her eyes widening.

No more. She was *not* a victim anymore, and like hell would she let him treat her like one. He had no right to come back into her life and threaten her. Threaten the ones she loved. He wanted a fight? He'd get it.

Phoebe clenched her teeth, grabbed the handle, and pushed open the door.

Gabby hurtled through the open doorway after a none-too-gentle push from Rick.

When he attempted to step in through the doorway, Phoebe pressed her hand against his chest and shoved him backward. The sight of a gun pointed at her almost did nothing to her nerves at this point.

"How dare you?" she hissed, eyes narrowed with rage.

He grabbed her wrist and jerked her out of the building, the door locking behind them.

The click of the gun sounded before he said calmly, "We need to—"

"Talk?" she finished and then shook her head. "I don't think so."

With a hook kick, she nailed his wrist, knocking the gun from his hand. It skittered across the parking lot.

With a howl of enraged pain, Rick dove for it. She just barely got the chance to kick it again, sending it spinning under a nearby car.

She misjudged him in thinking he'd try for the gun again. Instead, he whirled toward her, fists flying.

All too easily, she blocked the punches.

"Not this time." Lifting her leg, she delivered a solid sidekick to his ribcage.

Rick fell to the ground with a choked gasp.

"I am *not* a victim." *Never again.*

"You stupid bitch," he wheezed.

"You want your restraining order?" she asked harshly, pushing back the curls that fell into her eyes. "Here it is."

He sat up and reached for the gun. She let his fingers almost graze it, before delivering another front kick to his chest.

His face turned a sickly green, before he fell backward onto the concrete parking lot.

"Consider yourself served."

Police sirens wailed in the distance, growing louder by the

second.

She moved carefully past him and retrieved the gun, gripping it fiercely in her hands. Adrenaline still rushed through her blood, but the anger began to slip into shock.

Her pulse skipped and the gun wavered. Staring down at Rick and the fury blazing in his eyes, she knew she had to be a little bit nuts. Or maybe a lot.

The door to the office burst open. Gabby and several other workers rushed out, just as three squad cars squealed into the parking lot.

Gabby rushed to her side. "Are you crazy? Shit, Phoebe, he was going to shoot you."

"It was either me or you."

"I wasn't going to shoot her," Rick snarled. "This has nothing to do with her. This is between us."

"Just shut it, fucktard."

Phoebe tightened her grip on the gun and kept her gaze trained on him, hoping like hell she wouldn't have to use it—because if it involved anything more than pulling a trigger, she was S.O.L.

Slamming doors sounded and then people came running. She turned her head to look toward Craig and knew immediately it had been the wrong thing to do.

"*No.*" Craig's face crumpled in a mix of horror and rage, his hand already reaching for his gun.

The burning pain in her side seemed to come before the gunshot, but she knew that wouldn't have made sense.

She turned around gingerly, her head spinning, and saw Rick fall lifelessly back onto the concrete, a stain of blood blooming on his shirt.

Her gaze lowered to her abdomen, just as Craig came behind her and put an arm around her.

"Call a goddamn ambulance." he screamed hoarsely.

The knife sticking out of her side didn't seem real. It almost seemed like a prop in a play. And when she touched her side, her hand came away sticky and warm.

She looked at her hand, saw the blood, but it just seemed fake. The burning and tingling had begun to fade. In fact...everything was kind of fading.

Her legs wobbled and she staggered against Craig. He slid

another arm around her and the blue sky swung into her line of vision as he lowered her to the ground.

Craig's dark eyes watched her with intensity and alarm, barely anchoring her from getting sucked under.

"Stay with me, Phoebe."

"Not going...anywhere. Too tired to walk," she muttered and then closed her eyes.

Craig pushed a hand over his short hair and glanced down the white corridor of the hospital.

The churning in his stomach and the heavy knot that lay thick in his throat had yet to subside, even though an hour had passed since a nurse had come out to assure him and Gabby that Phoebe was in stable condition.

He'd almost been sick to his stomach, watching them rush her into the hospital, unconscious and pale.

"I know how you feel," Gabby said quietly from behind him.

Tension raced through his body and he straightened to his full height before turning to look at her.

"What made her do it?" he asked, his voice unsteady. "Run out there and confront him like that?"

Gabby wrapped her arms around her middle, guilt flashing across her face.

"Me. She was trying to protect me."

"I know. She's a regular hero, isn't she?" he muttered.

"She's impulsive. I tried to tell her not to open the door to him. Yes—I was scared out of my mind, but I really don't think he would've hurt me. Whereas her...I think he would have shot her point blank without blinking."

"Excuse me."

They both looked up as a nurse appeared in the waiting room again. She turned to Craig.

"She's awake, pretty lucid now, and asking for you."

He sucked in a breath and took a step forward, then glanced back at Gabby. She was Phoebe's close friend. Maybe she should have first rights...

"Go on." She gave an understanding nod and waved him away. "I'll see her when you're done. Besides, there's a reason she asked for you. I should call Delanie and give her an update anyway. I had to convince her *not* to fly down so close to her wedding."

"Thank you." He held her gaze and gave a soft nod, then turned again and followed the nurse back to Phoebe's room.

He entered the room, his gaze immediately seeking her out. She was semi-reclined in the bed, wearing a hospital gown and a sheet pulled up over her legs.

The minute she spotted him, her expression, initially stoic and hesitant, brightened.

"Craig," she whispered, his name a sigh on her lips.

"Hey, how are you feeling?" He pulled up a chair next to her bed and gave a slight smile.

It wasn't easy. Seeing her like this—so damn pale and weak—made him wish Rick wasn't dead so he could shoot the bastard again.

"I'm feeling pretty good." She touched her side and frowned. "A little tender, but they've got me on some stellar pain killers, so I'm not feeling much. They want to keep me overnight for observation."

"Good idea." He caught her hand in his, stroking the inside of her palm.

"And the doctor said I should be fine to drive up to Delanie's wedding next week." Her gaze searched his. "The invitation is still open if you want to come with..."

Craig gave a silent grunt. The invitation had slipped his mind with all the drama of the day.

The idea held more and more appeal, but he needed to make sure he could commit for sure before getting her hopes up. "We'll see."

She nodded, but disappointment flickered in her gaze.

"How are you really doing, Phoebe?" he asked softly. "Besides the physical pain."

"Okay...a little shaken up of course. I heard..." Her gaze sought his and she swallowed hard. "Rick didn't survive getting shot?"

"No. He didn't." His jaw flexed.

One less abusive asshole running around the planet. Unfortunately that meant he'd never be prosecuted for the disappearance and probable murder of his last girlfriend.

He debated telling Phoebe what the police had found in

Rick's apartment when they'd searched it this afternoon. Countless pictures of Phoebe, most taken years ago, but some looked to have been taken in the last few months.

Looking at the vulnerability in her expression now made him think that the conversation was best held at a later date.

Irritation flared deep inside him. That she'd been so foolish to even put herself in that situation.

"You shouldn't have gone outside," he muttered aloud, before he could stop himself.

Her gaze hardened. "I had no choice."

"The hell you didn't. I was five minute away. Tops."

She snorted. "Come on, Craig. We both know I'd never let my crazy ex hold Gabby at gunpoint for five minutes."

"Phoebe—"

"I had the skills to defend myself. I knew I would be okay."

"You got a knife buried in your side. Tell me, Phoebe, how is that okay?"

Her chin lifted. "I'm not the one who ended up dead."

"Because I *shot* him." He shook his head and his lip quivered. "*I can take him.*" He tried to keep his voice steady. "Do you have any idea the level of fear and helplessness that went through me when you said that? Knowing you were going out to face an armed man without a weapon?"

She looked away, but not before he saw the surprise in her eyes.

"You weren't thinking. Gabby's right. You're too damn impulsive."

Her head whipped back to face him, her eyes flashing. "I'm not impulsive."

"You are. You were impulsive when you faced Rick like that. And you were impulsive when you went to bed with me that first night."

She pulled her hand free, more color in her cheeks now. "Thank you. I love basically being called a reckless slut."

"Easy now, baby. I did *not* call you a—"

"You're right, Craig. I was a bit impulsive in going to bed with you. And that means you don't really know me, now do you? So please don't sit there and judge me."

Shit. He'd handed that argument to her on a platter. Her lips thinned and her gaze drifted away from him again.

Unease swept through him. The mood between them had grown colder. And he suspected she was damn close to resurrecting those same walls between them that he'd had to tear down the other morning.

"Do you want something to drink? Eat? Are they letting you eat?"

She shook her head and closed her eyes. "I want to rest..."

When she didn't say anything more or open her eyes, he figured she'd basically told him to get out.

"I'll come by tomorrow and pick you up. What time do you think they'll release you?"

"I think Gabby was planning on taking me home. I'm going to crash with her and Justin for a few days until I'm one-hundred percent again."

His jaw clenched and he looked out the window. She didn't want to stay with him anymore. Where was this all coming from? Could he have just blown any chance at long-term with her? All for calling her impulsive?

"Okay." He gave a slow nod and stood to approach the bed. "Why don't you give me a call tonight or tomorrow?"

She gave a wan smile, but didn't reply.

Craig leaned down to brush his mouth across hers. She tensed and then turned her head so his lips moved to her cheek.

Maybe the shock of everything had caught up with her and she just needed time. Biting back a sigh of frustration, he straightened and left the room.

Phoebe heard the door click shut, signaling Craig had left, and her stomach rolled with a mixture of relief and guilt—not to mention disappointment, if she let herself acknowledge it.

Maybe it's better this way. The fear of getting involved seriously with him had reared its ugly head a few minutes ago. And suddenly it was too much. The pressure of living up of to his expectations, of him living up to hers, of giving them that absolute trust. Then the fear of losing him...

The magnitude of Rick's death, and how close she'd been to dying as well didn't sit lightly with her. It cloyed her senses, took over almost all her thoughts.

"What's going on?"

Her eyes snapped open when Gabby appeared in the doorway, brows drawn together.

"What do you mean?"

"I didn't expect Craig to take off so soon. And when I passed him in the hall, he looked a bit bummed out."

"Oh." Another sharp stab of guilt. "Nothing's going on. I just told him I was tired."

"That's it?"

"For the most part." Phoebe shifted in the hospital bed, wincing as her stitches tugged. "They're keeping me tonight for observation, but I was hoping I could crash with you and Justin for a couple days."

"With us?" Her brows arched. "But weren't you already staying with Craig?"

"I was..."

"Not that we aren't happy to have you stay with us, but something totally happened between you and Craig." Gabby sat down on the edge of the bed and gave her a scrutinizing look. "Wanna talk about it?"

Phoebe hesitated, considering dumping her fears on her friends, and decided against it. "No. Have you figured out if you're...?"

"Pregnant?" Gabby glanced away, unease in her eyes. "I haven't had a chance to take a test yet. I've been at the hospital with you all day. Justin's picking me up when he gets off work."

"Have you told him you think you might be?"

"No."

"Think he'll freak?"

"Hard to say. I know I will."

"You know there's a drug store around the corner from the hospital. Why don't you run and grab a pregnancy test?"

"I probably should. Though I'm pretty confident what the results will be." Gabby gave a slow nod and then leaned forward to pat her hand. "When I get back, we're going to talk about you and Craig."

"Do we have to?" Phoebe closed her eyes again, trying not to think about the frustration on Craig's face as they'd begun to argue.

"Yes." Gabby gave her hand a squeeze and then stood up. "I'll be back in a few."

Chapter Ten

Phoebe glanced up as the buzzer to her apartment sounded. She went to the intercom and then pushed the button, asking who it was—though she already pretty much knew.

"Hey, girl, it's Gabby and Justin. Let us up."

"Okay. See you in a few." She unlocked the door to the building and then went back to her packing.

Pushing back a curl, she sighed and threw a few more things into her suitcase, before zipping it.

They were leaving today for Washington State, and she hadn't called Craig. Guilt stabbed in her gut, but she pushed it aside. It wasn't like he'd called her either.

There was a sharp knock at the front door and she grabbed her suitcase and dragged it to the living room, before turning to let her friends in.

They stood outside her apartment, Justin behind Gabby, chin on her shoulder and his arms around her waist, his hands cuddling the belly that indeed was carrying his child.

Phoebe bit back a sigh, envying how disgustingly happy they looked.

"Hey." Gabby grinned and stepped in through the door, pulling Justin with her. "So did you call him?"

Not even trying to pretend she didn't know who *him* was, Phoebe winced and shook her head.

Gabby's eyes went wide. "*Phoebe*. You promised."

"I'll take your suitcase down to the car, Phoebe." Justin grimaced and gave her an understanding wink, before disappearing again from her apartment.

"Call him." Gabby strode over to the cordless phone and handed it to Phoebe. "Now. Call him and invite him again."

She hesitated, and let her fingers drift over the wound in her side, which was almost four days old now.

"I know you're afraid," Gabby said softly. "Afraid to completely trust a man and get involved. But I also know how much you care about Craig. Even if you won't admit it. He's the only man I've seen you let into your heart—if even just a little bit. I really hope he comes with us, Phoebe. It'd be good for you guys to talk. Spend time together."

Phoebe swallowed hard, fear and doubt sending her pulse into double time.

"Call him."

She nodded and took the phone from Gabby, dialing his number with shaking fingers.

"He won't be able to come," she muttered. "We're leaving three days early. I'm giving him no notice."

Gabby folded her arms across her chest and gave her a pointed look. "You don't know until you ask."

On the fourth ring, his phone went to voicemail. Relief and disappointment mingled.

"He's not home."

"Leave a message."

"Gabby..."

"Do it!"

"Hey...Craig. It's Phoebe." She turned her back to Gabby, so her friend couldn't witness her discomfort. "I...I'm leaving for Delanie's wedding. I wasn't sure if you still wanted to come, and we're leaving early. Anyway...I'm sure you don't want—"

"Phoebe," Gabby hissed.

Phoebe's face flamed. "Ugh—I've got to go. Anyway, hope you're doing okay. Maybe I'll talk to you again...someday—"

"Maybe?"

"Goodbye." She clicked the off button and whirled around. "Okay, as if that wasn't awkward enough, having you standing there yelling your two cents *sucked*."

Gabby rolled her eyes. "That *message* sucked."

"Well, at least I left one," Phoebe muttered with a glare.

"Ladies, we ready to go?" Justin appeared in the doorway, bracing his arms high on the frame as he glanced around the room.

"Let me grab my jacket." Phoebe gave a quick nod and turned back to her bedroom.

Gabby sighed. "I guess it's just us three."

Which was probably better, Phoebe thought, tossing her jacket over her arm. There was a reason she hadn't called Craig before today.

Gabby was right, she *was* scared. And without Gabby there to encourage her, she may not have called him. Reached out to make that connection again.

Her stomach twisted. A connection that she probably waited too long to make.

Nothing to be done now...maybe she'd call him again after they got back. Her lips twitched into a humorless smile as the three of them left her apartment.

She knew herself too well. The chances of her calling him again were slim. By the time she got back from Washington, she'd be back in that *I'm better off single* mode.

So the ball was basically in his court...and after that crap message she'd left and the way she'd treated him in the hospital, she may as well just greet her single status with open arms.

Craig wiped the sweat off his face with a paper towel and stared at himself in the gym mirror. Damn, he still looked like ass.

After having the cold from hell for the last few days, he was finally feeling up to par. And having gone three days with his most strenuous activity being blowing his nose and getting out of bed to use the bathroom, he'd known it was time to workout.

A half hour on the treadmill had done him good. Made him feel somewhat human again, and had also helped him focus on something besides Phoebe.

She hadn't called. Which shouldn't have surprised him after her behavior in the hospital room. But it did a little. And it hurt. He'd planned to call her and hash it out—meet up with her even. But the cold had suspended those plans.

Tonight, he'd call her. The minute after he got back to his place and showered. He'd call her, or hell, he'd just go to her place.

Turning, he went and grabbed his bag from the locker and reached inside for his car keys. He grabbed them and his phone, leaving the locker room.

"Later," he called to the guy working the desk near the entrance.

"Have a good one."

His cell began to vibrate in his hand and he glanced down, noticing he had a message.

Flipping open the phone, he checked who'd called. His blood rushed through his veins and his brows drew together as he dialed the voicemail.

A minute later he closed the phone and climbed into his car, knowing what he was going to do and wondering if it made him a bit crazy.

"You look fantastic, Delanie." Phoebe hugged her friend again, before stepping back to observe the bride-to-be. She was glowing. Not to mention stylish and sexy like always. "Either the Northwest or being engaged sure agrees with you."

"Or both," Gabby piped up.

Delanie gave a soft laugh and twisted the diamond ring on her left hand.

"Being Grant's wife will agree with me even more." She rolled her eyes and sat down on the couch, curling her legs under her bottom. "I am so excited for our honeymoon in France."

"Umm, living here has got to be kind of like a honeymoon," Gabby pointed out, sitting down in a recliner and glancing around. "This resort is *fabulous*."

"It is. I'm so glad you both could make it up here for the wedding."

Phoebe gave a small smile. "We're in it, kind of hard to skip out."

"Well, it's so wonderful to see you both." She turned to Gabby with a sly smile. "And I really like Justin. You're an overachiever. Getting pregnant and engaged in one week."

Gabby's cheeks turned pink. "Yeah the engagement thing was being talked about. The baby thing sped up the process."

Phoebe averted her gaze as the two began to chat, her throat tightening up. God, she felt like the biggest downer. But seeing Gabby and Delanie both so in love and content made her really think about what she might have been able to have with Craig. If she weren't the world's biggest pansy.

"Where are the guys, anyway?" Gabby asked, yawning into her palm. "I haven't seen them since they left after dinner."

Delanie was quiet for a moment and Phoebe glanced over at her, noting the mischief in her gaze.

"I'm not really sure," she answered, fiddling with the coin on a chain that hung around her neck. "I think Grant mentioned wanting to go on a drive to show Justin a couple of the sites on the island."

Phoebe stared at the ancient coin, remembering all the trouble it had caused Delanie and Grant initially. But in reality, it had brought the two together. Her lips curled into a soft smile. And the day after tomorrow, they'd be getting married.

"So, you're doing okay, Phoebe?" Delanie asked suddenly. "I mean, I was so scared when I heard about Rick showing up in your life again. Thank God he's...well, thank God."

"Yes. And I'm doing okay." Phoebe nodded and looked down at her fingers, just manicured today for the upcoming wedding. "It feels a little surreal, but I'm coming to terms with everything that happened."

Gabby smiled. "Yeah, Craig totally protected her when Rick was out stalking her. And he's the one who shot Rick."

"So do you like this Craig?" Delanie lifted an eyebrow. "He seems like a good guy."

Phoebe shifted, thinking *like* was probably an understatement. "He's nice..."

"She's totally sprung on him, and don't let her try to tell you otherwise," Gabby inserted and took another sip of her Sprite. "She's just having a panic attack about getting serious with someone."

"I'm not—"

"It would be understandable if you were," Delanie said in a rush. "I mean you haven't dated since..."

"The stone age?" Gabby teased and then giggled. "Sorry, I'm not helping."

"No. You're not." Delanie shot her a warning look.

"I blew it, you guys. I really think I blew it." Phoebe finally confessed, fighting back tears. "He is a good guy. And I kept pushing him away emotionally. All the time he was with me. And then at the hospital...I think I just blew it."

"I don't think you blew it." Gabby shook her head and stood up, coming over to give Phoebe a hug. "It'll all work out."

Delanie leaned in and joined the embrace. "Me neither, sweetie. I don't think you blew anything. Or maybe you blew Craig at some point—"

"Delanie!" Phoebe gasped and then laughed, almost choking.

Gabby snorted. "Ah, see, she's still a bit of a dirty birdie."

"You guys are the best. I don't know what I'd do without you." Phoebe took the support of their embrace and bit her lip to hold back tears.

The last two weeks were catching up with her and fast. It fell heavy on her heart and moisture finally flooded her closed eyes.

"Oh." Delanie pulled back. "I hear Grant's car. That means the men are back."

The men were back. And once again she'd be the proverbial fifth wheel.

Car doors opened and slammed, and then the low murmur of men's voices could be heard.

"Delanie?"

"In here, honey," Delanie called back.

Gabby and Delanie stood, exchanging an odd look that Phoebe didn't miss.

She rose to her feet, her brows drawing together.

A second later, Grant strode into the living room, followed by Justin. Followed by...Craig.

Phoebe's heart slammed into her chest and her mouth went dry. He was here. Craig was here.

Delanie was talking, probably saying something to her, but she couldn't hear above the rush in her ears. Her vision was held by Craig's gaze, which hadn't wavered from her.

It was almost like an invisible beam locked them together, crackling with tension.

He crossed the room to her. It seemed to take an eternity before he stood in front of her.

"Phoebe." He reached out and cupped her cheek.

She blinked, snapping out of her daze and jerking her head around to see if her friends were watching the exchange. They'd all disappeared. She was alone in the room with Craig.

Craig. Who was here on Lopez Island, two states away from home.

"You came," she whispered. "But how...?"

"I flew up this afternoon and then took a seaplane to the island about an hour ago." His mouth curved into a slight smile. "I called the resort and mentioned I'd been invited to a wedding. Asked if someone could pick me up."

Her pulse raced and she ran her tongue over her mouth. "Why would you do all this? That must have cost you—"

"I don't care about the money, Phoebe. And right now I can afford it." His glance dropped to her mouth. "I care about you."

"Do you?"

"You know I do."

Her throat tightened with emotion and tears gathered in her eyes; she blinked them away. "I'm sorry I freaked out on you in the hospital. And I'm sorry I didn't call until too late."

"Shh, baby." He shook his head slowly. "It's not too late."

"I have a lot of baggage, Craig. I don't trust easily, I'm somewhat afraid of men—"

"But not of me."

"Not you," she agreed, soft with the realization. "I'm trying to say I've got issues though. I'm not an easy person to love, Craig."

"Phoebe." He cupped the back of her head and pulled her forward, touching his forehead against hers. "I think you'd be all too easy to love."

Tears spilled over her lashes now and she drew in a ragged breath.

"If you'd just give me the chance. Will you, baby?"

"Yes," she whispered, warmth exploding in her body and sending pleasure and a wonderful peace through her. "Yes, Craig. Of course I will."

This was right. This is what she'd wanted and was too afraid to take a chance on. But now she knew there would be no regrets. Because if any man could convince her to fall in love—and deep down, she knew she already had—then Craig was that man.

He lifted his head and relief and heat burned in his gaze.

"I'm willing to take it slow. Go at whatever pace you want."

"I don't think I want slow anymore," she admitted, surprising herself. "I spent too many years being afraid to love. And you're doing a damn good job at changing my mind."

"I've missed you, Phoebe. In more ways than one," he murmured on a growl, tucking a curl behind her ear. "Is your room somewhere around here?"

"They placed me in a cabin not far from the main house."

"A cabin. I like the sound of that. I need to touch you. Taste you. Hear you call my name..."

"Mmm. All of the above please."

He issued a soft a laugh and lowered his mouth to just above hers. "But I should warn you I just got over a cold."

"I should warn you...I don't really care," she whispered and sighed when his lips claimed hers.

About the Author

To learn more about Shelli Stevens, please visit www.shellistevens.com. Send an email to Shelli at shelli@shellistevens.com or join her newsletter for updates and contests. To sign up, visit www.shellistevens.com/contact/

GREAT
CHEAP
FUN

Discover eBooks!

THE FASTEST WAY TO GET THE HOTTEST NAMES

Get your favorite authors on your favorite reader, long before they're
out in print! Ebooks from Samhain go wherever you go, and work with
whatever you carry—Palm, PDF, Mobi, and more.

LaVergne, TN USA
28 June 2010
187669LV00003B/2/P